the medici dagger

ALSO BY CAMERON WEST

First Person Plural: My Life as a Multiple

the Medici Dagger

Cameron West

**Story developed in collaboration
with Seamus Slattery**

POCKET BOOKS

NEW YORK   LONDON   TORONTO   SYDNEY   SINGAPORE

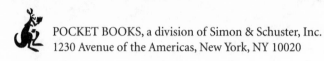

POCKET BOOKS, a division of Simon & Schuster, Inc.
1230 Avenue of the Americas, New York, NY 10020

Copyright © 2001 by Plural Productions, Inc.

Library of Congress Cataloging-in-Publication Data

West, Cameron, 1955–
    The Medici dagger / Cameron West.
      p. cm.
    ISBN 0-7434-2035-7
    1. Leonardo, da Vinci, 1452–1519—Contributions in military science—
Fiction. 2. Medici, House of—Art patronage—Fiction. 3. Americans—
Italy—Fiction. 4. Stunt performers—Fiction. 5. Arms transfers—Fiction.
6. Daggers—Fiction. 7. Italy—Fiction. I. Title.

PS3623.E83 M44 2001
813'.6—dc21   2001034024

First Pocket Books hardcover printing September 2001

10 9 8 7 6 5 4 3 2 1

For information regarding special discounts for bulk purchases,
please contact Simon & Schuster Special Sales at 1-800-456-6798 or
business@simonandschuster.com

Designed by Christine Weathersbee

Printed in the U.S.A.

a note from the author

Reb, the fellow who is about to tell you this story, was inspired by the man who wrote:

"Every obstacle yields to effort."

Prologue

−1491−

But for God and the bakers, all of Italy slept through the sultry August night and the moment of the great discovery—that is, all except the inventor, who stood back from the heat of his forging furnace, astonished, holding the cooling, practically weightless dagger in his palm. The piercing blade glinted in the orange light as beads of sweat gathered like berries on the hairs of the man's strong wrists.

Placing the dagger point-up in a vise, the man hefted a sledge and struck the blade's tip with full force. The hammer's iron mallet split like a ripe melon. Using his extraordinary powers of reason, the man struggled to account for this miracle. There was only one answer. An incalculable ingredient had been added to his experimental mixture of metals.

Gazing skyward out his window, the genius contemplated another question even more profound. Would his incredible discovery be used for good or for evil? As he solemnly watched the molten sparks from his furnace chimney race toward the velvety heavens, the man from Vinci made his decision.

And five centuries passed.

twenty years ago

One

I sank into the black leather sofa in my father's spacious office, leaning against a pillow that looked like a big, silky Chiclet. Tension rippled through the room. I glanced up at my dad, who was slumped forward in his chair, elbows on his leather-topped desk, forehead in one hand. His face was six inches from the speakerphone—a boxy thing, separate from the telephone, that sounded even worse than they do today. Wedged between the fingers of his other hand was a number-two pencil that he nervously wiggled back and forth.

The voice coming out of the phone belonged to Ensign Hector Camacho, a representative from the Coast Guard. "I'm very sorry, sir," Camacho said with professional dispassion.

My dad winced as if he'd stepped on a thumbtack. "You're saying he could have gone down anywhere within a hundred-mile radius?"

"I'm saying that—"

"Can't you find that plane? You cannot fathom the importance of this, the devastating consequences!" Sweat glistened on my father's upper lip.

"Try to calm down, Dr. Barnett," Camacho said. "I know how difficult this must be for you, losing, uh, Mr. Greer."

"Henry!" Dad shouted, and then, as if in an afterthought, he said, "Oh, God . . . Henry." I knew Henry Greer was the pilot and courier my father had sent to France to retrieve a page of Leonardo da Vinci's notes.

7

"Was he a relation?" Camacho asked.

My father ignored the question. "So there's no way at all to recover this airplane?"

"He went down in very deep waters, and probably at high speed, sir."

My father snapped the yellow pencil and threw the two halves on the floor. "Jesus!"

I squirmed in my seat and thought maybe I should take a walk. But I stayed.

"I know," Camacho said. "I'm very sorry."

My dad was silent for what seemed like a full minute before I realized that he was crying. That got me, and I felt tears welling up, too.

Out of the little box, Camacho's voice said, "Mister . . . um, Doctor?"

"You'll call me if anything turns up?" Dad said desperately. "Anything. A piece of paper. A scrap of paper."

"Of course, sir."

"A document of any kind. Anything with writing on it."

"We'll call you immediately if anything at all is recovered, sir."

My dad collected himself. "Thank you, Ensign," he said. "Goodbye."

"Goodbye, sir," Camacho said, and disconnected.

My father stared at the dead speakerphone. I got up and walked over behind him, my boot heels silent on the thick maroon carpet. When I placed a hand on his shoulder, I realized his shirt was damp from sweat.

"Dad?" I called softly.

He slowly raised his head and looked at me through watery eyes. "It's gone, son," he whispered. "It's gone."

On July nights the humidity in Georgetown was so thick it looked as if a plastic shower curtain had been hung in front of the moon.

Sometimes, after my mom and dad had kissed me good night and closed my door, I'd get out of bed and kneel down in front of my second-story window, open it up, and poke my head out into the night. I'd squint up at the hazy yellow face of the moon and feel the air-conditioning going one way and the hot, sticky air going the other, until I'd start to sweat or a mosquito would nail me.

The night of the plane crash I lay on my back in bed, propped up on my elbows. My mother leaned over me, dressed in her light blue cotton robe, scrubbed clean, no makeup. I breathed in the scent of her favorite soap—apricot from Caswell Massey—hoping to ease some of my worry. I watched Mom's eyes as she fluffed my pillow. *Her eyes are the color of acorns,* I thought. The serenity they normally radiated was absent that night. And my sheets were tucked in too tightly. I pried them loose with my toes.

"You did the wash today, huh."

"Nothing like fresh sheets, is there?" Mom said, managing a smile. "Okay, there we go. You can cozy up now."

There was no chance of that happening. I laid my head back and my mother pulled the covers under my chin.

"Is Dad coming up to give me a kiss?"

She sighed. "I don't think so, sweetie. I don't know when he's coming up. He's . . . you know, he's pretty upset." She covered her mouth with her hand. If she cried I'd have a nightmare for sure.

"But it was an accident," I said. "It wasn't his fault."

"I know, but . . ." She sat down on the edge of the bed and placed her hand on my chest. I wanted to hold it, but my arms were stuck at my sides like a mummy's.

"Dad feels responsible," she said. "If he hadn't bought the notes for the museum, or if he'd gone to get them himself, instead of sending the courier . . . He's really . . . upset."

"Is he going to feel better tomorrow? What about the museum party? Are we still going to have the party? We're not, are we?"

Just the low hum of the air conditioner.

"Maybe now nobody'll ever find the Medici Dagger." I sighed. "What would Leonardo think of that?"

"It was a tragedy today. For a lot of people."

"I could have helped. I could have done something."

"Honey, you're eleven. There was nothing you could have done. Now go to sleep. Everything's going to be all right."

She kissed my cheek and gave my earlobe a little tug. "Have swell dreams and a peach," she whispered in my ear. "Swell dreams and a peach."

"Big peach," I said, taking a last whiff of her. "Oh, Mom . . ."

"I know. The night-light."

She stopped by the door, clicked on the little light, and turned off the overhead. "Happy dancing shadows . . ." she began.

". . . in Reb's sleep-tight light," I murmured, finishing our little ritual. She padded down the hall, creaking the old floor in all the usual spots.

Everything's going to be all right. Everything's going to be all right. I wish I could have done something—flown the plane maybe. Everything's going to be all right. Everything.

I was dreaming about twigs crackling in a campfire when my mother's scream woke me. I bolted up in bed and looked out the window, surprised by the brightness. The campfire? A second scream shook me out of my dream state. I smelled smoke and realized the light was from a real fire creeping up the outside of our wooden house.

"Mom! Dad!" I shouted as a window exploded somewhere downstairs. Smoke billowed up from under my door like a ghost coming to get me. I jumped out of bed; the rug felt oddly warm under my bare feet. Running to the window, I threw it open and punched the screen out. All around me flames licked the house. Looking up, I saw the shake-roof shingles burning, shooting cinders like a million fireflies into the night sky. The whine of fire engines pierced the roar of the blaze, and I heard my mother scream my name from somewhere deep in the house.

"Mom!" I yelled as I crawled backward, feet-first, out the window. I hung on to the sill with an iron grip, looking into my room, waiting for something—I didn't know what. My hands began to tremble, but I held on tight.

Just as the first fire truck came racing down our narrow street, my bedroom door burst open and I saw Mom standing in the doorway, flames all around her. Our eyes met and she shrieked, "Reb! Jump!" Her nightgown was on fire. Men's voices shouted at me from down below—echoes from a distant canyon. As my mother threw her arms out and took two steps toward me, the house shuddered and the roof collapsed, with a sound like a thousand bones breaking, crushing her into eternity.

I froze for a second, suspended in a place where the claws of horror couldn't touch me. Then, scrambling my feet up the clapboard siding, a dozen splinters piercing my soles, I pushed off the wall and turned in midair, arcing over the walkway, going into a dive, reaching for the ground. I heard yelling as I hit the small patch of grass by the big elm near the curb and rolled smack up against the tree.

And then the world went black.

I don't remember the name of the doctor who told me my parents had died in the fire. I know it was a man, though, because the voice was deep and had come from somewhere above little gold sea horses that floated in an ocean of royal blue tie.

"Can you look at me, son?" he asked.

I gazed at the strange, curly-tailed creatures, envying their silken inanimateness. "I am looking at you," I replied flatly.

He cupped my face in his cold hands, swallowed audibly, and said again, softly, almost crying, "Can you look at me, son?"

I realized that he was probably thinking of his own kids. I felt sorry for him, having to be the one to tell me. I couldn't look at him, though. I just let him deliver the news while I mingled with the sea horses. It wasn't really news.

I'm nobody's son, I thought.

the Present

two

I crashed through the third-story picture window of the huge chalet at the exact moment the entire floor exploded. Landing on my stomach on the snow-covered, second-story roof, I did a "Superman" down thirty feet of steep pitch. Gunfire erupted from the nearby woods, breaking off chunks of slate all around me. I scrambled to get my body turned around before I ran out of roof.

I slid over the edge feet-first, latching on to the big tin rain leader with my fingertips. One of the men in the forest yelled something in Russian. I heard two bursts of gunfire and felt the metal rip on either side of me. The section of leader I clung to groaned and broke off, and I fell twenty feet, barely managing to get the jagged piece of tin under my boots. I hit the steep, sloping ground in a crouch and slingshotted down the hill like a snowboarder on a double-diamond trail. Four guys jumped on two snowmobiles, roared their two-strokes to life, and took off after me.

I yanked my gun out of its shoulder holster, pointed it at the snowmobile on my far right, and squeezed off three rounds. The driver grabbed his chest, and the snowmobile smashed into a tree and exploded.

With the second sled closing in, I entered a steep, bumpy clearing. Fifty yards ahead, a single red and yellow hang glider launched off a sheer cliff. I aimed for the glider and crouched, feeling the spring in my thighs and the stir in my belly as I prepared for the dive. In an instant, the ground disappeared and my board dropped off into space; the snowmobile driver behind me swerved to a stop at the edge of the precipice.

I arched my back and stretched every fiber in my arms and fingers toward the glider, shot by the wing, and grabbed on to the frame at the front. The glider took a sharp dive. Some biceps and body English would have snapped it back up, but I leaned forward and to the right and we went into a spin. One, two, three, four, five electrifying, corkscrewing seconds ticked by before I countered with my hundred and eighty-five pounds, yanked the frame with all my strength, and pulled the glider straight to sail out over the icy blue lake.

The second unit director's voice came over my earpiece. "Jeeeezusss, Reb! What the hell happened up there?"

I locked my harness to the glider frame. My hands were trembling, but not from the chilly mountain air. It was "the heights"—the shakes I get whenever I fly or take a fall. I don't make the heights public.

"Did you get the shot?" I said into my lapel mike, feeling the ebb of adrenaline.

"Of course I got it! It was gorgeous. But major heart attacks are happening here. Who said spin? Did anybody say—"

"Marty, nothing bad happened, right?"

"Uh, right."

"Then please just say 'thanks.' And 'that's a wrap.' Don't forget to say that."

"Okay, okay," he squawked. "Thanks, that's El Wrappo!"

"You're welcome," I said.

I'd nailed it—the whole scene. It was over the top. I knew it would be. Knew it when I talked Charlie, the hang-glider pilot, into going for the spins. He didn't want to, of course, but I swore to him it would be all right. "Think of the bragging rights," I told him, "and besides, you can always break off and pull your chute." Charlie didn't know I left mine in my trailer.

Nine cameras rolling—one take. A good morning's work and

the end of the picture for me. Later they'd punch in the close-ups of the star, the dapper and always cool Tom Sloane, apologizing to a beautiful hang-glider pilot: "Sorry to drop by unannounced." Meanwhile, Charlie was giving me the thumbs-up. I grinned, unclenched a hand, and pulled my earlobe, hoping he didn't see the heights.

There was major whooping and back-slapping when we got back to the set, followed by everybody thanking everybody and exchanging temporary goodbyes. I made the rounds fast, then changed out of my getup into a tight black T-shirt, faded jeans, brown leather bomber jacket, and custom-made Beatle boots.

I was getting ready to leave when the producer, a slim woman named Rhonda, all red hair and big lips, headed my way with the star himself.

Tom was about my size and looked remarkably like me—dark wavy hair and brown eyes—which kept me busy as his double. His best quality, though, other than his naturally good teeth, was his wife's spinach and mushroom quiche.

I heard Rhonda telling him, "Are you kidding me? With this in the trailer we could show two hours of you sleeping and still rake in a hundred and fifty mil. And that's just domestic."

Today I'd fallen *and* flown, and still had a touch of the heights. I slipped my hands into my pockets.

Tom flashed me his famous smile. "Jesus, Reb, how'd I do that?"

"You had no choice," I replied with a shrug. "They were trying to kill you."

"Good line," Rhonda said. "Very macho. But that spin, Reb. One of these days you're going down. Don't you know the meaning of the word 'danger'?"

"Danger's my maiden name," I said, forcing a grin.

She laughed. "C'mon, let's all go celebrate."

"Can't," I replied, turning in the direction of my '68 silver-blue Jaguar XK-E. "I left some wet towels in my washer." I could feel my gut churning and knew I'd better get out of there fast.

Tom turned to Rhonda. "Towels?" he bristled. "What's he talking about, towels?"

As I made my escape, I heard Rhonda smoothing him: "Stunt-men . . . strangers in a strange land."

I pulled off the road at the first deserted spot, sank to my knees, and threw up all over some wildflowers. *Rhonda had it almost right. But I'm not going down one of these days. I already went down.*

The warm western sun presided over a shiny sea as I pulled up the short driveway to my Malibu bungalow. I let the motor idle for a moment before turning it off, not wanting to hear the lonely crackle of the cooling exhaust system or the single cardinal singing to itself, as if it didn't matter that I was alone again.

I reluctantly entered the house, quickly stripped, and threw on my old Speedo shorts, a holey T-shirt, and my Etonic something-or-other running shoes. I had to get out and take a run. Didn't want to. Had to . . . breathe . . . sweat.

Sometimes when I run I forget where I am, even *who* I am, and become a jungle man in a loincloth and bare feet—a vertical streak of blood and muscle racing through tall grass and wet trees, with monkeys oo-ooing and a slinking panther catching my scent and salivating.

My mind is clear and still in that jungle, and I can spot the black beast before it lunges, and dodge it or, worst case, catch its eye and get one laugh in before it sinks its long white teeth into my neck. I dodge for a living, and I already know what dying is like. I knew the second the roof caved in on my life, the second I let go of the sill. The last time I died I didn't get to laugh. So getting the laugh in now, that's important.

I did the 4.2-mile loop through the Malibu hills, stretched out in the driveway till I stopped sweating, then went in and showered. I cooked some scallops in ginger and fresh chives, opened a bottle of wine, poured a glass, and moved into the living room carrying my dinner.

Beethoven's "Pastoral" played softly in the background. My eyes glanced across the room, past the rows of art books that lined my bookshelves, to the dents in the recently laid carpet where a heavy Morris chair had been. I tried not to look at the empty space, but free will had all but eluded me since Emily left three weeks earlier, taking her chair with her. I didn't ask her to leave, but we both knew our relationship was destined to fail. I came home from a shoot and found her packing her bags, dividing up the few things we'd bought together. Emily's dents weren't the first. At that moment I'd sworn, yet again, that they would be the last.

She'd said she wasn't mad at me, she was mad at herself—being a therapist—forever thinking she could nest in a tumbleweed. I didn't stop her from reciting the litany of my sins, though I'd heard them all before: risk-taking bordering on self-destruction, unresolved issues of pain and loss, fear of intimacy, inability to commit. Handing me the spare house key at the front door, she told me that I ought to look into my dreams, then closed with what she referred to as my "obsession with Ginevra de' Benci."

I apologized to Emily and meant it. I knew I wasn't right for her—or for anybody. She patted my cheek tenderly, saying she took full responsibility for her own mistakes. I listened carefully to the sound of her shoes on the slate pathway, then to her car door opening and closing and the engine revving once and fading as she pulled away. Then I heard nothing but the cardinal's song, to my ears forever the sad sound of being someone's mistake.

I stepped over to the carpet dents and sat down cross-legged on the floor between them, cushioned by new Orlon and old grief. Tears pooled in my eyes. My gaze shifted to my framed print of Leonardo's portrait of Ginevra de' Benci—my dear friend Ginny—the only girl I'd ever been able to hold on to.

"Ginny . . ." I said. "Help me." I squeezed my eyes shut, massaging my throbbing temples as tears trailed down around my nostrils and over my lip. Their saltiness saddened me even more. I began drifting back to before time had stalled, and landed in the National Gallery in Washington, D.C., where my dad had been the curator of Renaissance Art, and I'd strolled with my parents through the oak-paneled Widener Rembrandt Room.

In front of the luxurious paneling hung incredible treasures, each painting a burst of emotion, capturing forever the innermost feelings of the subject, rescuing all but the painter himself from the dust of time and forgotten bones. There among *The Lady with the Ostrich Feather Fan*, *The Philosopher*, *The Girl with the Broom*, and the portrait of his beloved wife, Saskia, sat Rembrandt himself.

We'd stand there, my folks and I, three feet from the great master's face—his doughy, wrinkled, sadder-than-the-weepiest-willow face—and my dad would point a long finger at different parts of the dense painting and tell us Rembrandt was fifty-nine at the time he'd painted it, Saskia had died, and he'd lost favor with the upper-crust, gone bankrupt, and was desperate. "But look at his hat," Dad would say. "How delicate and soft it is, how the black isn't just black, it's fabric."

My mom would grab my hand, as she always did when we stood in front of the self-portrait, and a sorrowful wind would sweep through us from three hundred years ago. Mom and I couldn't move our eyes away from Rembrandt's; we both knew we were staring into the old man's soul.

I raised my wineglass. "To pain and loss . . . and ruination," I said to Rembrandt and myself, taking a gulp. "And to you." I nodded to Ginevra de' Benci, remembering the many times I'd slipped away from my parents, my Beatle boots tick-tocking past all the tourists packed in like clumps of lobster roe, to see my Ginny.

Her portrait, the only one of Leonardo da Vinci's paintings in the United States, had been the greatest acquisition of my father's tenure as curator. He'd purchased her from the prince of Liechtenstein for five million dollars, at that time the largest sum ever paid for a work of art. To Dad she was very special. To me, she was more than special; she had captivated my inquisitive heart long before I could touch the gilded, glassed-in frame that protected her from humanity's grasp. And when I finally could reach her, Ginny became my sole confidante.

She listened patiently to my secret Christmas wish lists, never provoking the least nip of conscience. She was waiting to greet me the first day I soloed in on the bus, after third grade let out. And she was there every day after that when I came to meet my dad. Ginny and I hung out while he finished work, the two of us owning the whole place. We were a spectacle.

Leonardo painted Ginevra's portrait in 1474 or so, when she was already twenty-six years old. My father told me that she called herself a mountain tiger, though Leonardo's painting made her look as soft and sad as the last petal on a solitary rose.

I wondered what she must have talked about with him out there by the juniper tree. Leonardo had probably painted her hands—hands maybe even more beautiful than Mona Lisa's—and it made me furious to think that someone had wantonly sawed off the bottom seven inches of the oil-on-wood painting. No one had the right to commit an injustice to Ginny—or to Leonardo. Nobody.

My scallops cooled. I pronged one, but laid my fork down, no longer hungry. I slugged the rest of the wine and a little dribbled down my chin and onto my shirt. The telephone rang. Setting my plate and glass down, I answered it.

A raspy voice whispered, "Rollo Eberhart Barnett?"

My first thought was Publisher's Clearing House—a man with laryngitis.

"Is this the son of Dr. Rollo Barnett who was the curator at the National Gallery?"

"Yes . . ."

There was a harsh cough and some throat-clearing. "I knew your father."

"Who is this?"

"I have some things to tell you. Important things."

"What are you talking about?"

"There's a ticket waiting for you at the American Airlines counter at LAX."

"A ticket? Look, you'd better just tell me what this is all about."

"It's about the fire," he said.

Bitter-tasting bile rose in my throat. My mother's screams echoed through two decades.

"What about the fire?" I managed.

"At the counter," the voice rasped, "under Rollo Barnett. Open ticket, but you'd better come first thing tomorrow." The line went dead.

I stood for a moment with the receiver to my ear, looking blankly out at the backyard, confused and frightened.

A squirrel scampered up a tree by my deck. My eyes followed it. *Squirrel, tree, darkness, stars. Where's the moon? There it is.* I peered at it till I saw the familiar face. The air filling my lungs couldn't cool the embers in my mind. I realized I still held the phone to my ear and slammed it down.

I got the number for American Airlines and made the call. A sales representative named Kayla told me I had an open-ended, round-trip, first-class L.A.-to-Denver ticket waiting for me.

"Does it say who purchased it?" I asked.

"A Mr. Harvey Grant," she answered.

"Harvey Grant," I mumbled. "Who the hell's Harvey Grant?"

"Sir?"

"Sorry. I was talking to myself."

"Would you like to make a reservation?"

I finger-combed my hair; an uneasy tingle spread down my neck and shoulders.

"Sir?"

"Um, I'm just not that gung-ho a flyer is all."

"Actually, me neither. Can I help you with a reservation?"

"Well, Kayla," I answered slowly, "I guess you can. What's the earliest flight tomorrow?"

At eight-fifty the next morning, my car was parked in the short-term lot and I was in the terminal, with a ticket tucked in the back pocket of my jeans and an American Airlines envelope clasped in my hand.

I stood against the wall next to a nut stand with a red-and-white-striped awning and opened the envelope. My hand was shaking a little—early heights? Inside there was no note, just two faxes: directions to a Denver address and a photocopied article from the previous day's *Denver Post*. The article read:

> **Venice, Italy** In what is being called an extraordinary tragedy, Fausto Arrezione, the owner of an antiquarian bookstore, was killed today in a fire that destroyed his shop and all of its contents, apparently including a priceless page of Leonardo da Vinci's notes. Earlier this week Arrezione had placed a call to the Gallerie dell'Accademia, a venerated museum and art school, to report his discovery of the page that purportedly included a drawing of what Leonardo described as the "Circles of Truth," which he has, in several of his notebooks, referred to as the key to the whereabouts of the legendary Medici Dagger.
>
> Mystery has surrounded the Medici Dagger since 1491 when Lorenzo de' Medici commissioned Leonardo to produce the piece to commemorate the death of Medici's younger brother, Giuliano, fatally wounded by enemies of the Medicis in an attempt to overthrow the family from Florentine power. Leonardo never delivered the Dagger. The legend surrounding it began with the discovery in 1608 of a manuscript called the Codex

Arundel, in which Leonardo wrote the following words next to a drawing of a magnificent dagger:

Through the din of the bustling airport I heard my father's voice speaking Leonardo's words in my head—words I'd memorized at my dad's side, elbow to elbow on the living-room floor, his oxford cotton sleeve touching my flannel pajama top.

> "Something has occurred which I cannot explain. While casting the dagger for Il Magnifico I have chanced upon a mixture of metals which once formed became almost as light as the air. Try as I might I could not return it to liquid form nor could I cause it to be deformed or dented in any way. And there is an edge to this blade which is sharper than any man has ever seen. The world is little prepared to receive a material that could be transformed into indestructible weapons of death. No good purpose could come of it. War is bestial madness. But I see beyond us to a glorious future with science the benevolent ruler, when man, unencumbered by ill intent, could utilize this extraordinary discovery for the noblest of purposes. So I will hold the dagger for that man of the future. And the Circles of Truth shall lead him to it."

"The Circles of Truth," I repeated aloud. The man from Vinci, who'd bought caged birds only to set them free, had discovered an indestructible alloy and felt a responsibility to keep it a secret for a man of the future. He'd hidden the Medici Dagger somewhere, almost five hundred years earlier, and had left the secret to its whereabouts in some sort of cryptic message he called the "Circles of Truth."

I glanced at the remaining paragraph of the article, although I'd already guessed its content.

In 1980, another page, found in Amboise, France, thought to contain the "Circles of Truth," was tragically destroyed when the private plane transporting it to the National Gallery of Art in Washington, D.C., crashed into the Atlantic Ocean, killing the courier who was piloting the plane, traveling alone. Since that incident, all hope of recovering the legendary Dagger had been lost until this recent find, which experts say might have included a duplicate of the "Circles." A spokesperson from the Gallerie dell'Accademia maintained that while the notes had been viewed by one staff person, a photocopy had not been made. Apparently the notes were lost in the blaze.

I fingered the envelope. There was nothing else in it but air. I folded the directions and the article, tucked them into my jeans pocket, and bought a small bag of roasted cashews. The bag was red and white, like the awning. I drifted over to a deserted gate, took a seat, and popped a few of the salty nuts in my mouth, grinding them into paste till my jaw hurt.

Leonardo. My dad. The Circles of Truth. The Medici Dagger. Who was Harvey Grant?

three

Three hours and fifty minutes later I parked my rented Mustang convertible under the portico of a beautiful, turn-of-the-century gabled mansion in a quiet neighborhood near Cherry Creek Lake. A carved and painted wood sign read: THE WILLOWS ~ A PEACEFUL PLACE.

Three wide brick steps led to a huge porch with maybe a dozen flowering plants in glazed ceramic pots, standing like sentries. I rang the bell next to the double oak doors. Moments later a middle-aged woman with a freckled face and half-glasses perched on her pointy nose appeared. She wore a white nurse's uniform and rubber-soled shoes. Over her left breast was an ID tag that said PEGGY.

"Hi," she said. "Can I help you?"

"Hi, Peggy. I'm looking for . . . I don't know, a patient?"

"We don't think of people as patients here," she said politely. "This is a hospice. Mister . . . ?"

"Reb Barnett," I said.

"People come here to finish their lives in a tranquil atmosphere, Mr. Barnett."

"I'm looking for Harvey Grant. Is he here?"

"Mr. Grant. Yes. He's here."

"Who is he?" I asked. "What do you know about him?"

Peggy covered her nose and mouth, and sneezed. She asked if I'd excuse her for a second. Before I could answer she stepped around a desk and returned holding a Kleenex to her nose. "Allergies. Happens to me every year."

I stepped into the foyer and closed the door behind me. It was a large, cheery room that must have looked more austere at the turn of the century, when rich men in dark coats and derbies crossed its threshold. I repeated my question about Harvey Grant.

Peggy dabbed at her nose. "I'm not allowed to discuss our guests," she said. "Sorry. It's against policy. I'll take you to his room."

I accompanied Peggy up a wide wood staircase with lush gray carpet and an ornately carved baluster. At the end of a long hall, she stopped in front of a room with a partially opened door, knocked, and walked in. Her white nurse shoes squeaked on the wood floor until she hit the Oriental carpet. The shoes looked brand-new. I stepped in behind her.

The curtains were drawn, the room dimly lit. Fresh-cut flowers stood carelessly in a vase on a table next to an old man lying in a brass double bed in the corner.

He was mostly bald save for a few scattered tufts of silver hair; pallid skin covered the fragile bones of his face and shoulders like the membrane of a bat's wing. His eyes were closed and still. I thought he was dead until his rib cage moved and a wheeze issued from his open mouth.

"Mr. Grant?" Peggy said, lightly touching the man's shoulder. "Harvey?" The dying man's eyelids lifted like garage doors on rusty hinges, and he looked at her with a milky gaze. She said, "Your visitor is here."

Harvey Grant slowly turned his head till his eyes met mine. "Please go now, miss," he rasped.

She withdrew without looking at me, but I was grateful for the faint scent of her perfume. I moved closer to the man.

"I'm Henry Greer," he said. "The courier."

I shook my head as if a bug had flown in my ear, then swallowed hard. My throat was dry and there wasn't enough air in the room.

"You remember," he said.

"But . . . your plane crashed. You were . . ."

Greer drew a deep breath, summoning energy. Then he raised a hairless arm from under the covers and laid it on his chest. A thick scar sliced diagonally across his forearm. He pointed a long-nailed finger toward a chair. "Please sit down. I have some things to tell you."

I reached behind me, felt for the chair, and sat. Greer scanned me for almost a full minute.

I began to fidget. "I'm waiting."

"Have you ever heard the name Werner Krell?"

"German billionaire. Munitions manufacturer."

"Nolo Tecci?"

"No. You're supposed to be dead, Greer. I was there when my father got the call from the Coast Guard."

"Tecci worked for Krell," Greer said. "Still does."

I pulled the curtain back a little. A foot-wide band of sunlight cut across the bed. Greer squinted. His skin looked almost powdery in the light. I let go of the drape and it swished back in place.

"The day your father sent me to collect the Leonardo notes from France, Tecci approached me," Greer said. "Krell wanted those notes, was obsessed with them. Had been for years. Was convinced that the Dagger was out there, just like your old man. Tecci offered me a great deal of money for the notes. *Serious* money. It was my shot, kid. I took it and staged the crash."

"You staged the crash?" My mind flashed back to my dad on the phone getting the news. It was the first time I'd ever seen him cry. The last time, too.

"I met up with them on a train," Greer continued, licking his parched lips. "Krell had his own Pullman at the back. I was standing on the platform waiting for him to come out, but he didn't. Instead, Nolo Tecci was there. Black hair, cut like Caesar's. Tattoo of a cobra wrapped around his neck. He had the briefcase with the money. We were crossing a bridge—a high bridge in the Alps—through the St. Roddard

Pass. I was nervous. It didn't feel right. And it wasn't. Tecci pulled a knife and that was it; I knew I'd had it. I spit in his face and grabbed the briefcase."

Greer lifted his arm an inch and dropped it. "He slashed me, right through the artery," he said. "I kicked him, got a leg up on the railing, and jumped. Two hundred feet to the river. Crushed my legs."

I observed what must have been a twisted mess under the blanket as the man restocked his decrepit lungs.

"I'd spent two years in a prison camp in Nam," Greer said. "Knew how to survive. Got away down the river. They never found me. You were right, kid, when you said I was supposed to be dead. I stayed dead."

Greer coughed, a sound like coal spilling down a chute. Almost a minute passed before he caught his breath.

"So I'm here for the confession before you die?" I said, barely containing my rage. "Or did you just get the urge to cheer me up? You bastard."

Greer half-smiled. "Do you believe in destiny, Reb?"

"I'm here because you said you knew about the fire. What about it?"

"I believe in destiny," he pushed on. "I've been keeping track of you for a long time. I was glad that widow college professor adopted you after your parents died. Mrs. Tucker, right? Martha Belle Tucker. She must have raised you right."

"Yeah?" I seethed. "Why's that?"

"You haven't strangled me yet."

"The fire, Greer . . ."

Greer's smile vanished.

"I think Nolo Tecci came for your father and set fire to your house."

Instantly, time cracked and I was sailing toward the ground through the smoke-filled air. I squeezed my eyes shut trying to focus, to stitch it back together. Voices pecked at me—whispering voices from rooms in neighbors' houses. *Arson? Do you think? I don't know. Remote possibility, I suppose. That's crazy. These old houses, they go up like tinder. Besides, who in the world would want to harm the Barnetts? That's absurd. Shh. Quiet. We don't want the boy to hear us.*

I opened my eyes and breathed in through my nostrils, anger and disgust swirling in my belly.

"Why?" I demanded. "Why would he do that?"

"Just in case I'd survived," Greer said. "Gotten the notes to your old man somehow—double-crossed Krell. Your father didn't have the notes, but Krell and Tecci didn't know that. Tecci had to check. He probably tortured your old man before killing him and then burned your house down for fun. I saw the look in his eyes when he was about to kill me. I think he would have enjoyed it."

I stared at the pathetic, rotted out, worm-eaten log of a human being. "And the notes?" I asked slowly.

Greer sighed. "You didn't answer me when I asked you if you believe in destiny."

"You're playing me. Nobody plays me," I said, rising out of my seat.

"Mmm," he said. "No one's immune from that."

I headed for the door. "So long," I spat. "I'm out of here."

"No, you're not," Greer shouted after me. "This is your game now, Rollo Eberhart Barnett, Jr. Your parents' killer is still out there. You find the bookseller's notes, you'll find Tecci."

I stopped in my tracks.

Greer stared me down.

"But the notes were destroyed."

"There is no way they burned," Greer said, shaking his head. "No way. And whatever the bookseller in Venice found, they weren't the original notes. Maybe da Vinci made a duplicate. Maybe it's a second part of—"

"Leonardo," I warned. "His name was Leonardo. Don't call him da Vinci. It's not respectful."

"Mmm, just like your old man. That's even better."

My toes involuntarily curled in my boots; my palms began to sweat.

"Nolo Tecci killed the Italian," Greer continued. "Burned him down for his notes. Just as he did your father."

Something inside snapped and I sprang for the old man. I stood over him clenching and unclenching my fists, anger knocking the lid off the kettle. I drilled a look into his waxy eyes, my breath ruffling a wisp of his thin silver hair.

Greer arched his neck as if he wanted me to strangle him. After a minute he lay back and whispered, "Like I said, you were raised right. Your old man wanted that Dagger, but my greed got in the way. I'm not greedy anymore. Now what are you going to do?"

"I'm going to call the police," I said, picking up the phone next to his bed, pointing the receiver at him. "And you're going to tell them what you just told me."

Greer shook his head. "No."

I slammed the phone down. The little bell inside resounded in the dim room.

"For one, Krell is too powerful for the police," Greer rasped. "For two, you don't want police."

"Don't tell me what I—"

"The museum curator's kid gets a degree in Art History and what does he do? Becomes a stuntman—a high flyer with no net. No, you don't want to be a citizen," Greer said. "You want risk. You want action. Maybe now you even want payback. This is *your* quest, kid, don't you see it? You can find the Medici Dagger. Avenge your parents' deaths. This is your fate."

I closed my eyes and began to tremble. Bubbling rage awoke my demons and they began to dance on my soul, a furious, thundering dance of wrath that shook the dank walls of the cave where I'd lain in a death sleep since the fiery night in 1980. The howling heat of a thousand suns suddenly switching on, blazing through a stunned universe, lighting the word: *Fate!*

I pictured the pointy tip of Leonardo's dagger hurtling through history toward me. I felt crazy. Giddiness overtook me and for a

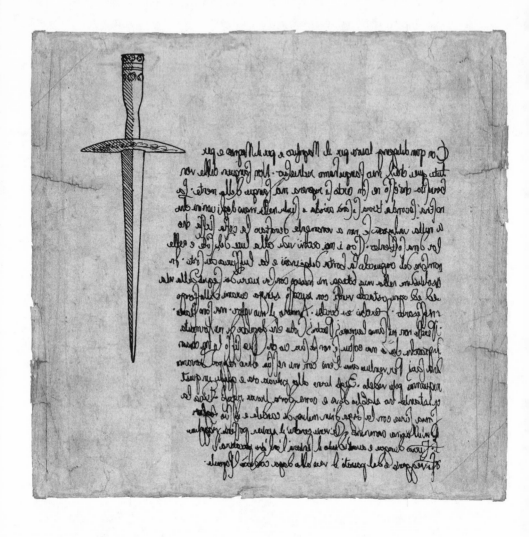

second I almost laughed out loud at the absurdity of the moment, the profundity of it. Coming from Henry Greer! The dead courier who wasn't really dead.

He was right. I wanted revenge.

I opened my eyes.

"What happened to the original notes?"

Greer turned his head to the side. At that moment I caught sight of

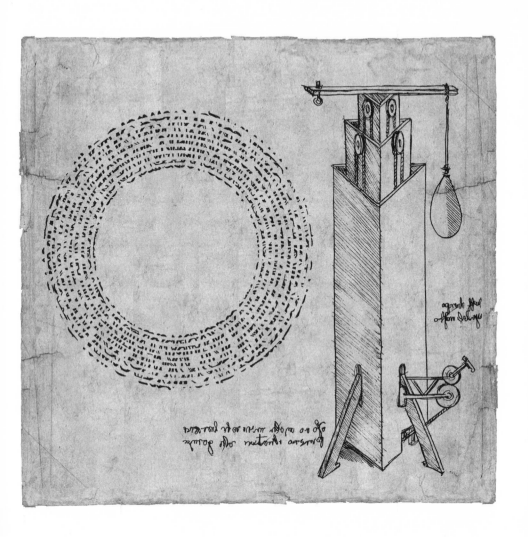

a corner of yellowed paper barely sticking out from under the edge of the pillow.

"Take it," Greer said, lifting his head with what little strength he possessed.

I gently removed the paper from under the pillow and drew a deep breath.

I was holding Leonardo da Vinci's notes.

Turning the fragile document over and back, I held it up to the light. To one side was a drawing of a sleek dagger and a paragraph next to it, written in Leonardo's precise backward handwriting. And on the reverse, a circular design that resembled a delicately drawn bull's-eye composed of ten individual rings in decreasing size, each ring made up of seemingly haphazard tiny marks. The Circles of Truth? Next to that, another drawing, this one of three triangular-shaped tubes nested together like a closed sailor's telescope interconnected with pulleys and supported by a leg on each side.

I pressed my fingertips to the dried ink—ink that had flowed from the quill of Leonardo's pen. The pen that had been grasped by the hand that gave the world *The Virgin of the Rocks, Mona Lisa*—that had given me Ginevra de' Benci.

I pried my eyes from the page, looked at Greer. "Why didn't you try to solve it? Why didn't you go after it?"

Greer surveyed the blanket that covered his ravaged body.

"You could have told *somebody* somewhere down the line," I said.

"I just did," Greer whispered, closing his eyes.

"Greer," I said, moving my face close to his. "Greer!"

The dying man opened his eyes; I could see a map of crisscrossing red capillaries.

"If it's true," I said slowly, "if this is all true . . . then you and Tecci are the ones who killed us."

Greer coughed a visceral, painful cough. "Resurrect yourself," he rasped.

I drove back to the airport with the radio off, one hand on the wheel, the other clutching Leonardo's notes. On the flight home, I studied the page, thoughts tearing at me like a thousand vultures. Greed. Fire. Endless questions. *My parents murdered? Werner Krell? A man named Nolo Tecci had been in my house? Burned down my life? For this? This is what we died for?* I remembered my dad's jubilation the day he'd sent

Henry Greer for the notes, certain that they'd lead to the Medici Dagger. Our conversations about the glorious things that could be done with the Dagger's alloy—indestructible bridges, automobiles lighter than air. And then his dreams reduced to smoldering ash in the wink of an eye—Nolo Tecci's eye.

It was ten o'clock when I arrived home. A suitcase-sized package with no return address sat by the front door. I brought it inside, flipped on the lights, and opened it. The night sky was clear, and moonlight mixed with the amber of my mica table lamps. In the box was a beat-up leather satchel, the kind that yawns open at the top. I felt its weight as I hefted it out and laid it on the living-room table.

Inside was a bulky laundry bag cinched together at the top. Loosening the rope, I discovered bound wads of cash—hundred-dollar bills in ten-thousand-dollar stacks. With clammy hands I counted two hundred bundles—two million dollars. I reach for the page of Leonardo's notes. His words, his thoughts, brushed my fingertips.

I called Denver information for The Willows. A woman answered after the second ring. "Hello, The Willows."

"Peggy?" I said.

"Oh . . . yes, this is Peggy."

I identified myself and asked for Harvey Grant. After a pause she said, "I'm sorry. Mr. Grant is . . . no longer with us."

"Ohhh," I said with remorse—not for his death, but at the loss of a resource. My utter disregard for the end of Henry Greer's life registered briefly, but my heart was busy pumping icy vengeance through my veins.

There was an awkward silence as the interstate phone line hummed; then Peggy said, "Reb, take care of yourself. And good luck."

I thanked her, hung up, and wandered back into the living room. A cool breeze swept in through the open window and mixed sweet night air with the foul smell of Werner Krell's money.

I touched Leonardo's notes to my cheek.

"Venice," I said to nobody.

four

Near morning, I dreamt I was playing checkers with Julius Caesar in the middle of the Piazza San Marco. He was wearing a black toga and had a snake around his neck that kept whispering in his ear, telling him what moves to make. And Julius, the son of a bitch, was winning—getting kinged all over the place, stacking checkers up like a bunch of Oreos while the tourists and pigeons watched.

I sat there, red-faced, in the middle of the vast square, trying to grab the snake's tongue when it stuck out and wiggled. Julius was throwing his head back, going "mwa-ha-ha" each time I missed.

It was a rotten dream. I woke up way too early, frustrated and pissed, thinking what the hell was I doing playing checkers.

The morning paper had the same article that had run in the *Denver Post*. I threw it out, fixed my usual breakfast of oatmeal with dried cherries and banana, and ate robotically at the kitchen table.

An hour later I was jogging through the foggy Malibu hills, moist, cool air filling my lungs, clearing my mind. *Breathe in, breathe out. Focus. Don't forget to laugh. At what? Life, death, fire, daggers, revenge, pain . . . searing pain. You've got a purpose. Get Nolo Tecci.*

"Hah!" I yelled as the beams of an oncoming car flashed through the murky whiteness. "Hah!" I yelled again, the sound of the tires dissipating as the car vanished around a bend in the road. Then I stopped thinking and things got still and clear; I finished out the run in the jungle.

After a shower, I called my travel agent, Leah, who had a sexy voice that hardly matched her size-sixteen body. She booked me on a flight that night to Milan—first class—with a jumper to Marco Polo Airport in Mestre, just outside of Venice.

I put on a Credence Clearwater Revival CD and listened, while I packed, to John Fogerty howl about being born on the bayou. A bunch of socks and Jockey underwear, jeans, shaving and tooth stuff, some black T-shirts, running gear, and a dripless candlestick in a small brass holder.

No matter where I am, what hotel, what country, I always light a candle on my way to bed. The softness of the flickering light reminds me of a painting in the National Gallery by Georges de La Tour called *The Repentant Magdalen*—a picture of Mary Magdalen sitting at a desk in a room lit only by a candle.

Leaning on the table, chin resting in one hand, the delicate fingers of the other caressing a barely illuminated skull, Mary stares into a mirror, absorbed in thoughts of mortality and forgiveness. The softness of the light playing on her pensive face and billowing sleeve has entranced me since I was a kid.

Lying in hotel beds that have been dreamed in by countless strangers, I watch my candle flicker and search for comfort in my nightlight. Happy dancing shadows in Reb's sleep-tight light. I can barely remember the sound of my mother's voice.

I closed the suitcase, turned Fogerty off, and called Archie Ferris. Archie owns a specialty gun shop called *Hoo-ah!* that caters to the film industry. He knows how to use every kind of weapon ever made and owns most of them, too.

In addition to running the store, Archie makes a good living as technical advisor on action films, providing weapons as props and showing stuntmen and -women how to look authentic. He's late fifties, five-ten, two-twenty, and stocky as a gorilla, with hairy arms and knuckles to match, and a five-o'clock shadow at eleven A.M.

Archie started out in South Boston. Joined the Army out of high school. Went into Special Forces and made sergeant. Did two tours in Nam. He was a victim of that war, that was obvious to me, though he never took a bullet in hundreds of firefights. He'd come back to a country that spit on his loyalty, almost the worst thing that could happen to any veteran, but particularly Archie. Archie Ferris and loyalty mean the same thing.

After returning to the States, he drifted out to L.A., became a cop, and married the first girl who didn't look sideways at the khaki T-shirt, battle fatigues, and jump boots he always wore. He wouldn't tell me her name. Couldn't say the word. All he'd said was "She was an empty-hearted woman who couldn't love anybody, not even her own son." This while sobbing into an Orange Crush.

The son he was referring to was Danny, who'd been raised mostly in the custody of Archie's ex-wife and a succession of losers.

Archie loved Danny more than anything or anybody, even though the boy had inherited most of his personality from his mother. There was nothing Archie wouldn't give him, even on the policeman's salary he got after leaving the service. Actually, he'd never really left the service; he'd just swapped protecting the people of the United States for the people of L.A. County. He was a born protector, and would have kept at it, but Danny got shot dead in a bar fight. That was when Archie quit the cops, after taking the one bullet he couldn't dodge.

He'd faded into security work on movie sets for a couple of years, his generosity, loyalty, and professionalism masking his depression and earning him nice credentials. At first, people were intimidated by him. His body was like a block of concrete and he had a look in his eyes that told the world he'd stood the watch few could stand.

A star-stalker pulled Archie out of his depression by making it through the rest of security and onto one of his sets—an action set with plenty of guns, all of them loaded with blanks except for Archie's and the stalker's. A foot chase, a screaming celebrity hostage, real gunplay, real heroism—a combat pro showing how it's done.

Everybody got rescued, including Archie. He ended up with a new job: teaching movie stuntmen how to use weapons. He had a new life and some of himself back, but not enough to fill the hole Danny had left in his big heart.

Archie got me started in the business by almost running me down in the street as I munched a vegetable burrito from La Cantina. I'd been thinking about getting into the movies and not getting salsa on my T-shirt when I'd caught him out of the corner of my eye, barreling down Santa Monica Boulevard in his black Land Rover, cell phone pressed to his ear. I was midstreet with the burrito sticking out of my face when I'd realized there was only one way to go to avoid becoming a tortilla myself, and that was up.

Archie had tromped on the brakes two feet from me. I'd jumped and rolled over his hood and down the back of his buggy, hitting the street in a crouch—all without dropping the burrito. Our eyes had met in his side-view mirror—his in horror, watching me chew and grin and pull my earlobe. He'd grinned back.

Over some blue drinks and a pu pu platter at The Golden China, he'd discovered I had a number of useful talents—hang gliding, rock climbing, karate, parachuting, and racing motorcycles—so he introduced me to some stunt directors he knew and that was that. I've been diving, driving, rolling, racing, flipping, and falling ever since.

On top of getting me my start, Archie gave me a Sig Sauer nine-millimeter handgun, taught me how to use it, and helped me get my carry license.

Because I was a fast learner and mastered every weapon Archie put in my hand, he quickly grew to respect me. But I knew it was more than that. We both did.

Archie answered the phone on the first ring. "Arch," I said a little tentatively, knowing he'd have heard about the hang-glider spin and wouldn't let it slide.

He blurted, "You want to kill yourself, you can use the Sig I gave you. That would be perfect. First Danny, then you. Aw, Christ. What's up?"

"You've been such a good friend to me," I said. "I need your help."

"Been a good friend, huh? That doesn't sound like a compliment. Sounds like last words. What is it—Emily? Come on over, we'll drive up to my joint in Big Bear, talk it all out. What do you think, you'll never fall in love again?"

"You know I wasn't in love with her."

"Yeah, yeah. You've never been in love with anyone. Me, too. So?"

"That's not why I called. Look, I'm going to Venice—not the beach, *Italy*—and I . . . um . . . I'll need a gun when I'm there." The second I said it, I wanted to go back in time and not call him.

I filled the painful silence.

"I'm sorry, but I know you've got that buddy from Nam who sells guns. I can't travel internationally with mine and I can't wait for the paperwork to go through."

"And?" he said. "You have my full attention. Don't hold back."

"It has to do with Leonardo da Vinci and my parents. That's all I can say."

"Come on," he said angrily. "This is the real goddamn world. People actually get *killed* with guns."

I knew it. I'd just triggered Danny memories. Archie would be watching a video of *Shane,* crying into a Crush, within ten minutes after we hung up. I hated myself for being so reckless.

"Look," I told him. "Just forget it."

"Forget nothing! Shit! Leonardo da Vinci and your parents . . . what the hell is this all about?"

"Did you get the *Times* this morning?"

He told me he had.

"You read it?"

"The Lakers lost. No, I didn't read it. Christ, cough up."

"Page three. Top."

He told me to hold on. I heard rustling, then mumbling for a minute, then, "Jesus! So what are you going to Venice for? It says the page was lost in the fire."

I told him everything—Greer, Tecci, the Dagger, the works.

There was a long pause.

I said, "So, will you set me up or not?"

"I'll do you one better. I'll come with you."

That stunned me. "You would do that?"

"You sound surprised."

I felt embarrassed, confused. It hadn't occurred to me that Archie, or anyone, might place himself in danger for me. On a film shoot, yeah. For money. But this had nothing to do with that. Loyalty, selflessness—these were precious things that were hard for a shaky hand to hold. I sensed their great value, perhaps for the first time. I wanted to say, "Help me out." But I couldn't knowingly put Archie at risk.

"Arch," I said. "Your offer means more to me than I can tell you, but I've got to do this alone. I need an answer on the gun."

Tension prickled over the line.

"Goddamn you!" he shouted. "You turn me down, then you want me to make up my mind right this second?"

"Yes," I stated flatly. "I'm sorry, but I need to know now."

I heard a deep sigh. "I guess we're both sorry, 'cause I can't do it."

Silence.

"Okay, then," I said. "I shouldn't have called. I apologize for getting you involved. I've got to go."

"Wait. Please don't go."

"Really, I've got a plane to catch."

"I mean don't go at all," Archie pleaded.

"I have to."

"You have a choice."

"No I don't. It's all there is."

The fog had lifted and sunlight created dust corridors where it danced in through the open living-room windows.

I took fifty thousand dollars out of the laundry bag, wrapped it in brown paper, and stuffed it in a red backpack I'd acquired in Boston when I was checking out the Museum of Fine Arts and the Isabella Stewart Gardner Museum.

On top of the money, I packed a leather portfolio containing Leonardo's notes and a handful of Boulder Bars, the one kind of energy bar that didn't taste like window putty. Then I cinched the laundry bag and returned it to the old leather satchel.

I said goodbye to Ginny, stashed my bags in the trunk, and headed for Bank of America in Santa Monica. A red-faced account representative converted five thousand dollars to lire and rented me a family-sized safe deposit box, where I stashed the satchel.

I got back in the Jag and turned the key. The throaty purr made my spine shimmy as I headed for the airport.

Somewhere over the Rockies my hands steadied enough to use the air-phone. I called Lois van Alstine, a redhead with green eyes and long legs who could have written *Who's Who* by herself. Lois had used her schmoozing skills to develop a lucrative public-relations business representing some of the biggest names in Hollywood.

We'd spent one night together a couple of years earlier—amusing until she'd dug her long nails into my back. I told her to stop and she did, but the fun was over. There were no hard feelings.

Lois answered her phone after the third ring. "Bobby, I'm in the tub. I'll be there in an hour."

"Lois," I said, "it's Reb."

"Spitfire! How are you? Tom's heartbroken. Says you like your towels more than him."

"It's true."

"Oh. So what do you want? I'm guessing not a date."

I told her I was looking for information on Werner Krell and Nolo Tecci.

"Krell, I know of, of course. Never heard of Tecci. Don't tell me," she said, "Krell wants to film you falling off his money."

I said nothing.

"All right, wait a minute. I'll check my database, see what comes up. Where are you? In a wind tunnel?"

I told her I was en route to Venice.

"You're kidding. What, is Krell on the plane? No, can't be. He's got his own jet."

"This call's costing a hundred dollars a minute, Lois."

"Uh-huh," she said. "Okay, let's see . . . I'm looking for Tecci. Is that T-E-T-C-H-Y?"

"Two c's and an i, I think. Try it both ways."

"I don't think so. Nope, nothing comes up. Give me a second on Krell. He'll come up. Here he is. Werner Krell. He's a baldy, you know. A Yul Brynner. Not bad-looking. Born in Berlin, 1935, only child. Papa was a weapons manufacturer, too. Came up with a revolutionary design—the Gewehr 41W—first semi-automatic rifle to go into wide use in the Second World War. Oh, and he was a Leonardo da Vinci fanatic."

"What?" I said.

"I said Papa Krell was a da Vinci fanatic. He had a museum-quality collection of models of Leonardo's weapons and tanks, catapults and things. Was showing them at the Gemäldegallerie right before the war. Got a picture of him here, little Werner in knickers next to him. Oooh, Mother was killed during an Allied bomb raid when Werner was eight. Rumor is, that whacked him and his old man out. Both of them real eccentric, to put it kindly."

I thought of the model that my dad and I had built when *I* was eight of an extraordinary bridge Leonardo had designed for Sultan Bajazet II to cross the Golden Horn in Istanbul.

Lois continued, "Uh . . . let's see . . . little Krell kept pushing. When he was twenty, he graduated magna cum laude from the Berlin Poly-technic Institute with a degree in mechanical engineering, and began designing weapons himself for Papa's company. By that time, he had taken over for his old man. Thought up the first submachine wrap-around bolt system. Made huge shekels when that gun became the rage. Bottom line, he's a billionaire with controlling interests or sole ownership of arms and munitions manufacturing companies in Germany, Austria, Belgium, Italy, Chile, and Mexico. Apparently sells to both sides. And he's ruthless," Lois added. "Whenever he wants something, like somebody else's company, he gets it. Quirky as hell and getting quirkier as time goes on."

"Is there anything else?" I asked her.

"When he's not in his jet, he travels in his own Pullman car on the back of whatever train he wants. Orient Express–type thing. Fabulous. Got a picture of it right here. Must have cost millions. Really Art Deco. Elegant . . . deck I guess you'd call it—on the back. Brass railing. Remember Dumbo? At the end he was out on the deck of his own Pullman?"

I didn't answer; I was picturing Henry Greer hopping the rail, plummeting into the St. Roddard Pass. I glimpsed a fragment of memory. I'd been through that pass myself, maybe ten years before, when I'd hitched a ride from Switzerland to Italy with a pasty-faced guy in a VW bus.

Lois said, "So . . . you're awfully quiet for a hundred bucks a minute."

"Sorry," I said. "I guess I was lost."

"And now you're found?"

"I don't know," I replied. "Thanks."

"Hey, Spitfire . . . before you go . . ."

"Yeah?"

"I'm, uh, tamer now. Maybe when you get back . . ."

A second's hesitation on my part and she knew.

"Well then," she finished. "I guess I'm entitled to hang up first."

Before I could answer, she did.

I replaced the phone in its cradle. . . . *Werner Krell and his father.*

Me and mine. Leonardo. There had been five men. There were two left. Under different circumstances, would Krell and I have drained an ale in honor of our dead fathers and Leonardo's genius? Would we have wept together for our missing mothers, whose forgotten voices would never comfort us?

And if we'd met on a battlefield in the middle of the century, who would have pulled the trigger first?

It was dark and raining when my plane fell out of the sky onto the tarmac at Malpensa Airport in Milan. An hour later I was up in the ether again, eastbound for Venice on a miniature version of the aircraft I had just deplaned.

I steadied my nerves on the short flight to Marco Polo Airport by thinking about those carved Russian dolls that open up one inside the other until at the center is a tiny doll that looks like something from a Barbie tea set. I pictured myself on a plane that opened to reveal smaller and smaller planes, me shrinking and boarding until, at last, I climbed into a plane the size of a mallard, which headed skyward and got into formation with a flock of other ducks. Damn, I'd been in the air too long.

Soon, my luggage and I were on the ground and in a private taxi cruising through choppy water into the Grand Canal. It had rained and the air felt thick and electric.

Leah had booked me into the Gritti Palace—a regal hotel that overlooked the grand canal and was a home of the doge, in the sixteenth century, Venice's most powerful official.

The door to my room was ajar, the bellhop just setting out a basket of fruit. The high-ceilinged suite was large and replete with antiques, a huge Oriental rug, and an ornate chandelier. I was pleasantly surprised, having stayed in hotels that boasted opulent lobbies but were otherwise ordinary. Leah had done well.

I slipped the bellhop some money and he backed out graciously.

After a shower I unpacked, lit my candle, and climbed into bed.

My mother and father would have loved Venice. We could have stayed right here. I would have dug my bare toes into the soft couch cushions, peered up at the patterns on the high ceiling, and listened as my dad delighted me and Mom with stories of the proud and the poor who had crossed these canals and streets, their splendid canvases tucked under their paint-stained arms.

My elegant room suddenly felt empty and the night too vast.

A piece of chocolate in the shape of a dove, wrapped in orange and white aluminum foil, sat on the oversized feather pillow next to me. I picked it up and sniffed: Grand Marnier.

I lay on my side flying the dove back and forth in the flickering light, aching for my stolen past, longing for daylight and a chance to lay a knee on evil's chest. Nolo Tecci. Werner Krell.

The candle's flame softened the chocolate bird.

Ahh, vengeance.

The next morning, I followed my only lead. At nine on the dot, I was standing in the marble-tiled reception area on the third floor of the Gallerie dell'Accademia, facing a sixty-year-old secretary with voluminous dark brown hair and thick eyebrows. Her excellent English accompanied a restrained professional demeanor that belied a tension which could not be concealed.

Though my pulse was pounding, I plowed ahead, smiling at her like I was hands-down the nicest guy she was going to meet that day. I explained that I'd come from California to speak to the person to whom Signore Arrezione, the bookseller, might have shown the page of Leonardo's notes.

"Are you a reporter?" she asked, her face taut.

"No," I answered. "I'm not."

She eyed me warily, her big brows almost touching.

I opened my jacket. "See? No recorder, no paper, no pencil. I'm not a reporter. I'm not even a good speller."

I detected a momentary thaw in her countenance.

"Are you with an official organization?" she asked. "The police?"

"Actually, I'm a stuntman."

She looked puzzled. "In the movies?"

"Bad spellers don't have many options," I said, smiling. She thawed a little more.

The secretary glanced behind her at a man's figure, still as a store dummy, curtained by a smoked-glass door. When her eyes met mine again I knew I'd lost my advantage. "I cannot help you," she said.

I leaned in a little closer. "Signorina Rossi—"

"Signora," she corrected, glancing nervously over her shoulder again at the figure behind the door, then back at me.

I had to get through to her.

"Signore Arrezione showed the notes to someone here. I'd just like to know his name, maybe have a word with him."

The ghost behind the door turned the knob.

"No, sir, there is no one here who has seen the notes. I'm sorry. Please go."

Anger and frustration began to surface. I forced myself to hide it. I knew she wanted to tell me, she was just frightened. I had to stay cool, find out why.

The glass door opened and a large, balding, grim-faced man wearing a brown suit and tan bow tie stepped out. He looked to be in his mid-sixties. Signora Rossi spun around in her seat. "Professore Corta." She bowed her head deferentially.

I sized him up. Edgy came to mind. Unlikely to be forthcoming came to mind.

"Signore," he said to me in a surprisingly high voice. "What is your business here? We have made our statements to the press and the *polizia*."

47

"I like your tie, Signore," I said. "I've got one just like it, only mine's more butterscotch than tan. I prefer yours."

"Thank you," he said, his face a little flush. "Now you will excuse me? I am late for a meeting."

He dismissed me with a glance and blasted some Italian at Signora Rossi. Then he brushed past me and left through the door I'd come in.

Signora Rossi nervously straightened her blotter and pen.

"I can see how concerned you are, Signora. I haven't come here to cause you more worry."

I offered her the Denver newspaper article and gave her a minute to read it.

"My name is Reb Barnett, Signora Rossi. My father was the museum curator at the National Gallery in Washington. He and my mother died in a fire that destroyed our house immediately after he tried to acquire the last 'Circles of Truth' notes."

That got her attention.

"You can look it up on the Internet," I continued. "*Washington Post*. July 23, 1980. His name was Dr. Rollo Eberhart Barnett."

"You could have looked it up also," she said, scribbling the name and date on her blotter.

I pulled out my passport and pointed to my name. "I didn't have to look it up. I was there."

We were both silent for a moment while she regarded the passport, then me again.

"What is it that's causing you so much worry?" I asked.

Her lips quivered. She put her hand to her mouth. I understood the feeling of having your foundation shaken and felt compassion for her. I waited, willing her to confide in me.

After a moment she said, "You are the second person who has been here asking to see . . . asking these things. And that is *after* the police and reporters."

I asked her who the other one was. She said she didn't know.

"What did he look like?"

Signora Rossi leaned forward and covered her face with her hands as if she were going to catch a sneeze. She peeped through her fingers. When I sat down on the corner of her desk, she didn't object.

"Whatever you share with me," I said, "I promise I won't tell the professore. I mean no harm at all. In fact, I'll help if I can. Look at my face. You'll know I'm telling the truth."

She lowered her hands, scrutinizing me thoroughly, introspectively, relying on a half-century of living to tell her whether I was the cup with the poison.

"All right," she said tentatively. "He was scary."

"In what way?"

"Every way. The way he dressed, the sound of his voice . . ."

"Was he American?"

"He spoke Italian, but not so good, and with an accent. American, maybe. He had the darkest eyes. His hair was brushed forward on the sides, like Caesar. And his hands," she continued. "I remember his fingers were long and delicate like a surgeon's, and his fingernails were—I don't know how you say it—polished, that's the word. Yes, they had clear polish on them."

My stomach muscles tightened. Nolo Tecci was real.

"Anything else?" I asked, pointing to the side of my neck.

"*Si, si,*" Signora Rossi confessed animatedly. "He had a . . . how do you say . . . *tatuaggio* . . . on the side of his neck. The head of a snake." I felt a tingling flush, heard my pulse in my ears.

Jesus. Tecci's still here, after the bookseller's fire. Did he have the notes or did they burn in the blaze?

"What'd you tell him?" I asked her as calmly as I could.

"Nothing," she whispered. "He spoke with Professore Corta in his office. Corta's been anxious ever since. Warned me not to speak with anyone regarding the notes. Has been trying to reach . . ."

"Who? The person who saw the notes? Did Professore Corta see them?"

"No. He never saw the notes. Only . . ."

"Who?" I prompted a little too strongly. She covered her quivering lips.

"You know where I can find him?"

She nodded almost imperceptibly. "Her. She is my friend. She is nervous since the fire. She feels in great danger and has ... uh ... taken a leave."

"Is she at her house? Or apartment?"

"No."

"But you can get a message to her?"

Frustrating silence.

"Signora Rossi, you said your friend thinks she's in danger? Believe me, if the man with the snake tattoo is here, your friend *is* in danger. Grave danger. Tell her I must talk with her. I'm staying at the Gritti Palace. Have her call me at noon. That's twelve—"

"I know what *noon* means," she blurted, her eyes narrowing, boring into me for any sign of deceit.

A moment passed.

"Noon," I repeated.

She nodded.

"Thank you, Signora Rossi." I offered her my hand.

"Francesca," she corrected, taking it.

As I turned to leave, a man ran right into me. He let out a loud "oof" and fell backward, dropping his newspaper and losing his hat.

"Oh, jeez, I'm sorry," I said, helping him up. "*Spiace.*"

He grabbed my lapels as I pulled him to his feet. He was short, maybe five-eight, and wore an expensive raincoat over a rail-thin body. As we both reached for his paper and hat, we clunked heads and I caught a whiff of Old Spice. He grunted as he picked up the paper, puffing out his sunken cheeks. His hat was a Borsalino, gray like his coat. He snatched it from my hand, scowling.

"Grazie," he said brusquely, and walked off, folding his paper.

Out on the street again, I pressed the side of my head where it hurt. A little punishment for being clumsy, out of my element. But I'd succeeded in getting Signora Rossi to confide in me. I was closer.

I looked down at my Beatle boots. The soles had touched the same floor Nolo Tecci had tread on. I felt the heat of anger spread through my feet, up my calves, thighs, and chest, into my throat and out to my fingertips. I'd never felt this way before. *I could snap. I could kill. Who the hell am I?*

I squinted up at the sky. "Is there more than bone and gristle, God?" I whispered. *Breathe, Reb.*

I walked back to the hotel scraping my shoes on the cobblestone streets, urging myself into an easier groove.

five

Soft yellow fingers of sun massaged my face and neck through the open window of my room as I sat waiting at an intricately carved desk, daydreaming, steeping in time. I wondered if some doge, in a robe and leather sandals, had looked out this very window the day Leonardo composed the words and drew the mysterious circles on the page I had in my possession.

Maybe the doge sat in this very spot, digesting pheasant and pasta, some fruit. Perhaps he was writing something himself, a poem about an apostle or the curve of a slice of crenshaw melon, a quill pen in his steady hand, ink stains on his noble fingers.

I looked at my own fingers. They hadn't written much poetry. Instead, they'd hung on to airplane wings and motorcycle grips, steering wheels, window ledges, rock walls, and elevator cables. Punched calculator keys, doing the physics of falls and crashes. Signed contracts and checks, even the odd autograph. *Decent fingers,* I thought, holding them up to the light. *An occasional tremor, but overall reliable.*

There was a knock at the door. I peeped through the brass fisheye: the maid—about four and a half feet tall, middle-aged, closely cropped salt-and-pepper hair, white gloves, light blue uniform. I let her in. She slid past me, eyes down, and hastily dusted the furniture with a real feather duster. I moved out of her way and stood at the window.

The splashing sun and aquatic activity drew me back to my daydreams, where I rummaged amid the spare parts of thought and fancy, unable to overturn anything resembling real cognition. The click of the door as the maid left brought me back from that intangible place.

I remained at the large window for a while, contemplating why Francesca's friend from the Accademia would be hiding out, when my phone rang.

A throaty voice, a little deeper than the average female's, spoke into the receiver: "Francesca Rossi gave me this number. With whom am I speaking?"

"My name is Reb," I answered.

"What do you want, Reb?" She spoke perfect English without an accent. It threw me.

"World peace . . . and a pony," I replied.

"I'm not laughing."

"Why don't you have an accent?" I asked. "I thought you were Italian."

"I'm going to hang up in three seconds if you don't tell me what you want."

"I thought maybe you could help—"

"*You* want help? Who's going to help *me?*"

"What do you need?" I heard the maid's hamper squeaking down the hall. A thousand dollars a day and they had squeaky hampers.

Silence. I was getting nowhere. "Okay," I offered. "I'll help you."

"How?"

"I know who's trying to find the Medici Dagger."

A gasp and then a whispered "Who?"

"Look," I said, "could we meet somewhere?"

I heard squeaking wheels again, closer. There was a knock at my door.

"How do you say 'wait' . . . in Italian?" I asked.

"*Aspettare.*"

I put the phone to my chest and shouted at the door, "*Aspettare, per favore. Um, cinquecento minuti.*"

The maid hesitated before saying, "*Si, signore,*" then squeaked away.

"I'm sorry," I said. "The maid was at the door."

"You told her to wait five hundred minutes."

"I did? I meant fifteen." We were both quiet for a few seconds while I figured out how to recover. Finally I said, "Do you think she'll do it?"

I heard a mini-chuckle over the phone.

"I may not be able to help you," I said. "But at least I'm not scared." That wasn't true, but she didn't know it. "Will you meet me somewhere? I promise nothing bad will happen. Are you hungry? I could buy you some lunch. How about . . . what's the name of that place on Torcello Island. That inn?"

"You mean Locanda Cipriani?"

"That's the place. A ferry takes you there from—"

"In front of the Hotel Danieli, I know," she said. I could feel her on the edge of commitment and didn't dare say a word. "All right," she said firmly. "I'll meet you there in fifteen minutes. That's not five hundred."

She hung up.

I combed my hair, brushed my teeth, threw on my jacket, grabbed my red backpack, and headed out.

It was a short walk to the Danieli, a huge place that looked like a cake that had won a bake-off for the most intricate icing. All of Venice looked that way to me, as though a giant pastry chef had gone wild with a frosting bag. Spires and arches and bridges, double- and triple-deckers with cutouts and dollops and swirls. I could picture the chef in his baker's whites leaning over his creation, eyes twinkling, squeezing the last of the icing out of the big cloth bag, then bellowing, *"Mia bella Venezia!"*

I took my post across the street from the Danieli, wishing I'd found out what my mysterious informer looked like, figuring that Francesca must have told her what she knew about me. I played a little game, trying to pick her out. Using the Sherlock Holmes method, I checked out the females in the crowd. Holmes just kept ruling things out until he arrived at a conclusion, and then, if there was only one thing left, it had to be right—no matter how improbable. I had used this method countless times to find missing socks.

The teenage girl with the platform shoes? The tour guide with the red umbrella? The fiftyish lady in the elegant suit? Maybe. One of those two girls striding arm in arm? No way. How about bushy brows, like Francesca? I kept looking.

Then someone tapped on my shoulder. She was a slight woman, maybe thirty, in a long print skirt, light-blue jacket, and dark sunglasses, with a scarf nearly covering her straight, shoulder-length black hair. She had high cheekbones, a thin nose, and a wide mouth with full red lips. The hair on the back of my neck stood up.

"Reb?" she asked, fingering the strap on her huge shoulder bag.

I swallowed hard and stuck out my hand.

She gave it a rigid shake. Her small hand was cold from fear. I wondered what had motivated this frightened woman to come out in broad daylight to have lunch with a stranger.

I asked her name.

"Antonia." Her voice had a smoky quality, like a young Lauren Bacall.

"Thank you for coming, Antonia," I said, attempting to see her eyes through her dark glasses. "If you want to stand here and talk for a while . . . if that would make you more comfortable . . ."

"I'm in danger," she whispered. "Serious danger."

"I believe you," I said, forcing myself to maintain eye contact, rather than check around for anyone who might be a threat. It was imperative to demonstrate that my real concern was for her safety. It was, but I was worried about me, too. And I needed to know what she knew.

"I want to know why you're in danger," I said. "So I can help you if I can. I'm not out to hurt you. Maybe you'd feel safer here than on a boat."

I could sense her stare though I couldn't see her eyes. She turned on her heel and started walking quickly across the street. "Let's go."

I noticed her running shoes as I caught up to her. Together we walked briskly to the boat dock. She looked nervously over her shoulder a couple of times.

After exchanging a few words in Italian with a uniformed hotel employee, Antonia said, "The boat for the restaurant left at noon. We can either take the ferry or get a private water taxi. A taxi is much more expensive."

"Taxi," I told the guy, handing him some money. One was just making its way in.

Antonia made a deal with the driver, a stocky man with a big nose and a cigarette hanging off his lower lip. We boarded and found seats at the back in the open air as we headed out into the lagoon.

"So . . . Antonia," I said over the rumble of the motor. "Would you take your sunglasses off? I can't see your eyes."

She stared at me. Though masked by her shades, the penetration was palpable.

I looked away, scanned the other boats. Taxi, taxi, taxi, ferry. Black and silver yacht maybe three hundred yards off to the right.

"Well . . . are you hungry?" I asked her, trying to break ground. "I'm starving."

"Who *are* you?" she asked, still staring. The disarming intensity of her presence cracked me wide open.

"I . . . I'm nobody." The words burst from the marrow of my being. I was stunned.

"Do you always ooze melancholy?" she asked matter-of-factly.

"What are you talking about, melancholy?" I recoiled. "You don't know me from the driver."

"Uh-huh," she said to herself. "All right, so tell me. What do you do?"

The yacht was closer now, maybe two hundred yards. Sharp-looking boat.

"I'm . . . a Hollywood stuntman. Please don't give me grief about that."

"What an odd thing to say."

"What?"

"You have no sense of value in what you do."

"I didn't say that. In fact I may be the best in the whole damn business."

"Oh great . . . an enigma. In Beatle boots, no less."

The wind picked up. Antonia cinched her scarf down, slid away from me.

"Enigma. I'm not the one hiding out under the scarf and shades," I said.

I needed to get what I could out of this girl and get the hell away from her. She was a pain in the ass. She hooked a finger over the bridge of her glasses and pulled them down a half inch. I still couldn't quite see her eyes, but she looked mad. Good, but mad.

"So," I said. "When Fausto Arrezione discovered Leonardo's notes, he called you at the Gallerie."

She pushed her glasses back with one finger. "That's right."

"But he died in the fire, which I think we can safely say at this point was not an accident. It had to do with Leonardo's notes and somebody who wanted them very badly."

The wind whipped up. We were accelerating.

"Tell me who," she insisted. "Wait . . . why are we heading into the gulf?" She pointed to the left. "Torcello's over there."

The boat picked up more speed. I glanced at our driver. He was looking off the starboard bow, a walkie-talkie to his mouth. I followed the direction of his gaze. The black and silver yacht. It was pointed at us a hundred yards away and our boat was heading right for it. I squinted. Three men in dark clothes and sunglasses on the deck. A guy in an Aloha shirt at the wheel. Someone next to him with a handheld radio to his ear, looking through binoculars in our direction.

I stood up. Antonia looked up at me, terrified. "What's happening?"

I made for the cabin.

"Reb!" she shouted after me.

"Get down on the deck now!" I ordered her. The yacht was fifty yards away.

"Oh my God!" she gasped. "What are you going to do?"

"Just get down!"

She hit the deck as I stepped into the cabin behind the driver. He spotted me and threw an elbow at my face. I caught it on my forearm, but he quickly launched a side-kick at my stomach. I saw it coming and stepped around it, laying a good straight-arm punch into his ribs. He groaned and dropped the walkie-talkie. It skittered across the floor, sputtering Italian.

I grabbed the wheel and started to spin it left. The driver swung a backhand at my nose and I caught it on the side of my face. My head rang for a second. He hit the boat's kill button, yanked a gun out from under his shirt. I grabbed his wrist with my left hand, slamming my right elbow into his mid-back. He yelped and arched forward, dropping the gun. I kneed him in the face and heard his big nose break before he collapsed in a heap.

The huge yacht was now fifteen yards away, dwarfing us. The man with the binoculars held them casually against his chest and I could clearly make out his Caesar haircut. It was Nolo Tecci, under the same sky as me, smiling like a coyote with a paw on a groundhog.

I fumbled for the start button.

Antonia screamed. Two men on the yacht moved to the bow railing. I caught the gleam of a handgun.

"Get in here now!" I shouted. The driver groaned and turned his head toward me, his face streaked with blood. I kicked him as hard as I could from two feet away.

Antonia burst into the cabin and hit the floor facedown as if diving for home plate. She held up her hand, covered with Big Nose's blood, and screamed again.

I found the black start knob and jabbed it; the motor roared to life. Turning the wheel left, I pushed full-throttle as the first bullets shattered the glass at the back of the cabin.

"Find his gun," I barked.

Antonia looked around frantically. "Where? I don't see it."

"Look *under* him." The big boat followed, its bow lifting out of the water like a shark about to take a seal. *No way we're gonna outrun them. Think. Smaller boat, sharper turns. Maneuver.*

Antonia reached around Big Nose but she couldn't budge him. "He's too heavy! I can't—"

"Take the wheel," I shouted.

She sprang to her feet and grabbed the wheel just as two more shots ricocheted off the roof. Instinctively, I put my hand on her head and pushed her down low. I hit the floor, pushed Big Nose over, and found his gun. A Beretta Tomcat, seven-shot. I lurched for the back door, grabbing the jamb. I took a wide stance, aimed at one of the guys on the bow, and squeezed off three rounds. He grabbed his chest and went over backward.

Our right window splintered. Antonia screamed and swerved the boat, covering her face with her arm.

"Are you hit?" I shouted.

"No, I don't think so!"

I spotted a ferry three hundred yards off to the left. "Head for the ferry!" I yelled.

More shots chipped wood off the stern. I crouched, squinted, and squeezed off two more rounds at another shooter on the bow. His leg burst red and he grabbed it, lost his balance, and fell overboard.

Antonia screamed, "Reb! What do I do?"

"Give me a minute. I'm thinking!"

"We haven't got a minute!"

Three more shots splintered the doorframe. I tore open a closet. A dented old gas can. I grabbed it, gave it a shake. More than half full. I spotted a screwdriver and quickly poked a dozen holes in the top of the can.

"What are you doing?" Antonia shouted.

"Give me your scarf," I ordered, spinning the cap off.

"Why?"

59

"Just do it!"

Shots tore through the cabin, exploding the windshield. Warm liq-uid splashed the side of my face and Antonia screamed again. I felt my cheek. Wet, but no pain. I checked out Big Nose. His neck was spurting like a burst garden hose.

Antonia glanced my way and saw the blood. "Oh my God!"

"It's not me." I pointed at Big Nose. "It's him."

Over Antonia's shoulder, I could see we were closing on the ferry; its horn honked loudly. A crowd of tourists pointed at us.

I stuffed most of the scarf into the gas can. I reached into Big Nose's pocket and found his lighter.

Antonia was at the wheel, crouching low, the wind whipping her straight dark hair. "What now?" she shouted.

"Go around the front of the ferry, close to it. Cut hard and come up behind the stern of the yacht, full speed."

"But they're shooting at us!"

"Full speed!"

"All right! Don't yell at me!"

We were bearing down on the ferry and I could see people waving and screaming.

"Cut around it now!"

I staggered my way onto the back deck, Beretta in one hand, gas can in the other. The third man stood at the bow in a shaky firing stance with what looked like a submachine gun tucked into his armpit. He was taking aim. I raised the pistol and fired the last two shells at his midsection. He fell back out of sight. I dropped the gun.

Antonia gunned the motor and arced around the ferry, our boat throwing off heavy spray. The yacht slowed and started to follow, but there was no way for it to compete with Antonia's tight turn. Just like that we were completing the circle, heading for the black boat's low stern.

Out of the corner of my eye I caught Nolo Tecci rushing toward the back of the big boat, one hand going inside his black leather sport coat.

I lit the scarf, swung the gas can around like a discus, and let go. It sailed up and over the gleaming rail of the yacht, the scarf in flames, and crashed onto the deck, exploding with a gigantic whoosh.

Antonia straightened our boat and headed full throttle for the open sea.

When we were about five miles from anywhere, she cut the engine and stepped back onto the deck. We stood there looking at each other, bobbing in the Gulf of Venice, awash in blood, sweat, and adrenaline.

"You promised nothing bad would happen, you son of a . . ." She balled a small fist and punched me right in the stomach. It caught me totally off-guard and half-knocked the wind out of me.

"Jeez, why'd you do that?" I groaned. "I saved you."

"Saved me? If you hadn't taken me out here I wouldn't have needed saving, you big jerk. Did that occur to you?" She rubbed her knuckles. "My hand hurts. What do you have, rocks in your stomach?"

"I guess I deserved that." I slumped back on the seat, massaging my gut. "I did save you, though," I huffed.

She placed her hand on my shoulder. "Well . . . maybe I shouldn't have hit you. Are you all right?" She removed her shades.

I looked at her face, framed by the shot-up boat and pale blue sky. Almond eyes. Just a little eyeliner and mascara that had streamed down her lovely high cheekbones like black rain.

From the cabin, the walkie-talkie crackled and squawked: "You still there?" There was a pause and then: "Hey, you still there?"

Antonia looked up with panic. We both scanned the horizon. Not another boat in sight.

I stepped into the cabin, trying not to tread in Big Nose's blood. It wasn't easy. I spotted the radio, picked it up, and stepped back out on the deck. "Hey," it squawked again, "Flame Boy."

The voice on the walkie-talkie was the last voice my father had ever heard. Those vocal cords had vibrated in my house as I lay upstairs in bed. I wanted to cut them out, hang them on a chain around my neck. I was hotter than the center of the fucking sun. *Get still. Now.* A deep breath, then I slipped into the thick, damp jungle.

I pressed the talk button. "Well . . . Nolo Tecci."

"Who? I don't know anybody by that name. Who are you?"

"One of your goons accidentally nailed your man here," I said.

"I have no idea what you're talking about, but if someone's injured on your boat, we'll come right over and pick him up. Procure him some restorative remedies. Where are you?"

"You mean you can't see us?" I said. "Must be all the smoke on your boat. We're right off your bow."

"Hey," he said, "I only wanted to chat with your lady friend."

"You're going to have to learn some manners first. The carabinieri will help you."

"Don't get too invested in them, Flame Boy."

"Then I guess I'll have to teach you myself," I said through clenched teeth. "So long, Nolo."

"For now," he said. I clicked the radio off. A sensation of relief flooded me. I understood it. I had asked Satan to dance.

Antonia was sitting on the backseat, her hands over her mouth, eyes wide and blank. I sat next to her.

She said softly, "That's the guy? Nolo Tecci?"

"Not just him. He works for Werner Krell," I said.

"The German with all the money? He's had a long affiliation with Professore Corta."

"Tell me."

"Corta knows Krell, brokers art for him, and did for his father before him. Both of them sought out Leonardo artifacts, especially the Circles of Truth and the Medici Dagger, which, of course, haven't been found."

"Of course."

"Krell will pay any price for Leonardo pieces. Corta brokers to him for a fat fee. The competition for Leonardo artifacts is brutal."

"I know that."

"Do you also know that Krell's father, and Krell, lost more than one piece to the National Gallery?"

I studied Antonia's eyes as the implication of that statement sank in. Werner Krell and my father had known of each other, had been adversaries.

I suddenly felt the need to defend my father. "He was an honest man. A good man. My father wasn't Werner Krell."

"I didn't say he was. I'm not making any assumptions about your father."

We watched a lone sea gull swoop down near the boat and quickly flap away.

"I wonder if my father and Krell ever met," I said. "Maybe not. Maybe Krell just sent Tecci to meet him. To exterminate the competition."

This had happened when my only dream was to be Luke Skywalker as I waved my Toys "R" Us lightsaber at a three-dollar poster. Now, here I was, six feet from a dead man; Fausto Arrezione, the bookseller, was also dead; and others had died, some of them at my hands.

Antonia's face had turned ashen. She grabbed her stomach. "Oh, God, I'm going to throw up."

She got to her knees and vomited off the back of the boat, then wiped her mouth on her sleeve. "God, they were trying to kill me! They're *going* to kill me." She turned her face to me, her hair wet with sweat. Pushing it back with a finger, she tucked it behind her delicate ear.

"No," I said, "they would have been glad to kill me, I think, but not you. You heard Tecci. He thinks you know something. Now tell me. What is it he thinks you know?"

I heard nothing but lapping waves while she stared at me for what felt like a week. Then she reached for her big leather bag, pulled out a blank manila 9 x 12 envelope, and handed it to me. Between two pieces of heavy cardboard was a cellophane sleeve.

Inside was a yellowed page that looked very much like the one Greer had passed on to me. My face flushed, the sensation rippling across the rest of my skin. The sound of the waves slapping the creak-

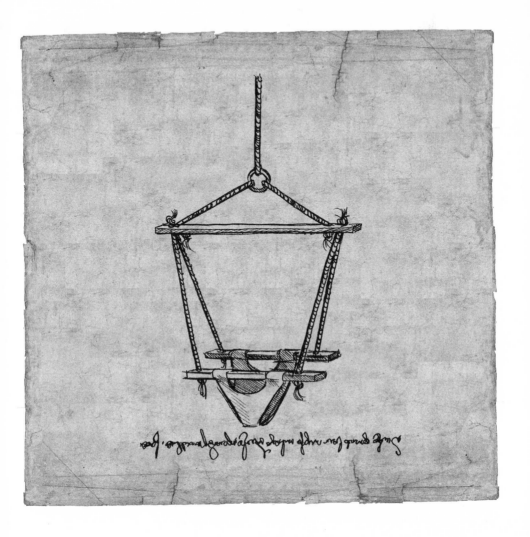

ing boat dissipated until they vanished, leaving Antonia, Leonardo, and me in the yawning breadth of time.

I opened my mouth to speak. My tongue felt dry and I had to clear my throat. "This . . . is . . . the page the bookseller found."

It was definitely different from mine. To one side, a large bull's-eye of tiny marks in concentric rings similar to the one on my page and a drawing of what looked like an astonishingly sophisticated system of pulleys. And on the other side, one line of Leonardo's backward hand-writing and a picture of a harness, like the kind of thing infants bounce up and down in to amuse themselves.

"Fausto Arrezione is my uncle. Was," Antonia confided. "He called me the day he found the page. Leonardo is my specialty. I told Corta about it right away, and we set up a time the next day for Fausto to bring in the notes. It would have been a major acquisition for the Gallerie. I wasn't really thinking much about the Dagger itself. But then something must have spooked Fausto, because he brought the page to me. He seemed unusually nervous and asked me to hold it for him. And later that night . . . oh God . . . Corta must have told . . ." She started to tense up, fear grabbing her, folding her in like a strand of rope. "Corta told Krell and Tecci and they . . . oh God. It *was* murder."

Antonia held her palms together, the tips of her index fingers just brushing her nose. She began to rock back and forth, staring intently at nothing, accepting that her uncle had been killed for the notes she'd been carrying in her bag.

"What am I going to do?" she muttered. "They want these notes and they'll kill me for them."

I wanted to grab her small wrists, feel her throbbing pulse, and tell her, "I've got you." But I didn't; I couldn't.

Instead I extracted the leather portfolio from my red bag and care-fully handed her my own page of Leonardo's notes.

Antonia's eyes went as wide as rainbows. Mouth hanging open, slowly shaking her head from side to side, she removed it from the large Ziploc Bag I had placed it in, turning the page over and back, the way I had with hers. She looked at me quizzically, awestruck.

It was my turn. I told her everything—Greer, Tecci, the Georgetown fire. I held the two pages of notes side by side. We sat silently, compar-ing what we hoped were the Circles of Truth.

"These pages could lead us to the Medici Dagger," I said. "Leonardo wrote that the key to the Dagger was in the Circles of Truth."

"They're definitely not duplicates," she said.

"No. They're obviously different. Two Circles of Truth. We've got them both and Krell and Tecci must have nothing."

"What should we do?" Antonia asked. "Should we go to the police?"

"Are you kidding me? Did Tecci sound scared of the police to you? Krell is connected. Besides, if you wanted to go to the police, why didn't you call them after the fire?"

"I . . . because it's Leonardo and I thought maybe I could . . ."

"Jesus," I said. "You didn't hand over the notes because you were working on them. You were hiding out and scared, but you didn't want to let them go, did you?"

"Well . . . no," she admitted.

I was impressed. I asked her if she'd translated the line on her page.

She nodded. " 'Let he who finds the dagger use it for noble purpose.' "

A shiver traveled through my body.

"He's talking to me," I whispered. "I can't explain it, but I know Leonardo is talking to me."

I could feel Leonardo's strong hand on one shoulder, my father's gentle one on the other. *I'm the "he" who will find the Dagger.*

I took a deep lungful of sea air.

"Well," Antonia said, "what do we do now?"

In my mind I saw a collage of splintered wood, broken glass, the dead driver spreading red, heard Tecci's threatening voice crackling on the walkie-talkie. I took in the sight of Antonia—the sunshine on her raven hair, the eager look on her face.

"Well?" she repeated.

"Simple," I stated flatly. "You translate my page and lend me yours, and I'll be on my way."

"What? What about me, you prick? You brought me out here, got me shot at. You think you're just going to send me home?"

She took her page of notes from my hand. "This stays right with me. And I stay right with you."

"Antonia, you don't understand. I can't . . . do this with you. I . . . don't . . . want you with me."

Every cell in my brain knew that was a lie. I did want her. In that moment it didn't even matter why. But I knew if I lost my focus one or both of us would get killed.

"Don't want me, huh? And you think I want you? Like a horde of locusts, I want you. Listen to me, Mr. Reb Barnett. I came out to meet you and this happened. Now you're *stuck* with me."

She was right.

A shiny fish with an emotionless eye surfaced, then plunked back under the water. For an instant I envied that fish.

Antonia opened her bag to slip Leonardo's page inside. "Hey," she said. "What's this?"

She held up a small, white envelope. On the front were three block letters: REB.

She looked at me suspiciously, her face flushing crimson. "When did you put this in my bag?"

"I didn't touch your bag," I said. "Not once."

"Oh my God. Outside the Danieli, right before I met you. This guy bumped into me, practically gave me whiplash. Then he disappeared into the crowd. What's going on here?"

"Did you get a look at him?"

"He practically knocked me down. Scared me half to death. No, I didn't get a look at him."

"Can I see the envelope?"

She gave it to me.

Inside was a small key labeled "104" that looked like it belonged to a lockbox, and an address written on a card.

"That's near the Gritti Palace," she said. "Do you have any idea who it could have been?"

"No."

"Maybe we shouldn't go."

"We have to."

"It could be a trap. Look, Reb, we have Leonardo's pages. We can leave town. Once we're safe, I can translate them. We can unravel the Circles of Truth."

"Antonia, I have to check this out, alone."

"Forget that! We both go. So . . . now what do we do, drive this damn boat back to the Danieli?"

Looking over at Big Nose I said, "I don't think so."

"Wait," she said. "I've got access to a car."

"Where is it?"

"In Chioggia. It's a fishing village a little south of Lido."

"Great." I stepped over to Big Nose and hefted him by his armpits. "Could you give me a hand?" I asked.

Antonia looked as queasy as I felt.

"I really don't think he needs to go to Chioggia today," I said to her. "Do you?"

six

We tossed Big Nose overboard and washed down the deck with a bucket. It was rotten work. Ten years in a slaughterhouse wouldn't have prepared you for it. I reluctantly threw the Tomcat in after him. Though I preferred to be armed, I couldn't afford to be caught carrying the weapon that had killed Tecci's men.

Antonia navigated us to Chioggia. As we wove our way through the collection of masts and booms, no one even noticed our shot-up boat. Ditching the water taxi at an open slip, we proceeded on foot into the crowded town.

On the way to where Antonia's car was parked, I asked if she'd told anyone where she was meeting me.

"No. No one," Antonia said. "You?"

"No." I thought for a moment. "Corta saw me at the Accademia. He had to have leaned on Francesca, or been eavesdropping from the hall. He must have told Tecci where I was staying."

"*Cazzo, porco Dio,*" she swore, waving her hand with an Italian flourish. "That son of a bitch!"

"No, wait," I said. "That's not enough. Tecci had the yacht in place, and the water taxi. How would he know we were going to take a taxi at the Danieli unless . . . damn . . . the maid."

"What maid? At your hotel? But you asked her to wait five hundred minutes."

I frowned at Antonia, winding my way to reason. "Not that one.

70

The first maid. She came in earlier. She must have bugged my phone. Right in front of me. I'm an idiot."

"You led them right to us!" Antonia shouted, slapping me hard on the shoulder.

I stopped in my tracks and faced her down.

"What's with you? First you punch me in the stomach, then you hit me."

She looked at me and laughed. "I thought you said you were a stuntman, for God's sake! Can't take a little hit?"

"You don't know anything about what I can take, and I suggest you don't make it your business to find out."

"But I have to," she said, a tear collecting in the corner of her eye. "I have to know."

I felt as if I'd eaten a bag of nails. "Let's both take it easy," I said. "We've got a lot to do. All right?"

She nodded.

At the next corner we took a left down a narrow cobblestone street. Each house in Chioggia was a different color, red next to blue next to yellow; they all seemed slightly off-kilter, as if the road had sunk in places. Venice was like that too. I never knew if it was me reacting like a landlubber to the watery feel of the place, or if everything was literally askew. Antonia stopped in front of a garage next to a faded red house and lifted a noisy tin roll-up door. There, in the musty old shed, was a small blue Fiat that must have been twenty years old.

Antonia walked around to the driver's door. "Good. The key's in there." She got in and started it.

"Shouldn't I be driving?" I said. "You could translate the other page."

"Reading in a car makes me sick. Come on."

I stepped around to the passenger side. The Fiat was as roomy as an egg.

Antonia flipped on the windshield wipers and stepped on the washer button. Now each of us could see out through a clear wet patch the width of an open book. She ground the shifter into first, lurched out of the garage, and swerved down the street in Keystone Kops fashion.

"Why do you keep your car out here?" I said over the whine of the engine.

"It's not mine. It was Fausto's."

"Oh . . . your uncle. Could you slow down, please?"

"You didn't mind my driving in the lagoon. Am I making you nervous?"

"Absolutely!"

She pulled over and hopped out. We switched places.

I scrunched in behind the wheel and pushed the seat back, practically into the trunk. The car still felt as if it were made for a Muppet.

We parked where everybody parks when they go to Venice and made our way by ferry into town. No one was overtly watching us. The address on the card was for a small Mail Boxes, Etc.–type shop.

We stopped across the street from the place. I pulled my Leonardo page from the red backpack and passed it to her.

"Why are you giving me this?" she asked, puzzled.

"I said before, you shouldn't be going in there, and I meant it. If I'm not out in five minutes, take off."

Antonia looked astonished. "You're trusting me with this?"

"Yes," I said. "I am. Now put it away."

It hadn't occurred to me that she might run.

"Here," she said, practically forcing the page on me. "Keep it. I'm going in there with you. Don't argue with me."

A half-dozen people were going about their business in the building, sifting through mail, filling out forms. Two old ladies badgered the clerk, a young man with long dark hair.

Box 104 was large enough to hold a good-sized toolbox. The key fit. Inside was a brown, corrugated shipping carton that almost took up the entire space. I slipped my fingers in around it and pulled it out. It was unmarked and weighed at least ten pounds. I gave it a shake.

Antonia just about jumped out of her skin. "Are you *crazy?*" she hissed, clutching my arm. "What if it's a bomb?"

"If it was a bomb, they'd be blowing up Leonardo's notes along with us. Now let go of me."

"No." Antonia looked at me pleadingly, her fingers bunching the fabric of my jacket. "I want to get out of here right now. We can open it at the car."

I glanced at the clerk, who was trying to calm the old ladies. He had three more people waiting impatiently in line. I had intended to press him about the renter of box 104.

We headed out the door and hustled over to the ferry, again watching to see if we were being followed. Though the boat wasn't crowded, Antonia stood right next to me, leaning against the rail and looking around nervously.

"Do you see that man over there?" she whispered. "The one with the windbreaker and black hat pretending to read the newspaper?"

"What about him?"

"He's been looking at me."

I checked him out as we chugged along the canal. He seemed like an ordinary guy reading a paper. I watched the other passengers. Either everyone looked suspicious—or I was just getting Hitchcocky. Out of the corner of my eye I caught the guy with the black hat steal another glimpse at Antonia.

"You see that?" she said. "He just did it again."

I immediately understood the look. "He's checking you out."

"That's it? That's why he's looking at me?"

"Yeah. He digs you."

"Digs me," she snorted. "Nobody says 'digs.' Not since the sixties. Where did you grow up, in a commune?"

"Almost. Berkeley, California."

The ferry docked. As we made our way off, I pushed past the guy with the windbreaker, giving him a little shove with my shoulder. I couldn't help it.

We caught the bus for the short ride to the parking lot. My pulse began to race as we approached the car. The second we got there, I tore open the package.

"Guns?" Antonia gasped.

"Guns," I repeated, feeling excitement mixed with confusion.

There were two Sig Sauer P-229s, my gun of choice, and a Miami Classic woven double shoulder holster with extra ammunition. Beneath them was a purple, velvet-covered case and a brown box. I opened the case first. It held an extremely small handgun. It was light, but substantial—super-modern-looking, mostly handle. I checked out the barrel.

"What *is* that?" Antonia asked.

"The tiniest bore I've ever seen," I told her, astonished. "Looks like it shoots mini BBs."

I opened the box. On top was a three-inch-long piece of rubber cut from a motorcycle inner tube. Under the tube was a word-processed note. Antonia grabbed it and read:

> "You are holding a prototype microchip-driven automatic weapon. The magazine contains two hundred exploding pellets. The gun defaults to single shot. Press the button on the side of the trigger guard once and it will switch to semi. Press it again and it will go to full auto. The rubber forearm band will serve as a holster."

"That's it?" I asked after a second. "Nothing else? No name?"

"Nothing. What do you think?"

My mind was clicking like a card spinning in a bicycle spoke. Then it stopped on the only reasonable explanation: *Archie changed his mind. Called Leah. Found out where I was staying.*

I cursed myself again for raking his coals. I made a mental note never to put Archie in any compromising situation again.

Antonia listened intently as I explained.

I waited for her to say, "That's crazy," or "Your friend must be nuts," but she didn't. She said, "Well, don't just stand there, put them on."

I loaded the guns, slipped the rubber inner tube over my wrist, and snugged the mini into it. I put on the double holster, then my jacket. With my sleeve unbuttoned I could reach right up and draw the weapon. I felt a sense of power and gratitude.

"Now let's get out of here," Antonia said, tossing me the car keys. "I've got some translating to do."

"Where's the best place for two people to be inconspicuous?"

She thought for a moment. "Milan. It's close. It's big. I know my way around. Milan doesn't care. Do you have money? I only have a little."

"We're covered," I said, getting behind the wheel, firing up the old heap. "Point me to Milan."

Antonia directed me to the A4 and we settled in for the three-hour trip. It was a sunny spring day, cool enough to keep the windows closed so we could talk.

"So," I said, my eyes on the horizon. "I told you about me; tell me something about you. You're American."

"What'd you tell me, that you used to live in Berkeley? Not exactly in-depth coverage. But I know plenty about you. You were going to ditch me."

"Well I didn't."

"But you wanted to."

My skin started to crawl. "Can't you start translating now? Oh, I forgot. You get carsick."

"And your glibness is a dodge, a protective device."

"No, *this* is a protective device," I said, opening my jacket to reveal one of the Sigs.

"There you go again," she said. "Being glib."

"Stop trying to analyze me. I'm not a painting. Analyze Leonardo's page, why don't you, so we can find the Medici Dagger."

"I intend to," she huffed. "When we get to Milan."

"And don't pick on me because you're scared. It doesn't help. Fear is . . ." I felt suddenly inarticulate. "Well . . . it's just fear."

"Something you know a lot about," she said to the window. She breathed on it and drew a little dagger through the condensation.

I checked the rearview mirror for Archie or any of Tecci's goons. Neither. I caught a glimpse of myself in the glass. *What the hell did she say, that I ooze melancholy? Brother.*

The motor hummed like a Singer sewing machine.

"So," I said again, "you're an American."

Antonia sighed. "I grew up in New York."

"Where?"

"Staten Island."

"Your parents are Italian? You look Italian."

"My father was. First generation. My mother, second. We spoke Italian at home."

"So, Italian neighborhood on Staten Island. Catholic school, right? Six kids?"

"Two brothers. Four and six years older."

"Close?"

"Not really. I kind of split off from the family."

"How come?"

A commercial van pulled up next to us on the right. I reached for a holster, checked the van. Two workmen. The driver blew Antonia a kiss. She responded with an expressive gesture involving her hand and her chin. He laughed and drove off.

"Italian men . . ." she grumbled. "Where were we?"

"Your family."

"My father was an electrician. Very traditional."

"And your mother?"

"A very bright woman. She went to college. Had big plans, wanted to be Jackie Onassis. They met while he was wiring her dorm or something and she just lost her senses. She's a hopeless romantic. He was too handsome and captivating. So she dropped out and started having children and misery. You know, the man she gave up a future for."

"And where did you fit in?"

"My brothers took after my dad. I was my mother's great hope. The delegated academic with a scholarship to Vassar."

"That's an all-girls school."

"So?" She looked annoyed.

"I thought girls who went to all-girls schools, you know, aren't that into men."

"Hah! Myth. Besides, it was a scholarship, to *Vassar*."

"What'd you study?"

"History, until I came to visit my uncle Fausto. I fell in love with art in Venice. That's when I decided I wanted to be a museum curator."

Just like my father, I thought, smiling at the coincidence.

"So you graduated and moved to Italy?" I asked.

"I went to graduate school here, got my Ph.D. I took a job at the Gallerie, where I've been under the sweaty thumb of Sergio Corta ever since. The man just keeps on not retiring, and instead of letting me do research, he has me giving lectures to visiting graduate students. It's about a half-step away from handing out rental tape players for the museum tour. That imbecile."

"What about men?"

"What are you talking about, 'What about men?' "

"You said 'Italian men'—they're what? Too traditional for you, right?"

"They're very romantic . . . at first."

"I see. After the flowers stop coming, the apron's next."

Antonia didn't answer.

"So what do you do for fun, other than drive boats?"

"Oh, scathing wit. You're centimeters from me, practically a total stranger, and you're engaging in repartee. That's really good."

"Okay. Can I just ask a real question, then? No snappy retort."

She raised her eyebrows.

"What *do* you do for fun?"

She paused a second and said, "I sing occasionally. Don't laugh."

"That's so cool. Like in clubs?"

"One. An out-of-the-way place, where no one from the Gallerie would ever go. On amateur night."

"What kind of music?"

"Anything soulful as long as there aren't too many notes. I don't have much of a range. I wish I did."

"You have a smoky speaking voice."

"Three cigars a day. Going on twenty years now."

"Everybody needs a vice," I smiled. "So, what's the first tune you ever sang in public?"

Antonia said boldly, " 'Like a Virgin.' "

I pictured her cooing that song—a good image of her full lips against a microphone. "Hot number," I said, trying to clear my head.

"Madonna or 'Like a Virgin'?"

"Yeah," I replied.

"It's not the song you sing or the notes you hit, it's how you hit them," she said, absently smoothing out her skirt. "It's soul that counts."

That made me smile. She was looking out the window and didn't notice.

"It's not the same with painting," she continued.

"No. Of course not."

"Painting requires soul *and* skill. Infinite soul, finite skill," she said animatedly. "The two have to mix in just the right balance, which varies widely from artist to artist."

"Definitely. Varies widely. Why are you looking at me that way?"

"Because you're yessing me."

"I am?"

"You're no longer paying attention. I hate that when someone repeats what you say so you won't think they're really ignoring you.

That's so vapid. You don't even know what I mean about soul and skill in painting."

"No?" I said. "I think what you're referring to is most evident in portraits. Let's compare, say, Franz Hals and, um, John Singer Sargent. One splashes color into everything, brings out the nobility in the bar-maid and the beer-swiller in the duke, and the other daintily goes about his business making the rich look richer. Both had amazing skill. Who had more soul? Tragic that old Franz died in the poorhouse, wasn't it? Show me a vapid stuntman, I'll show you a Vassar graduate in a tor-pedo bra."

A quick sideways glance revealed Antonia's surprised look. She began to speak, then sank back in her seat, folded her arms, and stared out the windshield.

"I've spent my life in museums," I said.

"Touché," she said softly. "One car ride, two myths dispelled. God I'm tired."

She weakly waved a hand, signaling me onward.

After three hours, Milan was in sight. Antonia had slept the whole way, mouth open, face wedged in between the headrest and the window.

I had no intention of searching for a hotel without consulting her. As we closed in on the city I gave her a gentle shake. Sitting up, she wiped a little drool from the corner of her mouth with the back of her hand, then turned toward me, lids half open.

"We're here," I said, trying not to breathe on her. My mouth tasted like a gym towel.

Antonia blinked hard. "Where?" she asked, coming to.

"Milan. Remember?"

She squinted in the low afternoon sun and looked out the window, checking the signs. "Oh, yeah. Milan."

"Pick a big hotel. A nice one."

"How nice? Gritti-nice?"

"Sure. As long as they have a bathroom."

She directed me to the Four Seasons, a medieval-looking manor surrounded by ancient walls. It was situated in the shopping district, Via Montenapoleone—the Rodeo Drive of Milan. I parked by the entrance, and extricated myself from the torturous little vehicle. A man in a white uniform and hat opened Antonia's door for her. I tipped him and we headed into the building.

The lobby was not medieval, although impressive frescoes and columns intermingled with shiny new bronze, thick glass, and Murano chandeliers. In my soggy jacket I felt underdressed.

"I attended a day seminar on Leonardo's influence on Raphael here once," Antonia pointed out. "I always wanted to stay at this place."

"Well," I said, stuffing a wad of bills in my front pocket, "maybe today you'll get lucky."

We both did. In spite of having no luggage and looking as if we'd crawled out of a Dumpster—we had, albeit a small, blue one—we were offered adjacent rooms, the price of which Antonia was able to haggle down to just under five hundred dollars per night per room.

I pulled out the cash and gave the clerk what I thought was a pretty convincing line about having had our belongings stolen. He went right for the manager; ID is big in Italy. I repeated the story to him, grumbling about the two whole days we were going to have to suffer through before our new identification would arrive. "Thank God," I told him, waving the thick handful of bills, "we're prepared for anything."

"Except for having no place to stay," Antonia added.

It was a nice touch.

We signed in under assumed names. I was Chet Cook. I always thought Chet was a cool name, and Cook came to me because I was starving. Antonia's nom de plume was Lisa Gherardini, which, she explained to me, was the maiden name of the woman many art historians thought to be the Mona Lisa.

I didn't mention that I knew that.

Asking the Gritti to forward my clothes didn't seem prudent. So, after converting some more dollars to lire at a money exchange and stopping for a pizza, we proceeded to pick up the things we needed at a couple of shops on Via Montenapoleone.

The busy city felt preoccupied with itself, but I couldn't shake the feeling that we were being watched.

"Here," I said, handing Antonia four million lire, about twenty-five hundred dollars, along with a thousand in U.S. currency.

She looked blank-faced at me, then at the money.

"Where'd you get it?"

"Just take it," I said. "When you get low you can have more, no questions asked."

"Just like that? I ask for money, you give it to me?"

"As often as you need it."

She hesitated a second then took the bills, folded them, and stashed them in a change purse. She continued walking.

We stopped at the first men's store we came to, where I purchased a change of underwear and some new running gear. Antonia stayed close by. A few stores down the road, she stopped at a lingerie boutique.

I said I'd wait outside.

She opened the stainless-steel and glass door, pausing. "Hey," she said a little pensively. "Are you sure you don't want to come in?"

"I'll be right here," I answered. "Go in. Panties await."

She shrugged and entered. An eager clerk approached her.

I loitered under an expensive awning, watching Antonia through the window. A few hours ago she was a total stranger to me, someone I couldn't pick out of a crowd. Since then I'd seen her drive a getaway boat with people shooting at her, cry and vomit, and snore in a beat-up car. I was chest-deep in the most profound adventure of my life with the very girl who was browsing through lingerie.

I recognized her now. I'd internalized the way the muscles

bunched when she clenched her narrow jaw, memorized the tiny scar peeking out from the top of her right eyebrow. I had been hit by that girl—hard—and not just in the stomach. And I didn't know what to do about it.

I shifted from foot to foot, hoping she wouldn't spot me spying on her. I saw her pick out a bra and a handful of thong underwear.

I tried not to, but I began to fantasize. Alone in the store, illuminated by soft lamplight, Antonia stood behind the cash register in a lace-trimmed teddy. Her chin was down, her eyes in a lover's gaze as she curled a beckoning finger at me. I locked the heavy door behind me.

She moaned my name as I approached her. The sound of her voice, the sight of her hard nipples behind the thin satin made my breath soft and my erection hard. She uncapped a cherry-red lipstick and slowly applied it, never taking her eyes from mine. Replacing the cover, she sensually ran the stick over each breast and then south and out of sight.

I stepped behind the counter, feeling the heat radiating from her damp desire. I heard the lipstick clink against the floor, felt her hot hands slide up under my shirt, then down to my belt, deftly unbuckling me, hungrily unzipping me, and then . . .

Someone tugged at my sleeve. A short, old Japanese lady stood practically toe to toe with me, breathless with excitement.

"Pahdon me," she said in a heavy accent, thrusting a pen and paper in my face. "You are famous Amelican actor Tom Sroane?"

She might as well have thrown a bucket of ice water at me. "No," I said firmly, backing away from her. "Definitely not."

The woman looked devastated, as though her dream of a lifetime had just been dashed.

As she walked away, I wished I'd given her Tom's autograph.

At least one of us would have been happy.

seven

Back at the Four Seasons, Antonia and I adjourned to our respective rooms, agreeing to meet in an hour to give her some time alone to translate the page. I dropped my things on the bed and tried Archie's phone number, though I didn't expect him to answer. He didn't. *Where is he? What's he thinking? Is he hunting Tecci himself?*

Pulling back the heavy Fortuny curtain, I looked out my window at the dots and dashes of cars and people, then over at the spires atop the Sforza castle, where Leonardo had lived at one time during the Renaissance—the rebirth—before floss and phones and mini machine pistols. Images of Greer and Tecci, Antonia and my father lay before me. Feelings poured on top of them, mixing too quickly for me to identify. The amalgam became a quicksand of thought and emotion into which I began to sink.

I jump out of windows this high. Pinocchio, diving into the whale's belly for adrenaline wages and a chance to become a real boy. Well, today this puppet killed. No blanks, no director shouting "Cut! Great, Reb, let's do it again." In this moment, I feel . . . everything. Fear, hatred, lust. Who am I? I'm still your son, Dad. I'm more than wood and vengeance.

My phone rang, startling me like a fire alarm. It was Antonia telling me I was late. I splashed water on my face, tried to collect myself, sighing into a thick towel. Stepping into the hall, I knocked on her door.

"Antonia, it's Reb."

The door opened a crack, still on the sliding double lock. A vertical strip of Antonia was revealed.

"It's me," I repeated, "your boating buddy." She closed the door, unlatched it, and let me in.

She was barefoot, wearing a man-sized, plush white terry-cloth bathrobe, courtesy of the hotel. Hair pulled back, with a couple of tendrils dangling. She looked like an angel.

Slipping my jacket off, I slung it around the writing-desk chair and plunked down on an overstuffed sofa.

"You, uh, translated?" I asked.

"The first half," she answered. "It's backward, you know. It takes time. We'll get to it. Hey, anyone ever tell you Reb sounds like it's short for rebel?"

"Nobody," I lied. "Could we get to it now?"

As Antonia sat on the edge of the bed, the collar of her bathrobe fell open at the top, exposing the slope of a breast. She let me look for a second before bunching the lapels together. She was working me, and I suddenly felt trapped.

"I ordered up something to eat," she told me. "Be here any minute."

"Please tell me it's a potato knish and a corned-beef sandwich from the Carnegie Deli. Light rye, heavy mustard."

"Fifty-fifth and Seventh Avenue," she laughed. "Bowl of matzo-ball soup . . ."

"Are you kidding me?" I said with mock derision. "You're at the Carnegie Deli and you order broth?"

"With those big matzo balls," she said defensively, showing me the size with her hands. "They're the best!"

"You're saying you'd actually go to the Carnegie Deli and *not* order corned beef?"

"Yeah, that's what I'm saying."

I got to my feet, threw my hands up. "Well . . . then I think I'll leave."

"What? Sit down, buster!"

I made for the door. "Later."

"I said *sit,* you son of a bitch!" she screamed.

I turned. Antonia's lips were tight, her face lobster-red now. Then her composure crumbled and she started to cry. "Goddamn you," she sobbed.

Shocked, confused, and embarrassed, I took a step toward her. She gestured with her hand for me to stop. "Don't you come near me! Don't you threaten to leave me."

"Really, I was just—"

"All your guns and money—a magic fucking dagger!" she shouted. "I just want my life back!" She sobbed into her hands, her small shoulders shaking inside that big robe.

I stepped over to her. She sniffled, wiped her eyes, and grabbed my hand. I felt a spark, suddenly needing to kiss her to put out the fire or fuel it. Letting go, I backed away.

"I don't like this either," I said.

"Bullshit! You should have seen your face when you were talking to that Nolo Tecci on the walkie-talkie. Something was turned loose in you. And when you put on Archie's guns? This is your world, and you . . . dig it!"

I pointed at myself, incredulous. "*I* dig it?"

She wiped her nose on her sleeve, leaving a trail that glistened in the lamplight. "Yes," she stated emphatically. "There's something about this you like, Reb—don't deny it. I'm intuitive. I look at a painting and see every color, every nuance. As if I was standing there when the painter painted it, one stroke at a time, one color at a time. And you, you're—"

"Here it comes . . ."

"Complex, multi-textured, totally abstruse. But the one thing that's clear is you *like* this."

I started to speak but all I could do was just stand there, pointing at myself, with my chin hanging down as if it were too loose a fit for my mouth. Antonia wiped her tears off on her other sleeve, glaring at me with an accusatory smile that said, "See, I'm right."

I shut my mouth and made for the bathroom, more than a little confused. She asked where I was going. I didn't answer, just closed the door. I turned on both gold spigots, put my hands on the edge of the sink, and leaned in toward the spotless mirror. There I was looking back at me, two semi-automatics hanging under my armpits.

But this time the cameras weren't rolling, and the ammunition was real.

I closed my eyes, seeking sanctuary. The sound of the tap water summoned up images of a camping trip I'd taken with my folks in the White Mountains of New Hampshire. It was the Fourth of July, 1976. I was seven and the United States was two hundred. The temperature was half that and the air was as gummy as rubber cement.

We'd carried our packs for what seemed like two years up a steep grade and pitched our dome tent on a flat spot with a long view by a bubbling stream. I was picking my way from rock to rock to cross the creek when I heard what sounded like gunfire off in the distance. I looked up to see where it was coming from, forgetting what day it was and that you've got to pay attention when crossing streams. My boot slipped off a wet, mossy rock, and I sank halfway up my calf in the cold mountain water.

There was something about that scene I'd liked. The icy water enveloping my leg, the slippery rock that got me when I wasn't look-ing, the unavoidable irony of humanity, blasting off fireworks when it was supposed to be quiet. It was nature, all right—unstoppable—totally imperfect in all its perfection.

Opening my eyes, I saw myself in the hotel mirror: imperfect, absolutely unstoppable, probably abstruse.

Antonia had changed back into her clothes, for which I was grateful. The dinner cart had arrived, too. It was laden with fruit, a silver bowl of cold jumbo shrimp that were fanned out side by side, leaning over the lip like tired tourists, a loaf of bread, a chunk of cheese, and a bottle of Chianti.

I poured us each a glass of wine, which Antonia immediately slugged down. She wagged her glass at me, without looking up. I filled it again and she knocked it back. I quietly fixed myself a plate of food. Antonia did the same, avoiding my gaze. She was a professional eater, digging right in with the delicacy of a pit bull.

"You know," I said, trying to get back in her good graces, "I just realized I don't even know your full name."

"Antonia Ginevra Gianelli," she said, a little chunk of cheese shooting out of her mouth onto my knee.

"Excuse me?"

"Antonia Ginevra Gianelli," she said, brushing the cheese off my pants.

My knee felt warm where she'd touched it. "Ginevra?"

"Yeah, Ginevra. You've got a problem with that, too?"

"Ginny?" I repeated, closing my eyes. I was on a fault line over a heartquake.

"What's the *matter* with you?"

Antonia stripped some grapes from a stem, popped a half-dozen in her mouth, and offered me a few. I took them, still avoiding her gaze. "Ginevra de' Benci," I said to the grapes.

"Born in 1475," she recited, "the second child of banker Amerigo de' Benci. Wrote poetry, called herself a 'mountain tiger.' "

"Leonardo's friend," I said. "*My* friend, too." My face flushed.

"What do you mean?" Her eyes were on me, penetrating.

I looked away, slurping my wine. "What does the first half of the page say?"

Antonia pulled two pieces of lined paper from her pocket, and handed them to me.

The first looked like this:

Con gran diligenza lavorai per il Magnifico e per tutti quei che'l mio sangue hanno richiesto. Non sangue delle vene beninteso ch'esso ne son certo si rigenera ma sangue della mente.

La nostra feconda terra si farà arida e sterile nelle mani degli uomini che pare a nulla valgan se non a vanamente devastare la cosa stessa che lor dona sostento. Con i miei occhi vidi alla luce del sole e nell'ombra del crepuscolo la bontà degl'inani e la lussuria dei forti.

In solitudine nella mia bottega mi misurai con la ricerca dei segreti della vita ed ogni ostacolo vinsi con successo senza curarmi dello sforzo necessario. I cerchi e i cerchi. Ammiro il mio valor, ma sono stanco.

On the other piece of paper was her translation, which she read aloud.

"I worked most diligently for il Magnifico and for all those who have demanded my life's blood. Not the blood from my veins for that multiplies I am certain but the blood of my mind.

"Our fruitful earth will unavoidably become dry and sterile at the hands of men who it seems cannot help but wantonly destroy the very thing which gives them succor. I have witnessed in the light of day and dimness of dusk the goodness of the weak and the lust of the mighty.

"Alone in my workshop I have sought to discover the secrets of life and have met with success for every obstacle no matter how great yields to effort. The Circles and the Circles. How clever I am but tired."

No cars beeped in the city below, no hotel toilets flushed. The brilliant passion of Leonardo's heart had been unleashed from the rusty cage of time to a man and a woman, in close proximity, eyes fully engaged.

"The Circles and the Circles," I said. "See, the Circles *and* the Circles, right? He's talking about two sets, One and Two. You agree?"

"Yes. And you intuit from that . . ."

"That Circles of Truth One and Two go together somehow. And that Krell and Tecci have nothing." I picked up both pages, studied the two sets of ten concentric rings. "There must be some kind of pattern here." At the word "pattern" some association poked at a memory that didn't reveal itself. I ignored it. Nothing else jumped out at me save the limitations of my intellect.

"Leonardo was amused by his own genius," Antonia said. "Ponder that for a second."

"He doesn't say anything about the Dagger."

She yawned. "I just couldn't keep going, had to give my eyes a rest."

"Well, can I coax you to do a little more now?"

"Hey," she snapped. "Using a compact mirror to read tiny backward handwriting takes time and a clear head. I haven't exactly had a peaceful day. I'll finish it in the morning, unless, uh, you want to." She faked going for the compact, turned toward me, and smirked. Then she flopped into the desk chair.

"Leonardo sounds depressed," I said.

"Definitely. And 'alone in his workshop' and 'secrets of life' sound to me like he's referring to his anatomy studies."

"What does that tell you?"

"By itself, not much." Antonia studied Leonardo's notes, pointing to the two drawings on the back of her page. "What do you make of these?"

"Well," I said, "this one is a harness—you know, like for rock climbers or bouncing babies. But the other one, this complex hoist, is incredible. I'm sure this didn't exist in Leonardo's time. It couldn't have."

"That's fabulous," she said. "Did you see the picture of his bicycle in *Atlanticus?*"

"The one that Pompeo Leoni pasted on the verso, the back side of the page?"

"Your father taught you well," she said.

"Well, actually I have a degree in Art History, too."

"You do?" She looked surprised.

I didn't respond.

"A stuntman with a degree in Art History? Hmm." She moved from the desk and flopped onto the bed.

"A bicycle," I said emphatically. "Leoni must have seen it, but he didn't know what it was, and nobody else saw it until they took the book apart and turned the page over. If there were nothing else on these pages, we'd have Leonardo's hoisting system. I wonder if it had anything to do with the Dagger?"

"Got me. Leonardo wrote and drew all kinds of things, many objects on the same pages, that had absolutely no relation to each other."

I regarded the translation. "Il Magnifico was Lorenzo de' Medici. At least we've got Medici on the same page as a set of Circles of Truth. Doesn't exactly point us to the Dagger, does it?"

Antonia covered her face with a throw pillow. From under it she mumbled, "First thing tomorrow morning I'll take a quick run and get back to the translation."

"A run first?"

"Yeah. Helps me think."

eight

I took Leonardo's notes and, stopping in my room to grab most of the money and the extra ammunition, went down to the lobby. Renting a box in the hotel vault, I placed everything in it for safe-keeping. I returned to my room with the deposit-box key in my hand and Leonardo's words repeating in my head: "Every obstacle yields to effort."

Leaving the guns on my nightstand and my clothes in a heap on the floor, I climbed into bed.

It occurred to me I hadn't bought a new candle when we'd shopped. No dancing shadows tonight, only the outlines of those in my own frozen heart.

I breathed in slowly through my nose, counting to four, and breathed out through my mouth to a count of eight. Soon my eyelids began to sag. My thoughts became syrupy and dripped into the waiting night.

I dreamt I was an abacus, or a billiards scorekeeping rack, I don't know which. Faceless fifteenth-century soldiers, with dirty fingernails and knee-length tunics of chain mail, kept sliding my alabaster Life Savers over, keeping track of something. It hurt every time, but I had to take it, their grubby mitts, greasy with chicken fat, sliming up my counting stones. I knew I couldn't ever get clean.

I woke up early with my face pressed into my pillow, my cheek and lips wrinkled like the crotch of a linen suit. The gray morning light peeked in around the curtains as the dream replayed in my mind. I rolled onto my back and scratched my head, trying to figure out what the hell it meant.

What would Freud have said, or Emily, my ex? That I was involved in a dirty business. That everyone was counting on me and somehow that hurt. Like Antonia, I wanted my life back. But I couldn't get it back without going forward. Maybe that Dagger was out there. As far as counting on me, well, there was Antonia "Ginny" Gianelli for sure. My parents, or at least my dad, waving his virtuous fist. There was the late great Henry Greer, peering at me with rat eyes from memory's trench. Then there was Leonardo. I was certain the master himself was counting on me. And who was I to say "I'm busy" to Leonardo da Vinci?

And what about Nolo Tecci?

Ah, yes, Tecci. We'll dance.

The phone rang at a little past six-thirty. "Ginny?"

"That's what you plan to call me?"

"Um . . . yes," I said. "Ginny."

"Do I have any choice in that?"

"I don't think so."

"Well, do you want to take a run with me or not?"

"Sure, sure," I said, throwing off the covers. "I'll be ready in a couple of minutes. I'll come knocking for you." I hung up and plodded into the bathroom, brushed the stench out of my mouth, and took a look in the mirror. Whoa, a Tony Roma's onion loaf on my head. I splashed some water on my hair, ran my fingers through it until it was passable, and toweled it dry.

I threw on yesterday's T-shirt and my new running stuff, and did some stretches on the floor. I folded four five-hundred-thousand-lire notes into the top of each sock and doubled them over. Then I slung on the Miami Classic with the Sigs, and tucked the Mini into its holder. With roughly two thousand dollars and a small arsenal, I figured I was ready for a run.

Opening my window, I placed the key to the deposit box out on the granite ledge, and closed the window tight. Unless a tidal wave or a hurricane hit, the key wasn't going to move. It's one of those things about flat metal keys. Mass versus surface area, or something like that. Throwing on my new sweatshirt, I stepped into the hall.

A janitor with a small, pinkish ski-jump nose and a John Travolta chin lingered by the window across the hall, holding a spray bottle and a cloth. I said, *"Buon giorno."* In a series of seamless moves, he took two steps toward me, pointed the spritzer bottle in my face, covered his mouth with the cloth, and sprayed me with a sweet-smelling mist. I blinked once, gave my head half a shake, and disappeared into a velvety black hole. In the distance I heard the janitor reply, *"Buon giorno."*

My eyes were sightless, my mind gooey, stretchy gum. I heard the unmistakable sound of metal being tapped against metal. A coin? A voice followed—that of a cultured Englishman. It said, "I believe Mr. Barnett is just now reentering our atmosphere."

I breathed in deeply through my nostrils, whiffing a hint of Old Spice, feeling my rib cage expand as if on spring-loaded hinges. The English voice called out again, with a musical lilt, "Oh, Mr. Bar-*ne*-ett. We eagerly await your arr-*i*-val."

My nose itched, and I pawed it, but my hand felt like a catcher's mitt.

"That's it," Old Spice said. "Open those eyes, Dorothy. You're back in Kansas."

Someone shook my shoulder and another voice, also English, though younger and more regional, added, "And we want to talk about your ruby slippers." Liverpool? Blackpool? One of the pools. Ringo wants to talk to me about ruby slippers. Slowly, neurons began firing again.

"The janitor," I mumbled, somewhat surprised by the deep, anesthetized sound of my voice. I opened my eyes, seeing only a blur at first.

"That would be me," he said, wiggling his brows once with pride. "That Windex'll get ya." He scrunched up his nose.

"Where's my friend?" I managed.

"Friend!" the janitor snorted.

"That's quite sufficient, Mobright," Old Spice said. I turned toward the source of the voice, surprised to find I wasn't restrained.

Sitting in a wingback chair, one thin leg draped casually over the other, dressed in an immaculate blue, double-breasted suit, was the short, slender man I'd klunked heads with outside of Francesca's office at the Accademia.

The fog in my mind began to lift as I looked him over. He was only about fifty, but had thin silver hair that he'd combed up over the dome of his head from an inch above his left ear, and shellacked. His nose was long and straight, his face gaunt. His eyes were intense and matched the slate gray raincoat and Borsalino hat he'd been wearing when we collided. I speculated that the coat and hat were hanging neatly in a nearby closet.

The man absently tapped a coin against an engraved silver money clip that held a wad of bills.

"The Accademia," I said, my voice still thick.

"Excellent," he replied.

"Where is she?" I demanded.

"In the next room. She's perfectly fine, other than being under anesthesia. So rest easy."

I cleared my throat. "You have good taste in hats."

"I agree," he replied, an amused smile on his lips.

"If not cologne," I added. His smile remained.

The one called Mobright poked me hard in the chest. "Shut it or I'll shut it for you."

I turned to him and did my best to scrunch up my nose like he'd done. He leaned in toward me with a look of menace. Actually, a little more Dennis than menace. The collar of his white shirt was too big for his pencil neck, and although it was buttoned behind his black-and-red-striped tie, there was enough room for me to reach my hand right in and rip out his chest hair, if he had any.

I returned my gaze to the man in the chair, who withdrew a monogrammed hanky from his breast pocket. *AB*, it read. He dabbed his thin lips and tucked it back into his pocket. On his third finger, he wore a gold ring with an emerald in the shape of a parallelogram. "Mobright," he said, "I believe some tea would do nicely."

"Yes, sir," Mobright said with deference. He did the nose thing again and stepped over behind AB.

"Do you take tea, Mr. Barnett?" AB asked delicately.

I wiggled my fingers. They tingled, normal sensation returning. I ran my tongue across my teeth and sat up slowly. "I want to see her now."

"That will be one Earl Grey," AB said to Mobright, shooing him away. "Two sugars." Mobright left the room through a side door.

I regarded the settee I was lying on. Red and tufted, it matched the decor of the room, which could have been the lair of a count.

My captor gently patted his caramelized hair. I stood up, carefully. "I said *now*, Mr. B."

The name caught him off-guard for a second, and he gave me a puzzled look. Then it dawned on him. "Ah, you noticed the handkerchief. Excellent. Identifies me as a thoroughbred, don't you agree? Although my father would take exception, damn his rectilinear, blue-blooded soul. Oh, don't fuss, she's not going anywhere," he said, nodding toward the door Mobright had exited through. "Although I do suspect she'll be coming to before very long. The latest central-nervous-system depressant. Extraordinarily effective. Twelve syllables or so. Don't ask me to pronounce it."

I made my way over to the door and turned the round brass knob. Locked. I listened. Nothing. I turned back to Mr. B, leaning against the wall for support. "Who the hell are you?"

He flicked an undetectable piece of lint from his sharply creased slacks and ignored the question. "If I do say so myself, Reb, you handled yourself quite well out in the Adriatic. I regret that we were unable to be of any assistance. Failed to anticipate your boat ride. I can say with certainty," he continued, "that Mr. Tecci will actively seek retribution for being bested. Deliciously nefarious fellow, that one. Would you like to know his history? I found it quite fascinating."

"Who *are* you?" I repeated.

"Why, an unnamed Englishman, of course," he laughed. "Oxford man. So," he plowed ahead. "Nolo Tecci. Born 1955 in Brooklyn Heights, New York. His father was Bruno Tecci, an executioner for one Nicky Arno until they both met their early demise in a steak house in Queens in 1968. Young Nolo turned juvenile delinquent as soon as he turned juvenile, and at the tender age of twenty was invited to Attica State Prison for five years for assaulting a bartender with an ice pick."

Mobright reentered the room carrying a silver tray with a small teapot, matching sugar bowl with tongs, and a china cup and saucer. He closed the door behind him and set the tray down on a small cherrywood table next to Mr. B, accidentally kicking one of the table legs. "Sorry sir," he said. "Here you are." He eyed me. "Is he giving you any trouble, sir?"

"None, Mobright. Be a good chap and leave us now, would you?"

"Yes," I copied, "be a good chap, Mo-dim."

He glowered at me, then faced his boss. "Yes, sir," he said, turning on his heel.

Mr. B called to him, "Oh, Mobright . . . do check in with Pendelton about our other guest. That methoxy et cetera et cetera should be wearing off presently."

"Yes, sir," Mobright repeated, shooting me one more look before leaving the room.

Mr. B picked up the tongs. "I told him to sugar the tea, did I not? And no spoon, to boot. Ah, well," he sighed, pouring the tea, "bunglers all." He removed a pill organizer from his pocket, opened a compartment, and popped half a dozen multicolored capsules in his mouth. He gulped some tea, knocked them back, and grimaced as he swallowed. He snapped the organizer shut and returned it to his pocket. "There," he said disdainfully. "They don't help, but at least they're expensive."

I peered around the room impatiently, looking for my guns.

Mr. B cleared his throat. "Now, while Tecci was in prison, he was suspected of killing fellow inmates on several occasions. Each of them had his throat cut in the shape of an 'N.' Nolo's signature, not unlike Zorro. Gruesome, but one must express oneself to the fullest, I suppose. The authorities knew he had committed the murders, but none of the inmates were willing to inform on him. Two months after Nolo's release, the pub in which he'd committed the initial assault was set afire, along with the bartender."

Fire.

AB continued. "The only witness met his untimely demise before he could testify. He was found stabbed, the initial 'N' carved in the nape of his neck with a tiny surgeon's laser. Tecci surfaced in Las Vegas, an enforcer for the Carbone family, but his disregard for authority and inability to play by the rules—even mob rules—made him a poor fit. So he moved on."

"Who the hell are you guys?" I interrupted.

"Tut tut, Reb, language," Mr. B chided, waving his ringed hand at me. He pressed on with his lecture. "Nolo Tecci is a sociopath. Devious, remorseless, clever, and very dangerous, as I think you'd agree, although I have it on good authority that he can be quite a charmer when he wants to be. He's been implicated in half a dozen international murders in the last five years, although there has never been enough evidence to convict him."

He returned the teacup and saucer to the silver tray. "Tecci is suspected of being a paid assassin for Werner Krell, an interesting if irksome man of deep pocket and shallow soul of whom you may or may not have heard. Krell shared an interest in Leonardo da Vinci with his father—a striking resemblance to your family situation, albeit with opposing motivations. Art versus power, if you will. Uneven parallel bars. One black, one white."

The effect of the drug had now waned, and was replaced by anger. "What do you know about my family?"

"Not much," B said casually. "But to continue, Krell has spent a lifetime in the munitions business. Recently, however, he shifted his focus to satellite communications. That is, he's building satellites. Through his old KGB connections, he's arranged to have the Russian Space Agency deliver his satellites into orbit."

"So?"

"It's a suspicious move from someone we believe has for some time been designing a new weapons system to use against a few of the more powerful English-speaking countries."

"Why would Krell do that?"

"Oh, certainly profit, but also individual and family history, personal associations, psychological profile, genetics. Mother had a frightful case of borderline personality disorder with paranoid schizophrenic tendencies. Werner was suckled too long at a tattered tit, I would say. Mother died in an Allied bomb raid, and Father, whose fanatic footsteps Werner followed into the munitions industry, died an early, angry death." B paused for a moment, then added, "Effectively, young Werner was orphaned at an impressionable age. Ironic."

I savored my growing anger, locked eyes with him.

B continued, "Werner was misshapen by both design *and* circumstance."

"So you're suggesting Krell's the new Hitler; he wants to rule the world?"

"No, Krell's not Hitler, we don't think he wants to *rule*, although we believe he would certainly take satisfaction in exacting personal

revenge against certain of our friends. Krell has been secretly develop-
ing a prototype laser-guided smart bomb, a number of which could be
hidden within and launched from a satellite. Targeted with impunity
from the ground, the bombs would be impossible to detect due to
their unprecedented small size and extraordinary velocity, making the
system the perfect terrorist weapon. Free-falling from space, these
bombs could whip past any defense, thereby placing the bombee in
great peril. Krell's bombs could rain terror from the sky whenever he
wanted rain, and no one on earth could do anything about it except tip
St. Peter at the gate."

"Go ahead," I said. "Enlighten me as to how this involves me and
my friend."

"Krell's primary munitions customer for the past few years has
been Soon Ta Kee, premier of Taiwan, who has literally built his army
with Krell's products. Tacky—as we fondly call him—was apprised of
Krell's bomb design, became convinced Krell could actually deliver,
and invested considerable assets to support its development.

"Tacky's political conflicts have dramatically increased of late, to
say the least. China wants control of Taiwan back, and because of
China's new PCL system . . . do you know what that is? The Passive
Coherent Location system," B said. "It's an impenetrable air defense
system. It cannot be jammed, unlike radar, and no missiles can be
launched at its beams to destroy its transmitters, because there aren't
any beams or transmitters. This takes away the United States' military
advantage over China. The F-117 and even the futuristic stealth F-22
fighter are no longer invisible to them. Bravo, China.

"You see," he continued, "Tacky feels that, with this sudden disad-
vantage, he can no longer rely on the United States to intervene mili-
tarily in a crisis. Tacky has his back against the wall and he's miffed. So
much so that he has dramatically increased the pressure on Krell to
ready the weapon. Krell—believing he was millimeters away from success—settled on an actual date on which he would provide Kee with
the bombs. Chap made a promise which he cannot possibly keep."

I was sick of this pretentious prick and his outrageous story—if even a shred of it was true. "That's a terrible shame," I said. "I repeat my question."

"Ah, but why can't Krell do it?" B said to the room. "Why can't he possibly come through?" He paused for effect. "I'll tell you why. Because he's completely stymied by the final ingredient—a material in which to house the bombs that would be capable of withstanding the extraordinary heat of high-speed atmospheric friction." B sat back in his chair, smacked his lips.

Suddenly I was transfixed. My captor knew it, winked at me.

"Your eyes just said, 'Aha, the Dagger.' Excellent. Listen to me now. There can be no doubt that Werner's father told him wondrous bed-time stories about the Medici Dagger, as your own father did you. The indestructible alloy, stronger that any other, lighter than air. When Werner attained great wealth, he sought the Dagger as the ultimate trophy, not only his, but his dead papa's as well—the Excalibur for the Knights of Krell's Round Table. Here's where the plot thickens. Intelligence informs us that Kee has vowed to destroy Krell should he not keep his word, and Kee has not one Nolo Tecci, but an army of them—each one caked with zeal—glad to carry out his wishes."

"So what?"

"You casually say 'so what' but your words belie your interest. Here's what," B said, rubbing his palms together. "Werner Krell placed himself in a situation where if he doesn't deliver his bombs he will be assassinated. And he cannot possibly deliver functional bombs. So what happens in his precarious mind? He leaps off the quivering lip of logic into total lunacy and begins to believe that Papa Krell's bedtime stories were not fable, but irrefutable fact. And then presto! Out of a dusty old architectural anthology pops a page of Leonardo's notes—possibly containing the Circles of Truth. Krell was foiled twenty years earlier when the first page of notes went down with the courier. Now he has a second chance and believes not only that the Dagger is out there, but that its alloy will provide his bomb with the necessary indestructible housing that will save his miserable skin."

B clapped his hands together. "If that's not drama," he said, "well then I just don't know what is. Raise a glass for Werner bloody Krell and every last one of us for whom the bookseller's bell tolled."

I felt a bitter chill. "But no one really knows if the Dagger even exists," I said. "Or if the alloy has the qualities Leonardo claimed it had. Maybe the man just discovered aluminum before Reynolds."

"Perhaps," B conceded. "But if it is as Leonardo stated and Werner Krell is able to obtain it, analyze its components, and duplicate it, he'll complete his weapon system and the world will be at his mercy—and of course, that of Soon Ta Kee."

"You think I give a shit about Soon Ta Kee? Or bombs free-falling on this or any other world in the stinking solar system?"

"Apparently not."

"You're damn right."

"How about individual liberty?"

"That's what I'm interested in," I said. "Individual liberty. Mine."

"You do have a rather myopic view considering your genealogy. Your father was a bit more a man of the people."

"What do you know of my father?" I bristled.

"Oh, that he was the curator of one of the world's greatest museums, while you take risks for money. Let me rephrase that. I can certainly appreciate taking risks for money, so I appeal to you on another level. You wouldn't want your films to say 'Made in Taiwan,' would you? No need to reply, but tell me this: Have I not woven a spellbinder? Your baby blues tell me nothing, but inside I believe you're having a little chat." He sat back in his chair, drummed his fingernails on the gold-painted arms.

I wasn't chatting; I was screaming like the signs in Las Vegas. The slot machine in my mind spun helter-skelter, finally stopping on the three familiar words it landed on so very often: *Trust. No. One.*

I stood and stretched. "So . . ." I said, feigning unconcern, "you're quite a perceptive person."

"Oh, I do enjoy praise."

"You want to find the Dagger first, whoever the hell you happen to be."

B pulled out his hanky and polished his ring. "It's my turn for a compliment. You're as perspicacious as you are handsome."

"You want our help," I said.

"Certainly."

"You think we know something?"

"Let's not be coy."

"How much is it worth?" I asked.

"You wish to be compensated?"

"The Medici Dagger. What's it worth?"

"Oh. That depends on to whom it is sold. An art collector would pay a substantial sum. Recall what the Japanese paid for a single Van Gogh? But Kee? What would he pay for a laser-targeted, nondetectable, satellite-launched smart bomb? Think of a large number. So . . . let us have a go at the Circles. We know you've got two pages of notes, two sets of Circles—"

"How'd you know—"

"Bugs. Electronic insects. A tiny microphone on your dinner cart. 'Our fruitful earth will unavoidably become dry and sterile at the hands of men who it seems cannot help but wantonly destroy the very thing which gives them succor.' Leonardo was quite a poet, wasn't he? I'd like to have a look at those pages. Perhaps your lovely friend would be kind enough to translate the rest for us, although she is by no means critical to the translation. Coded Circles, hoisting system? Fascinating."

"I want to see my friend right now," I insisted. "I want to know she's all right."

"Your Ginny?" B said with a wry smile. I glared at him. He shrugged. "We bugged your phone at the Four Seasons as well."

"So," I said to the pompous bastard, "you're the FBI or the NSA or no, MI-5, right? You're a Tea Bag. MI-5."

"Tea Bag, how homespun," B said, remaining unruffled. "A South-ernism you picked up from your mother? She was from Tennessee, was she not?"

I gnawed the inside of my lower lip.

"Reb," he said, "I'm simply the best man to tidy up Dodge, now that John Wayne is deceased and you've been relieved of your six-shooter. Very interesting, that. Never saw the likes of it before. We should discuss its origin."

I heard the sound of muffled voices emanating from the next room.

"I'm keenly interested in the Medici Dagger," B went on. "I know you are, too. Cooperate with me now, won't you? The key to your deposit box in the hotel vault would be appreciated, if something of interest lies within it. Rummaging through a room is one thing, including popping the odd wall safe. But opening safety deposit boxes, well, keys make the job so much more civilized. Be my buddy. Your father would most certainly have considered his Uncle Sam."

"Why did you drug us? Why didn't you just ask nicely? I'm a rea-sonable guy."

B thought for a moment. "I admit Mobright got a bit overenthusi-astic in bringing you in. The opportunity to have a look at the notes outweighed his more humane sensibilities. However, I pose to you this question: Would we have had your full attention otherwise?"

I paused and then gave him three looks: contemplation, convic-tion, concession. "I could be Doc Holliday," I said, showing some team spirit.

B stood, looking self-satisfied, and walked confidently over to me, all five feet seven inches of him. Offering me his small, manicured hand, he said, "In answer to most of your questions, my high-flying friend, I am Inspector Arlen Beckett, chief of Global Affairs, Gibraltar."

"And just what is Gibraltar?"

"Following the collapse of the Soviet Union, a specialized task force made up of senior agents from several Western members of the NATO alliance was formed for the purpose of preventing the proliferation of weapons of mass destruction. Catchy name, Gibraltar. Come now, my boy, you're bordering on being tardy for the inevitable handshake."

I grinned and stuck my hand out. Then I balled a fist and gave him a quick stiff uppercut to the jaw that knocked him up, back, and out. He hit the thickly carpeted floor, feet flat, knees sticking up. His hair didn't budge a centimeter.

"I'm not your boy," I said.

There were more sounds from the next room. I checked Beckett for a gun. Nothing. I dropped his seat cushion on top of the teacup and stomped on it as quietly as I could, then picked up a piece with a nice sharp edge to it. I walked to the door, cinched my face like a proper Englishman, and, trying to sound like Beckett, called out, "Oh, Mobright?"

The door opened and Mobright stuck his face in. "Yes, sir?" he inquired. I grabbed him under the knot in his tie, hoping it wasn't a clip-on, and jammed the shard against his throat. "Sir's not necessary," I said. "You can call me Reb."

"Reb. Please, I—"

"Another fucking word and you bleed. You know I'll do it."

His pinched mouth opened as if he were about to speak and then shut again. I spun him around, and, with his body as a shield, stepped into the room where they had stashed Ginny.

She was sitting upright on a puffy satin couch, looking much as she had when I woke her up in the Fiat, only groggier. A wide-shouldered man I presumed to be Pendelton towered over Ginny with his back to me.

She spotted me through glassy eyes. "Reb," she mouthed. Mobright kicked the door, either on purpose or because he was a klutz. Pendelton turned at the sound. He didn't pull a gun, for which I was grateful. I patted down Mobright for his and maybe mine. Nothing but a small spray bottle.

"Anything left in there?" I asked.

He looked at me pleadingly. "You don't understand."

"You're right," I replied, then double-dosed him. "Sweet dreams and a peach, Mobright."

nine

I double-dosed Pendelton, and Beckett, too. That gave us maybe four hours to do whatever we were going to do before Gibraltar was back on the snoop. I was confused and pissed, but at least I was in control. I had no idea where we were, but if Beckett was telling the truth, then we had to be in some sort of official building with other Gibraltar agents around, so I stripped Pendelton and put on his clothes to increase our chances of blending in.

Ginny was semi-anesthetized and couldn't have cared less about clothes; she was still trying to figure out why we weren't jogging. I got her to do some deep breathing, which seemed to clear her head some. Then I ran my knuckles up and down her spine and massaged her shoulders like she was the champ. This recharged her enough to prevent her from bumping into things while we were escaping.

When Ginny asked what was going on, I instructed her to just do what I said and everything would be all right. For once she put up no argument.

Before we left the room, I inspected the closet. Beckett's raincoat and hat were in there, all right. I slipped the coat on Ginny and with our chins down, we entered the hall. We appeared to be in a hotel after all, and made our way down two flights of stairs, passing half a dozen people, none of whom seemed interested in us.

By the time we made it out to the street, adrenaline had replaced most of the evil stuff in Ginny's system, and her eyes were clear and purposeful. We quickly melted into the throng of Milanese and tourists on the sidewalk.

"All right," Ginny barked, "what the hell was *that* about?"

She's back. "Check where we are," I said. "Can we walk back to the hotel or do we need to get a cab?"

She regarded the street sign. "It's two streets over. That way."

I took her by the elbow. "Let's go."

"Hey, give me a second, will you? I'm dizzy."

"Sorry," I said, slowing down a bit.

"Who were those people?"

"Gibraltar," I said.

"Gibraltar? That's a rock . . . and a mutual fund."

The lunch crowd provided us great cover. "It's also some kind of government intelligence agency," I said, "unless Beckett is an amazing liar. I don't know. I've never heard of Gibraltar. How can we be sure they're not working for Krell? And how'd they track us to Milan. Is Tecci here?"

"Who's Beckett?" Ginny asked, way behind me.

"The top dog. I knocked him out with a tasty uppercut."

Ginny stopped dead in her tracks. "You socked a government intelligence agent?"

"I don't know. Maybe. An international one, actually."

I tugged on her like a Central Park pony. She stumbled forward, staring at me. "And by the way," I added, "nobody says 'sock' anymore. Not since poodle skirts went out."

"Who cares?" she said. "The government will protect us from Krell. Governments protect people."

"No they don't. And besides, he called me homespun! The smug son of a bitch."

"So, naturally, you socked him."

"And drugged him. Mobright and his buddy, too."

Ginny looked at me as though I had committed a grievous error. A tour bus honked loudly as it maneuvered toward us through the heavy traffic.

I shrugged. "Listen, I'm improvising, all right?"

We passed a busy fruit stand where a lady called out, *"Mele, ciliegie, banane!"* The deep red cherries caught my eye.

In my peripheral vision I spotted two grim-faced guys in wrap-around shades, charging up the street, coats open.

Damn!

"I'm really sorry," I said to Ginny, shoving her hard into a group of people, knocking over the stand, sending fruit flying. I whistled loudly at the two guys, waving at them with my other hand.

The bus was thirty feet from me. I dashed into the street right in front. The driver went wide-eyed, honked his air horn, and tromped on the brakes just as I dove under, watching the squealing tires to see if they were going straight or fishtailing. If they fishtailed I was dead. They stayed straight.

I heard screams from the crowd as the bus passed over me, stopping while I was still under it. The floor above reverberated with the tromping of feet and shouting passengers.

I feigned a scream of pain. Horrified faces appeared through the tire smoke. I scanned them for the two grim ones. I saw one. Then it disappeared. I watched his brown shoes rush toward the back of the bus. I spun my body around like a break-dancer and pulled my knee up for a karate kick. The shoes stopped. One big-knuckled hand touched the pavement. I saw a gun with a silencer in the other; then the emotionless face angled over. I launched the kick as hard as I could, heel out.

I heard the satisfying crack of bone, teeth, and sunglasses, as blood spurted from his nose and mouth. Then his unconscious head smacked on the pavement. The gun lay in his limp hand. I scanned around me. More faces.

I caught sight of the second guy, midway up on the fruit-stand side. He saw me look at him and smiled, then disappeared. His black shoes headed for the back. My only thought was to get to the other guy's gun. As I lunged for it, the shoulder of Pendelton's big jacket snagged on a piece of the bus frame. I tugged at it frantically, once, twice, a third time before it tore loose.

The black shoes stopped next to the rear tire. I dove for the gun, but someone picked it up. I looked back at my pursuer. Sunglasses, sideways smiling face. Gun with a silencer pointing at me, finger on the trigger. *Too late. It's over.* Then a "poof" sound like a fist hitting a pillow. For an instant I thought I was shot; then I saw the smile disappear, the face hit the road, the silvery glare of sunlight on spreading blood. Someone had killed him.

Rolling out from under the bus, I sprang to my feet, looking for the shooter, and saw Ginny. Then through the throng I saw a male figure wearing a cap and a big coat rushing toward her in the midst of confused people and scattered fruit.

"Ginny!" I shouted. "He's got a gun!"

She turned toward the sound of my voice and covered her face in terror. The man reached into his pocket. Then, as if in slow motion, I saw him press something into Ginny's hand and rush off, disappearing into the milling crowd. Astonished, I dashed over and dragged her away.

We ran as fast as we could, zigzagging through the tangled streets until we were out of breath and certain that no one had followed.

Sweat pouring, we stopped in an alley and leaned side by side against a dirty brick building.

I took in the sight of Ginny—drenched hair, heaving chest. I wanted to hold her and smother her with kisses.

Ginny wiped perspiration off her face, leaving a bright red streak.

"Are you cut?" I asked desperately.

"I-I don't think so. I . . . it's . . ." She checked her hand carefully and licked the red liquid. "Cherry juice. You pushed me into a goddamn fruit stand, you asshole!"

"Yeah," I said, breathing a big sigh of relief. "I did."

She frowned at me. "Please tell me what the hell just happened."

I did, although I refrained from admitting that I would have let the bus flatten me or taken a chestful of bullets if it would have kept her safe.

"So the third guy—the one who ran toward me—he shot that other one who was going to kill you?"

"He must have."

"And you thought he was going to shoot me? You know how much you scared me?"

"Yes I do. Did you get a look at his face?"

She shook her head. "You think it was your friend Archie?"

"I don't know. I couldn't tell. What did he put in your hand?"

"This," Ginny said, handing me a crumpled business card.

I flattened it out. A phone number and the handwritten name Dracco.

The wail of police sirens several streets over made Ginny shudder. "Dracco?" she said. "Who the hell is Dracco?"

"I have no idea."

Crammed into a telephone booth, Ginny standing on tiptoe next to me, leaning in to listen, I dialed the number. A gruff voice on the other end of the phone said, *"Cosa vuoi?"*

"Dracco?" I asked.

Silence.

"Sono un amico di Archie Ferris."

Nothing, then click. He'd hung up.

Ginny and I looked at each other, puzzled. I dialed again.

Same voice. *"Cosa vuoi?"*

"Dracco? Um, io sono un amico di—"

Click. I was starting to get mad. So was Ginny.

"Give me this," she said, ripping the phone out of my hand. She jabbed in the number. The same voice answered, *"Cosa—"*

"Ascolti, idiota!" Ginny yelled. *"Qualcuno mi ha dato un biglietto da visita col suo nome. Io sono con un ragazzo chiamato Reb."*

I got the *"Listen, you idiot"* and *"Reb"* parts.

Ginny covered the mouthpiece and whispered to me, "I told him about the card."

"Reb?" I heard the man on the phone say.

"Si," she said into the phone. "Reb."

"Hollywood Reb?"

"Si."

"Well, put the fucker on, for chrissakes."

Ginny raised her eyebrows, passed me the phone.

Everybody loves Hollywood. "Dracco?" I said.

"The same."

"Why did you hang up on me?"

"Policy."

"Uh-huh. Listen, a guy shot somebody on my behalf and then gave your card to my friend before taking off."

"Shot a guy, gave the girl a card. I see," he said flippantly. "How 'bout that."

"Yeah. Then I say Archie Ferris and you hang up on me twice."

"I've seen all your movies, Hollywood Reb."

"Ar-chie Fer-ris," I repeated slowly.

"You say those words like you wanna win something."

"I'm hanging up," I told him.

"Okay by me."

"Come on, Dracco. Give me something."

After a pause he said, "All right. Somebody knows me thinks you got cash and a reason to leave the country without a trace. Don't bother asking me who."

"So you're in the travel business?"

"I got a Gulfstream Five and a forty-thousand-dollar opening in my schedule right now," Dracco said. "Anywhere you wanna go. It doesn't say so on my card, but it's implied."

"I see," I replied, looking at Ginny. "Anywhere."

"Pretty much, yeah," he said.

His offer sounded good to me. "Can I call you back in a couple of minutes?"

"Why not."

We rang off.

"Did you hear all that?" I asked Ginny.

"What do you think? Is this a setup?"

We both whipped around at the sound of footsteps behind us. An old man wearing a dirty apron emptied his trash and disappeared into his store.

I looked into Ginny's eyes.

"I think these things: The two men at the bus must have been Tecci's. Somehow they picked us up; I have no idea how. The man who saved us and gave you the card must have been sent by Archie. We're in danger here and we no longer have any weapons, but unless someone's broken into the hotel vault, we still have Leonardo's two pages, which you need to finish translating. And, I believe we're the only ones with the Circles of Truth."

"Right. Well, whatever the rest of Leonardo's writing says, I don't have the first clue about the Circles themselves. They just look like elaborate graphic designs to me. I mean it would take a—"

"Whoa!" I said, a strange feeling washing over me. Thoughts snapped like thumbnails on wooden match heads. *Mona Kinsky!* Last night at the hotel with Ginny, something had sparked a memory when we'd talked about searching for a pattern in the Circles of Truth, but I hadn't been able to identify it then. Now I did. Patterns, graphic designs. *Mona Kinsky! Of course!*

"What you just said," I told Ginny excitedly. "Graphic design . . . the Circles of Truth are a graphic design. What we need is a computer graphics expert."

"It's got to be someone we can trust."

"It is."

"Who?"

"Mona Kinsky." I fished a coin out of my pocket. "This is so weird . . . Mona . . . dear old Mona."

"Dear—old—Mona?" Ginny asked, incredulous.

"I'm calling Dracco back. I'm booking him."

"We're hiring Dracco?"

"And his plane," I added, my stomach getting queasy at the thought of flying. "As much as I hate to say it, we're taking to the sky, Ginny."

"You have forty thousand dollars?"

"Yes I do."

"On you?"

"On me."

"Wow. Okay, where are we going?"

"California." I picked up the telephone receiver.

Ginny sidled up to me, looking anxiously around her. "What about Gibraltar?"

"Another excellent reason to get out of here," I said. "Beckett and his bunch will be after us as soon as they come to, which is going to be sooner than we'd like."

I was suddenly aware of how close our bodies were to each other, how her musky scent drew me in. I needed clarity, not inebriation.

"But they could be good guys," Ginny argued.

"What?" I said, snapping out of it. "I thought we went over this."

More police sirens Dopplered by us, heading for the bus scene.

"I'm dialing now," I told her. "I'm booking the flight nonstop to L.A. It's the same fare for one as for two."

Ginny slapped me on the shoulder as Dracco's gruff voice answered, *"Cosa vuoi?"*

He told us to meet him in an hour at Linate Airport in his private hangar. Forty G's American, two passengers.

Ginny and I made our way back to the Four Seasons, where we changed and gathered our clothes, which had obviously been rifled through by Mobright. As I'd suspected, my key-on-the-window-ledge trick had worked. I thanked God and my high-school physics teacher. Retrieving Leonardo and the sundries from the vault, we were off.

Dracco was where he said he'd be. A swarthy, muscular man with a huge handlebar mustache, he wore what looked like an Armani pilot's suit and mirrored aviator sunglasses.

I showed him the business card, which he glanced at and handed back to me. "Tell me about the guy who wrote your name on that card."

Dracco smiled devilishly, revealing a gold canine tooth. "Relax," he said. "There's an old saying that everyone can keep a secret, it's the people they tell who can't. Only the first part applies to me. That means you don't find out who gave her the card and nobody else finds out I took you to Tinseltown. Now show me some cash. I'm a busy man."

I forked over the money. Dracco counted it, stating matter-of-factly that he had filed a phony flight plan, the jet was fueled, there was plenty of food and drinks, and we had nothing to worry about.

I could feel my hands begin to shake. Stuffing them in my pockets, I followed Dracco and Ginny onto the plane. He told us to enjoy the flight, then stepped up front and closed the pilot's door. Ginny and I strapped ourselves into the luxurious leather seats. Within five minutes we were airborne. Within six, Ginny was dissecting me with her stare.

"What are you doing there, balling your fists in your pockets?" she prodded. "Are you cold?"

"Shouldn't you start translating now or do you puke on planes, too?"

She crossed her legs, waited.

"Look," I said. "I don't like flying. That's all."

"That's obvious. Why not?"

"Ginny," I pleaded. "Leaves catch fire when you put them under a magnifying glass."

"That's an interesting reference," she said. "All right, we'll change subjects. Who's dear old Mona?"

I looked out the window at the dwindling city below.

"Mona was Martha Belle Tucker's best friend."

"Who's Martha Belle Tucker?"

"I knew it. After the fire there'd been no one to take me, so—"

"No one?" Ginny interrupted. "No aunts or uncles?"

"One uncle on my mother's side. Dell. And he didn't want any part of me."

"Why not?"

"The only thing I knew about him was what my mother had told me. That he was a wild kid, had run away from home at sixteen or so to race cars, which hadn't panned out, so he became a truck driver—a rambling man. My mother hadn't seen him in years. Anyway, when they dug Dell up, he wasn't . . ."

"Interested in rambling with an eleven-year-old."

"No."

"That must have felt terrible, to be unwanted."

"By Dell? I didn't know him. Besides, I was in shock. I didn't feel . . . anything, I guess." I hadn't said those words before. They sounded solitary, like the single bounce of a basketball in an empty gymnasium.

"Of course," Ginny said. "I'm sorry."

"You don't have to be sorry for me," I told her, shutting the door on my emotions. "Anyway, it looked as though I was going to end up a ward of the state. Then, out of nowhere, Martha stepped in."

"And she was . . ."

"A mathematician. A college professor. My mother's favorite teacher at Vanderbilt University. After my mother graduated, she kept up with Martha, called her every so often and sent her letters and pictures—first of my dad, then me."

"And she just showed up?"

"Martha heard about the fire on the news, found out about my situation through an ex-colleague who lived in D.C., and decided to have a look at me to see if there was something she could do."

"Was she married?" Ginny asked.

"Her husband had died of a heart attack, and she was living alone;

she'd relocated and was teaching at the University of California at Berkeley. Martha hadn't been able to have kids of her own, even though she'd wanted them, and she and George never adopted because he was against it."

"So at eleven years old you became Martha Belle Tucker's kid?"

"No! I was nobody's kid," I snapped. "I just lived in her house. Kept her company. That was it."

Ginny didn't seem satisfied.

"We had the same address," I clarified. "That didn't make me her son."

"She was good to you?"

"She was a cranky old buzzard, though it wasn't her fault. Her body ached from rheumatoid arthritis. Terrible thing to have. Make anyone cranky."

"Was she strict, lenient, what?"

"Only strict about geometry. That was her passion. Shapes. Deducing their properties. Turning postulates into theorems. She made sure I got pretty good at it myself. That's why she was friends with Mona Kinsky, you see. Because Mona was fascinated by shapes. Now you want to know about Mona."

"No," Ginny said. "What happened to Martha?"

I sighed. "After high school, I went on to Berkeley, majored in Art History. Martha died two weeks before I graduated. That's it."

"That's it . . ."

"Well, yeah."

"So when you swung your tassel, there wasn't a single soul in the world to clap for you?"

I didn't answer. Couldn't.

A minute, then: "How did she die?"

"Heart. She just fell over in the backyard while taking the kitchen tablecloth down from the laundry line."

"You found her?"

I fidgeted in my seat. "Can we talk about something else?"

"Martha was taking the tablecloth down and died."

I looked out the window, touched it. Cold. "It was draped over her chest," I said. "The corner of it was bunched up in her hand. She looked so serene lying there in the grass."

"What did you do? I mean, right then."

I felt a flush of embarrassment. I'd never spoken about my past with anyone, not even Archie, but this girl, this quirky pain in the ass, was scooping out my innards, sifting, exploring. Me—the guy with the shaking hands.

Closing my eyes, I was back there in the yard with Martha. The grass had needed cutting and I'd told her I'd do it on the weekend. She was lying on long grass.

"I sat down cross-legged," I said. "Put her head in my lap, ran my fingers down her hair, and stroked her cheek with the back of my hand. It already felt cold."

"Did you say anything to her?"

I whispered, "Now you're going to be with George."

I couldn't bring myself to tell Ginny that I'd cried. Rocked and cried and stroked that silver hair I used to braid when Martha could no longer do it herself. Then after they'd taken her away, I'd cooked her favorite meal and laid it out for two and cried at the kitchen table until long after the food had gone cold.

I dragged myself from that dark place, straightened up in my seat, and opened my eyes. "So . . ." I said, "that was that."

"What do you mean?"

"I mean 'cut and print.' The end. Anyway, you want to know about Mona Kinsky. Graphic artist. Nice lady. Very sharp. Good calligrapher, too. Always had state-of-the-art equipment. Like I said, Mona was good with patterns. I'm sure she's still designing things. You know how some people just never give up? Like Renoir, seventy-five, in a wheelchair with his brush strapped to his wrist? Hell, Mona couldn't be more than mid-sixties at the most."

Ginny eyed me silently. "Cut and print," she repeated. "The end of Martha. I'm beginning to understand."

116

"What?"

"Nothing. So . . . Mona. How do you know she's even still alive?"

"When I left Berkeley I asked her to write in her will that I be informed when she dies. What? Why are you looking at me that way?"

"Reb, you're not kidding, are you?" Ginny gaped.

She leaned forward, laid her chin on her palm, her eyes probing me. "Martha died so you just deleted that section of your past? You had Mona, someone who cared about you, write that in her will?"

I didn't answer.

"Jesus," she said. "How do you know where to find her?"

"She sends me cards. They have a return address."

"Which you, of course, don't answer." There was no malice in Ginny's tone. Just rueful comprehension. I hated the feeling of being ruefully comprehended.

"Where are Mona's cards postmarked from?"

"Outside of Mendocino."

"You've never been there," she added. It wasn't a question.

"Okay, now say something clever and pithy," I said, trying to regain control. "Like you would if you were analyzing a painting. Be literary and poetic. Tell me the seeds of connection lay unsown on my barren soil."

There was a pause.

"I don't have to, Reb," Ginny said softly. "You just did."

The whine of the jet engines was the only sound. Carefully removing her page of Leonardo's notes from her bag, Ginny abruptly swiveled her seat away from me and set about her task. Lying back, I closed my eyes and pictured burning leaves and barren soil. I fell asleep.

Somewhere over the Atlantic I heard Ginny laugh. "I ought to be bronzed."

She slapped two pieces of paper in my hand and clicked her compact shut, dropping it into her bottomless bag. "Now, why couldn't I have finished this last night? Read it, Reb."

I blinked, shaking myself clear, and looked first at Ginny's Italian.

Perché non mi fanno lavorare? Perché? Colui che dovrebbe di me fare tesoro mi nega i miei preziosi studi ché si rivela debole di stomaco. E ciò m'ha fatto male e mi tormenta giacché chi è mai costui se non sa fare ciò che Dio stesso lo ha chiamato a fare?

Per ventun anni l'ebbi con me e nessun altro neppure Giovan giammai poté vederla. Egli tornò alla polvere ora e giusto in quest'istante ho stabilito dove e come dovrà trovar riposo.

Brucia la mia furia con la forza d'un milion di candele e il suo baglior m'illumina'l cammino. De'venti cerch'il sentier che il possente viaggiatore ed egli solo giammai potrà veggente e del passato il vero alla daga condurrà'l sapiente.

I focused my overhead light on the second page and read her translation:

> Why am I not allowed to work? Why? He who should treasure me denies me my precious studies for his stomach is weak. And this has made me ill and how that vexes me for what is this man if he cannot do that for which God has tasked him?
>
> For twenty-one years I have kept this thing and no other man has seen it not even Giovan. He is gone now back to dust and in this moment I have just determined where and how it shall rest.
>
> My fury burns as the light of a million candles and its brilliance illuminates the way. The twenty circle path which none but the most mighty traveler will ever follow. Out then in back and forth one to the other the seer will wander the path and the truth of the past will lead the wise one to the dagger.

I felt my skin prickle as the ghosts of Leonardo's innermost thoughts fluttered across my mind. "The twenty-circle path," I said. "Circles of Truth One and Two do fit together somehow."

"Yes they do, mighty traveler," Ginny said. "You were absolutely right. But that's not all. Do you get it? Do you see what I see?" She was jumping in her seat.

"Who's Giovan?"

"Aaagh, Melzi, of course," Ginny blurted. "That was his first name. Giovan Francesco de' Melzi."

"Leonardo's adopted son," I said.

"Yes, now c'mon, move along. God, I'm so cool I want to kiss myself."

"Okay," I told her, "But I'm confused. 'Gone back to dust'? Died? Melzi didn't die before Leonardo. He outlived him by, I don't know, fifty years."

"That ain't the meat of the matter," she said, resting her chin on her palm Jack Benny style. "Don't get hung up there. Melzi was obviously still alive, so we can only infer that Melzi actually went to dust—like the furniture."

"Get out. Leonardo would write about that? Right next to the Circles of Truth?"

"This was a free-form journal," Ginny said impatiently. "Leonardo wrote about everything. Grocery lists next to sketches for *The Adoration of the Magi,* okay? So, sure, Melzi could literally have been dusting. You're missing the big point. Move on. Look, we know Leonardo made the Dagger in 1491, and he says here it's twenty-one years later so—"

"He was sixty," I said.

"There's the math," she said, chiding. "And that means . . ."

I thought hard for a minute, mentally leafing through my art history. Then I got it. "Jesus," I said, "Leonardo was in *Rome.*"

"Bingo!" she said, slapping her thigh. "In 1512, Pope Leo the Tenth had Leonardo summoned to the Vatican. Leo was Lorenzo de' Medici's son, and he wanted to follow in his father's footsteps and usher in a new

Golden Age of Art—only in Rome, not Florence—making Rome the art capital of the world with him as pope. But Leo was a hedonistic loser. Nobody wanted him to be pope, and that stirred up all kinds of trouble throughout Italy. Twelve Franciscan friars took it upon themselves to spread out over the country and preach like crazy that Leo was the Antichrist and that if he was made pope, the end of the world would come. These twelve had a profound effect on the mood of the Italians. Everyone was thinking doom and gloom, including Leonardo."

Excitement stirred in me. "Lust of the mighty, wanton destruction," I said. "So we know how he was feeling when he arrived in Rome."

"Yes. That explains the first part of the translation from yesterday. Now add that once Leonardo got to Rome, Leo didn't give him a single commission. That's where this part picks up. 'Why am I not allowed to work?' Leonardo asks. Raphael had been given *The School of Athens*, Bramante was building everything in sight, and Michelangelo was painting the Sistine Chapel."

"That had to hurt. Leonardo's archrival getting the cream of commissions."

"Sure," Ginny said. "They hated each other. Michelangelo called Leonardo a man who could get nothing accomplished, and Leonardo said Michelangelo had no business painting—the Sistine Chapel notwithstanding."

"Right," I said. "Leonardo thought sculptors were fools for spending their lives hip-deep in marble chips, said they looked like bakers or snowmen, while painters walked around dressed in fine clothes."

"So," Ginny said, "Leonardo, the greatest of them all, has nothing to do except dissections for his anatomical studies, and on top of everything else, Pope Leo orders him to stop the dissections because the thought of it makes him queasy."

I sat up straight, right in the pipe with Ginny. "So you're saying the 'he' of 'he who would treasure me' is Pope Leo."

"Exactly. You can feel Leonardo's frustration. He knows God gave him these incredible gifts, tasked him, but he's not allowed to complete his work. Million-candle fury, Reb. Now," she said, hunching over toward me, tenting her fingers, bouncing the tips against each other. "Any idea where Leonardo was staying in Rome when he wrote these words, when he devised the Circles of Truth?"

I simultaneously wanted to punch her out for making me work for it and kiss her for translating the page and knowing what it meant.

"The Belvedere Palace," Ginny said, clapping her hands. *"And* do you know where the Belvedere Palace is?"

I grinned and pulled by earlobe. "The Belvedere Palace is on top of Vatican Hill."

"My hero," she said, holding me in her gaze.

"So," I cleared my throat, "we've got Leonardo at the Belvedere Palace, deciding where and how the Dagger shall rest."

"That's my best guess."

"It's a very good guess. Nice work."

"I know. And isn't it slightly incongruous that we're at this very moment flying to California. We're going the wrong way, Reb!"

She jumped out of her seat and headed toward the cabin. "Tell Dracco to turn around right now!"

I grabbed her arm. "Forget it!"

"What are you saying?"

"Up till this second your thinking was stellar."

"Don't patronize me. You're telling me California, not Rome? Are you nuts?"

"Ginny," I snapped, squeezing her arm. "The Vatican. Take one. 'Pardon me, Pope, could you please cancel the Mass, we're checking under the pews for the Medici Dagger. Oh, and don't tell anybody we're here because all of Europe wants to capture us or kill us, or both.' "

The color drained from Ginny's face. She shrunk back into her seat.

"Yes, we have to go back there," I told her, "but not before we figure out the Circles of Truth. They're going to tell us 'where and how it shall rest.' Till then, we play it safe."

Ginny frowned absently. I was sorry I'd reminded her of the danger.

I picked up Leonardo's two pages and examined the Circles of Truth. The shape of the markings triggered a memory. For my twelfth birthday, Mona had given me a book of Sherlock Holmes adventures. She'd recommended one of the stories to me and it became my favorite.

"Do you remember Sherlock Holmes's 'Adventure of the Dancing Men'?" I asked Ginny.

She shook her head.

"The messages were written with pictures; stick figures of dancing men with their arms and legs in different positions. They were an alphabet that only two people knew. Secret messages were written in the dancing-men alphabet. We've got a bunch of concentric rings of lines and squiggles here. Maybe all these little marks on the Circles of Truth are some kind of alphabet, or a pictograph—broken up, cut apart."

"Could be," Ginny said, peering at the Circles. "I'm an art historian, not a cryptanalyst. Look, I got us to the Vatican. Maybe we should just go there and give the pages to the pope. He could, I don't know, call Gibraltar and—"

"Call Gibraltar?" I shot, stunned that she would give in so easily to her fear.

"They'd get us out of trouble."

I slapped my forehead. "Maybe you're right, I should tell Dracco to turn around. Pick a spot in Europe. Any spot. I'll let you off."

"Why?"

"Because you don't have a goddamn clue what this is all about, that's why."

Tears welled in her eyes, but I didn't care; I was boiling. "You're saying million-candle fury—translating it for chrissakes—but you don't get it. You know all the history, but you don't know what this is really about." I waved the pages at her.

"What's it really all about?" she said, tears falling now. "Illuminate me."

"It's about getting something right for Leonardo, Antonia! One thing right! You know Leonardo's Sforza Horse was used as target practice, the bronze melted down for cannonballs. *The Last Supper* hung for years in a stable, then got painted over a dozen times. And here Leonardo was in Rome at the Belvedere Palace, sick to death because he knew he was the greatest genius in the history of geniuses and everybody let him down. He creates the most amazing thing, perhaps of all time, and has to hide it from everyone for his entire life and on into the future. *This* can't be another Sforza Horse or *Last Supper*. I won't allow that to happen. Leonardo was alone in a rotten, lousy, cruel world he couldn't trust with his Dagger. And if that Dagger is out there somewhere . . . in the Belvedere Palace, or wherever . . . if Leonardo wrote its location down on these pages, then locating it is exactly what I'm going to do! I'm not about to let some billionaire bastard and his tattooed sidekick put the vise grips on Leonardo." I was pumped now, pacing the tiny luxury cabin, pounding my fist in my hand. "Or for that matter some steel-haired, tea-sipping elitist with a Gibraltar ring. The hell with all of them. Nobody uses Leonardo. Not in this century, not on my watch."

I stopped and shot a look of single-minded purpose into her tear-laden eyes. "Let he who finds the Dagger use it for noble purpose. That was my father's plan. And now it's mine. Me. The 'mighty traveler,' that's *me!*" My hands were trembling again.

Ginny looked from them to my face. "I see, Rollo Eberhart Barnett, Jr."

I turned away, took a deep breath, then let it out slowly. "Are you in or out?" I said. "For Leonardo."

"Look at me," she urged. I reluctantly acquiesced. The overhead cabin lamp cast a reddish hue on her dark shiny hair as the jet engines hummed through the heavens. Ginny swallowed once, her small Adam's apple vanishing and quickly reappearing.

"I'm in," she said. "For Leonardo. And for you."

"Okay, then," I told her. "California."

ten

After landing where the smog meets the sea, Dracco slid us through customs as if we were invisible. As we parted, he told us to think of him the next time we needed special travel arrangements.

We bought my Jaguar back from the long-term lot and eased onto the freeway. Up above, the sky looked cloudless and forgiving, offering grace to all the Southern California sinners. The familiar sights of the city freed my tired mind to focus on the immediate tasks ahead.

First stop, the bank. I squirmed in my seat, keeping to myself the fear that Krell's men might have cleaned out my account electronically and even gained access to my safe-deposit box. Another possibility: They had somebody staked out waiting to attack the minute I walked out the door.

I parked around the corner from the bank. I asked Ginny to wait in the car and explained why. Reluctantly, she agreed. As I approached the building, I could feel my heart begin to pound. Everyone looked suspicious: the two Armani suits peering into that old Mustang; the couple whispering in each other's ears; that shopping-cart lady. Like the maid who'd planted the bug at the Gritti, anybody could be anybody.

I entered the building fully vigilant, my boot heels clicking noisily on the marble floor, alerting everyone to my presence. I checked for the guards. The one by the vault with a red-veined nose hitching up his belt buckle looked like a retired cop. The other, stifling a yawn, kicked something off his thick-soled orthopedic shoe. Neither seemed interested in me.

I stepped over to a familiar-looking woman sitting at a customer-service desk. She had me sign the register, and then I followed her into the vault, checking over my shoulder.

It looked like business as usual, but it was hard to tell. I hadn't suspected anything at the Gritti or at the Four Seasons. Self-doubt pawed at me. The customer-service woman left. I watched her go, half-expecting the door to close, the spoked steel handle to spin, locking me in for eternity. *Get a grip.*

I opened the safe-deposit box. The satchel was there. I pried its jaws apart. Wads of cash. *Yess!* I closed the beat-up case without counting the money. I knew how much was in there: one million nine hundred and fifty thousand dollars. I took the satchel with me and left the bank.

Outside, I looked for the young whispering couple. Gone. Nobody by the Mustang. The shopping-cart lady. Still there, sitting on a bench now, holding out a paper cup to a man in a suit who was giving her spare change.

I hustled around the corner back to Ginny. Just as my anxiety was starting to dissipate, I spotted the two Armanis standing on the curb leaning against the passenger door of my car, talking to her. *Shit!*

The car was facing away from me and one of the guys partially obscured my view of her. I picked up my pace, moving a little closer to the shops in the hope that they wouldn't see me in their peripheral vision. They had to be armed. All I had was a satchel of money.

I stayed low, gaining speed. Throwing the satchel to the sidewalk, I sprang up right behind them, balling my fists and raising my elbows, and dropped down hard on each of their shoulders. They both yelped and fell to their knees.

"Oh man!" one of them moaned. I threw a forearm into the side of his head and he went down silently.

"Reb!" Ginny screamed as the other guy grabbed me by the back of my jacket. I spun around, took his hand with both of mine, and twisted. To keep his arm from breaking, he went with the force of the

125

momentum until he was facing toward the back of the car with me behind him. I let go of his wrist with one hand and pushed on his elbow. He groaned again and fell back to his knees.

"Where's Tecci?" I shouted, wrenching his arm higher. "Tell me or I'm going to break it right off!"

"Oh, shit, no, please!" he moaned.

"Where's—"

"Reb!" Ginny yelled, jumping out of the car. "Let go of him! They were just asking about the car. Jesus, you're hurting him!"

"We were just looking at your fucking car, man," the guy groaned. "Lemme go."

I did. He crawled away, sat against a light pole, and massaged his shoulder, glaring at me. His buddy started to come to and held his hands over his ears, shaking his head as though something very loud was happening in there.

"I'm at UCLA Law, pal," the lamp-post boy threatened. "You just committed assault and battery on two people. It's just a fucking car. She called you Reb? Give me your last name now, you animal."

"Animal," I gulped, comprehending what I'd done. I removed two ten-thousand dollar packs from the satchel and handed them to the law student. "Here," I told him. "Take these. One is for your friend. Consider it an out-of-court settlement."

I threw the bag in the trunk and opened the door for Ginny, whose expression had changed from astonishment to veneration. I had saved her, again, or at least thought I was saving her.

I hated feeling unhinged.

"Where are you taking me now, animal?" she asked as I pulled into traffic.

"I'm not taking you anywhere," I said flatly. "And please, please don't call me— Hey, that's Archie's car!"

"Where?"

"Four cars up," I said, pointing. "The black Humvee. He's just turning on Wilshire. Goddamn!"

I threw on my blinker to follow.

"How do you know it's his?"

"I know. Can you see the license plate?"

"HOO-AH!" Ginny read.

"That's the name of his business," I told her as we got caught at a red light. "He's heading there now. I can't believe this."

Archie's specialty gun shop, *Hoo-ah!*, was in a small, freestanding purple building off Wilshire Boulevard. It had at one time belonged to a movie production company that started off big, but went toes-up after a couple of major flops. Inside, among the standard assortment of guns and paraphernalia, were glass cases with memorabilia and a couple hundred signed pictures of movie bozos, including me, although it was hard to tell it was me because I was wearing a motorcycle helmet and sliding under a burning semi-tractor-trailer on a police motorcycle.

In the store the opening credits of *The Philadelphia Story* were running on a big-screen TV that usually played action films. Archie sat in a steel and leather chair wearing his customary getup—battle fatigue pants, jump boots, and a green army T-shirt that was a size too small. He had a bottle of Orange Crush in one hand and a fistful of popcorn in the other.

I approached him while Ginny hung nervously by the door, taking in the spectacle of the place. Archie didn't see us.

"Hey," I said.

Archie jumped out of his chair, looking like a parent who just spotted his lost kid at the mall. He lunged for me, his face bunching up as though he was going to cry. He hugged me so hard I could barely breathe, the popcorn in his huge fist crunching behind me.

"Jesus, Rebsky," he whispered in my ear, "I've been so worried."

I finally got free, picked up the remote, clicked it off, and tossed it on the table.

Ginny approached cautiously.

Archie looked at his mashed handful of popcorn, then stuffed it in his mouth. He offered his buttery hand to Ginny and mumbled, "Hi. Ahee Feh."

"Don't tell me you don't recognize me," Ginny said.

He chewed the popcorn as fast as he could, washing it down with a slug of Crush. "Uh . . . no," he said to the bottle. "I'd remember seeing you. Who are you?"

"Archie," I said. "What the hell's going on here?"

He jabbed a thick finger at me. "You first."

I was getting angry. "The bump into Ginny outside the Danieli? The note in her bag? The box full of guns? Shooting the guy when I did the bus gag in Milan? Dracco's card?"

Archie looked at me like I was crazy. "You're Ginny?" he said, smiling at her.

She nodded.

"What's he talking about, Ginny? Notes, guns. What bus gag? Who's Dracco?"

"Archie!" I shouted. "I *know* it was you. Wasn't it you?"

Archie pointed his thumb at his massive chest. "*This* is me."

I was totally baffled. "You didn't set up the guns?"

"What guns?"

"Come on. Two Sigs. Mini machine pistol."

"Mini machine pistol?"

"We've known each other a long time," I said. "I know my phone call got you thinking about Danny. I can picture you hanging up after turning me down, replaying what happened to him over and over. Don't tell me my call didn't stir up all kinds of stuff."

Archie swallowed.

"Please tell me the truth," I implored.

He plunked down in his chair, took a big swallow of soda.

"I did the guns," he confessed to his jump boots. "Had to. Ginny, I hope I didn't hurt you in the square. I never put the bump on someone your size before."

Ginny said, "How did you know to give it to me?"

"I could tell Reb was searching for somebody. And you, well, you were dressed like . . . the scarf and goggles, head down, scoping everybody in the piazza? I used to be a cop. Come on. Stevie Wonder couldn't have missed you."

"Why didn't you just come to me?" I asked.

Archie spat, "You're damn right you stirred things up, asking me to make that kind of decision in a second. The whole flight over, I didn't know whether to help you out or shoot you myself. I got you the guns, didn't I? Sue me. But what the hell are you talking about? Who got shot? Reb, you shot somebody?"

"No, *you* did!" I shouted, confusion digging into me like barbed wire.

"The hell I did! I'd remember if I shot somebody."

"That's the same phrase you used about seeing Ginny! And five seconds later you confessed. So what the hell?"

Archie sprang out of his chair. "Look," he snapped, "I decided to help you out. I made a call to somebody I know from a long time ago. I got the guns stashed. I tracked your ass, put the bump on her, planted the card, said two Hail Marys, and caught the next plane out of there."

"Why didn't you follow us?"

"I didn't, okay? I just didn't. May Moses smash my nuts with the Ten Commandments if I'm lying. I've been holing up at my place in Big Bear two days grinding down my fillings, thank you very much. I don't have a damn clue what you're into. And then what happens? Your place gets torched."

"What?"

"Oh my God!" Ginny gasped.

"Your house burned to the ground yesterday."

My heart froze.

"Oh . . . Jesus, Reb," Archie said. "Gimme a hand, Ginny. He's losing it."

I felt the room telescope. I was slipping down a funnel. *Mom's on fire. Who's gonna put her out? Where's Dad? I'm just a kid. "Jump, Reb! Save yourself." Oh no . . . Mom . . .*

My eyes came into focus. *Ginny's hand's on my chest. She's saying my name.*

I struggled to a sitting position, took two deep breaths. Archie and Ginny knelt by me, the air heavy with their concern. "I'm all right," I said as calmly as I could. "Really."

"You just had a flashback, is what you had," Archie said. "I'm a combat veteran. I know."

Ginny checked my pulse. I shook my hand free of hers and got to my feet, feeling acrid and defensive.

"I'm all right," I said with vinegar. "Tecci . . . he burned my house down."

"Who's Tecci?" Archie said. "What the fuck is going on here?"

In a burst of rage I grabbed Archie by his shirt, bunching it in my fist, getting right in his face. "That's what I want to know, Archie!" I screamed. "What the fuck is going on here? Are you telling me you weren't in Milan? You didn't shoot that asshole by the bus?"

"Reb," Archie said quietly, covering my hands with his much stronger ones. "My boy—"

"I'm not your boy!" Instantly I regretted saying that.

Archie closed his eyes for a few seconds, as if in prayer. "My *friend*," he corrected. "Please let go of me."

I smoothed out his T-shirt, shivering from cold sweat trickling down my back.

A moment later Archie said, "Now . . . tell me about the asshole I didn't plug in Milan."

An hour later we had told him everything. He had listened carefully, staring bug-eyed at Leonardo's notes and the Circles of Truth. When we finished, he shook his woolly head.

"I'm one of those people who didn't think *Alice in Wonderland* was strange. The Mad Hatter? No problem. But the Medici Dagger and

Gibraltar? Beckett and Tecci? And you have some guardian angel in Milan puts you onto some guy named Dracco who drops you in L.A. for forty big ones? Tell me you don't take drugs."

I showed him Dracco's card. "He knew what I did for a living."

"He called him 'Hollywood Reb,' " Ginny added.

"And he knew I could come up with a lot of cash, Archie. You're the only person I told I had money. You and Ginny."

Archie shrugged. "So? What's that worth? If he knew you were a stuntman, he'd know you're the best. So he'd figure you're not working nights at Chuck E. Cheese."

"Mm-hm. But how'd he know I'd be carrying it?"

Archie shrugged again. "C'mon. I didn't tell anybody anything about any money."

I mulled that over.

Archie raised a brow. "A guardian angel's a handy thing to have."

I rested my elbows on the table, wondering who it was.

Archie broke the silence.

"Here you are back in California to see Mona. I tell you, that's somehow fitting. You know what I mean? It's . . ." He turned to Ginny. "What's the word I'm looking for?"

"Symmetrical?" Ginny said.

"Symmetrical, sure. Like these circles. So, Reb, you gonna call her or just show up on her doorstep?"

The hanging lamp's light cast shadows on Archie's and Ginny's faces. I left the room to make the call.

Thirteen years. Three presidents. How many unanswered cards? What would Mona say? What would she think? What would she sound like?

She answered on the fifth ring, out of breath.

"Whew! I hope it's a client because if this is a sales call I'm going to be very petulant. I was outside at the car just about to leave."

I took a deep breath to calm myself. "Don't be mad, Mona. It's a client."

Silence.

Then, "This voice sounds familiar. Where do I know this voice from? The past, that's where. Oh my . . ."

I told her it was me.

Silence came from her end. All the anxiety was mine.

"Martha's Reb . . ." she said softly.

I didn't reply. My throat felt tight. I massaged it with one hand, aware of the pressure of the receiver against my ear.

"I can feel your hesitation," Mona said. "There is nothing casual about this call. Something's brought you to me. Something powerful."

"I . . . need your help."

"Help," she repeated. "You're saying I'll get to see you?"

"Right away, if possible."

"What about?"

I hesitated to answer.

"It's all right. It can wait till you're here. Are you coming alone?"

I told her no.

She asked if I was coming with family. That threw me. I had no family. I closed my eyes, sensed the moat I'd built around my life. "No," I confessed.

"Well," Mona said. "I'm a ride up from anywhere. If you plan on staying over, you should go to the Hollister House Inn in Little River, just outside of Mendocino. I'd offer you my couch, but the last person who slept on it woke up needing a chiropractor."

The Hollister House sounded faintly familiar, but I didn't know why. "What's a good time?"

"Tomorrow. Eleven. Ask directions from the man who owns the inn. His name's Pop. He'll send you my way."

I wanted to say something, but didn't know what. "Mona . . ." I began. "I'm sorry for—"

She interrupted. "Whatever it is that brought you to me, it's something to be thankful for. I'll see you tomorrow."

She rang off.

I kept the phone to my ear for a moment, surprised by the calming effect her voice had had on me. I rubbed my eyes too hard so when I opened them everything was slightly out of focus. Now I was off-center again. That was better.

I reentered the room where Archie and Ginny were waiting expectantly.

"I want guns, Archie," I announced. "Same stuff you got me in Venice."

Ginny slapped the table. "Just a minute!"

"What?" I asked, surprised.

"I'll bet that's pretty much the same way you asked Archie last time."

She was right. His silence confirmed it.

"Take two, Reb," Ginny said. "This time with a little respect. Maybe even open with telling us if you reached Mona."

"I reached Mona," I answered.

"Would you like to embellish that?"

"What I'd like is guns and to get going. We've got some driving to do."

I turned to Archie. "I apologize for being abrupt. I'd very much appreciate if you'd please loan me some handguns. Preferably of the same variety as the ones you planted in Venice."

Archie stood up. "The Sigs I can do. But that mini, that was a special thing I got as a favor. A prototype. It's a bitch you lost it to that Buckett guy."

"Beckett," I corrected. "And I'll get it back."

"I bet you will," he said, walking into the storage room. He returned a minute later with the weapons.

As I was strapping on the Sigs, Archie said to me, "This time I'm coming along."

"I don't want you involved."

"Don't want me involved? You're wearing weapons licensed to me, for chrissake. I'd say that's involved."

"Arch, I know you went way out on a limb for me, and you're still out there. That means . . . much more than I can convey to you right now. Much more. Maybe I shouldn't have come here today."

"What are you talking about? Your house got burned down. There are some bad-ass motherfuckers out there."

"Yeah?" I said, my anger fanned. "Well the baddest-ass mother-fucker that ever drew a breath is standing right in front of you. Now I'm telling you, lay out."

Archie's face flushed. "Step in here any time, Ginny," he urged. "He seems to listen to you."

"That was manners," she said. "This is . . . personal. I don't think I can influence him about this."

"I need to do this alone," I told Archie.

"Then what the hell are you doing with her? Answer that."

"I . . . I don't know how to answer that."

Ginny looked disappointed.

"I can't answer any more questions today," I said. "Not one."

He didn't reply, just stood in the doorway and watched us walk over to the Jag.

We slowly pulled out of his lot. When we hit the interstate I leaned on the gas.

After fifteen minutes of eighty-mile-an-hour silence, Ginny said, "So . . . aren't we festive."

eleven

Cruising up I-5 at warp speed, I pulled my portable phone out of the glove compartment, called information for Little River, and got the number for the Hollister House Inn. As I dialed, I recalled where I'd heard of the inn. My mom had taken me to see the movie *Same Time, Next Year,* which had been set in a quaint cottage that stood off by itself on a bluff overlooking one of the choicest views of the California coast.

She'd grabbed my small hand in the theater while we watched. "Dad and I went there in '65," she'd whispered. "The Hollister House. Stayed in that very cabin. We ate smoked oysters and thought big thoughts, and, Reb, it was the ultimate place to rejuvenate."

Mom, Dad, and the Hollister House in '65. Mom, me, and the Hollister House in '78. Ginny, me, and the Hollister House, tonight. Big thoughts.

With one hand gripping the wheel and both eyes on the road, I rang the inn. A pleasant woman answered the phone. I asked her for two separate cottages. She reserved White Pine and Beechnut, just across from each other, under "Arthur Holmes." Giving my real name didn't seem prudent.

I checked Ginny for a response. "You know what I think, Art?" she asked.

"What's that?"

"I think you're the most enigmatic man I've ever encountered."

"I don't want to hear this."

"We'll bookmark that for later. Do you want to know what else I think?"

"Does it have to do with the Medici Dagger?"

"I think your friend Archie may be our guardian angel—not just for the guns but in Milan as well."

I tromped on the gas till the speedometer read 92. Interstate 5 didn't care. The Jaguar didn't care. None of the L.A. motorists seemed to either.

Ginny grabbed the dashboard. "Slow down. We're illegally in the country and you're wearing guns registered to Archie."

I backed it down to eighty although I really wanted to punch the pedal through the floor. "You may be right about him being the angel," I said. "Damn it. He was disturbed enough to plant the guns, write me a note, and then lie about it when we showed up at his office. I made him lie to me, Ginny."

"Guilt. Good. A little introspection is a good thing."

"Oh Christ. I'm talking about Archie, not me. I told you how his son got killed. I put Archie's tail in a crack the second I asked him to fix me up with a gun in Venice. I don't feel good about it."

"I'm guessing Archie doesn't want you to know that he killed someone to save you. We are alive right now because of that man."

"He's my best friend."

"Say that again."

We were passing vineyards, miles of them. I wished I were one of those billion dusty grapes. "What the hell do you want from me?"

Out of the corner of my eye I saw Ginny watching. "Have you ever told Archie he's your best friend?" she asked.

I thought about it. "No."

"Why not?"

"It's complicated."

"That's a given. Can you think of a single relationship that really meant something to you that wasn't?"

"No," I admitted. "I love Archie as a friend, though. I do. I'm telling you I would do anything for him."

"I believe that. You'd spend your only day off for a year to help him fix that goofy car he drives."

"It's a Humvee. You're heading to the bookmark, aren't you?"

"So you're lifting up the front of his Jeep with one finger while he's under it with the wrenches and the two of you are talking about stunts . . . women. And everything is great until the conversation turns personal. At that very moment you drop the car on him, without even knowing it. Drop it right on his feelings."

"I don't have to listen to this."

"Well, you can block your ears and scream, 'Woop, woop,' but I'm saying it anyway. On one hand you have all these amazing capacities—you can squash tall cities and leap locomotives—and on the other hand, you're utterly and completely out of touch with human emotions. It's not your fault," Ginny added. "I'm not attacking you."

"Oh really? Because that's exactly what it feels like to me."

"I hoped you'd say that."

I felt trapped. I was driving through Ginny Gianelli's hall of mirrors and I couldn't find my way out. "Why'd you hope I'd say that?"

"Because you're *not* being attacked. You just believe you are—that you're going to get hurt at any moment, especially by people you care about. Right down to your bones, you believe it. It's written all over you. Can you see it, Reb?"

I was doing eighty on the interstate, but was stopped dead in front of Ginny.

"I can see it," I admitted.

Ginny sighed with relief. "Now . . . you won't like what I'm going to say next."

I gripped the wheel.

"For a boy who lost his parents so violently, it was totally natural and even helpful for you to expect to be hurt at any moment. But tell me . . . how well has it worked for you as an adult?"

I took a deep breath. Ginny did the same. I considered her question for another billion grapes.

"You're not to blame any more than Archie is for lying about being in Milan," Ginny said. "Look at him. Here's this resourceful person, a Vietnam vet. At eighteen, nineteen years old he probably saw and did absolutely atrocious things. When the war was through with him, he came out a changed man. Maybe got involved with some disreputable people. Somewhere down the line he had a son whom he probably didn't know how to father, but whom he loved with all his big heart. Then, in a senseless tragedy, he lost him. And ten years ago, through a set of circumstances that involved nearly killing someone with his car, he began to project all of his unspent parental love onto an enigmatic young stuntman orphan. I ask you, can you blame him?"

Ginny pulled her hair back and stretched in her seat as I considered her insight into Archie, and me.

She looked out her side window and said, "My God, that's a lot of wine."

Clicking on the radio, she started scanning stations. She stopped on Aretha singing "Respect," and joined in for the backup vocals. Damned if she didn't hit all the "sock it to me"s with soul. Awful lot of soul for an Italian girl from Staten Island. Sang in tune, too.

As we crossed over to the coast road nine hours later, an untroubled moon illuminated the landscape. Redwoods reached toward the pinpricks of yellow in the distant galaxies, and crickets and crows scratched and swooped. We rolled on, ignored by all except for the odd raccoon whose retinas reflected our passing headlights.

Finally, Little River appeared on the bluff, the shiny black ocean bobbing behind it. Though the full effect was lost in the darkness, it was still spectacular—the Mendocino coast.

We pulled down a long tree-lined road to the Hollister House and staggered out of the Jag. We checked in at the main building, a little dazed and buzzing from the ride.

A jovial old man with a yellow Ben Hogan cap, a weatherworn face, and tan hearing aids welcomed us warmly.

"Rodney Norcross," he said, brushing dandruff off one shoulder of his brown sweater, "but everybody calls me Pop. Even the codgers who've been coming here since just after the war. That's World War II, Harry S. Truman's triumph, or his catastrophe, depending on how you look at it." He inspected the registry log. "You must be . . . uh . . . Arthur Holmes," he said to me.

"That's me," I replied. "Art Holmes, sir."

"Thanks for the sir, son, but just Pop'll do. Popadoodledoo." He laughed a grab-your-suspenders laugh, showing well-made false teeth. Turning to Ginny, he asked, "And you are . . ."

"Watson," Ginny offered, filling in the blank. "Ginny Watson."

Pop slapped the book and laughed again. "How 'bout that? Holmes and Watson. You two answer an ad in the personals?"

Pop winked at me. "I 'spect you're gonna pay me in cash, Art, aren't ya?"

"Yup," I said, pulling out my wallet, sharing the laugh. It was hard not to like the old barnacle. I handed him a thousand dollars. "We don't know how long we'll be here, Pop. Will this get us going?"

"Sure, sure," he said, taking the money. "I'll hang on to it for ya. But what are you getting two places for anyway? Did you have an argument? Hell, I shouldn't be asking. At least get a little closer while you're here. How about Same Time and Next Year?"

"You named them after the movie?" I asked excitedly.

"What, you think I'm a dope?" Pop answered. "Course I did. Used to be one cabin, then I separated it down the middle. Now there's two of 'em. One's Same Time and the other's Next Year. They're adjoining. Real nice. Way off over there by themselves on the cliff overlooking the water, and they just happen to be vacant. Only four hundred a night each. For you, seven-fifty for both."

Ginny gnawed her finger, waiting. She sidled six inches closer to me.

Pop threw me a grin. "She's hooked," he said. "You got no choice, Holmes."

I agreed.

Pop slapped the register again. "I'm a born salesman," he said to the world. "P. T. Barnum got nothing on me. Better heavy up the down payment, Mr. Holmes. Another grand ought to do it, just in case you stay a while or wreck the place. You wouldn't do that, would you?"

"Which one?" I asked.

"Course you wouldn't. We haven't had trouble here since Baby Face Nelson hid out in the old cabin."

Ginny's eyes widened. "The gangster?"

"Oh, I was a rooster back in those days," Pop said, reminiscing. "I let him hole up here for a while just for the fun of it. Hell, he couldn't have set foot on the property without me knowing about it, though naturally I never said that to the buttons. Yep, this place is Fort Pops, all right, the whole thirty-seven acres of it."

I handed him another thousand, which he fanned out like a cardsharp before stashing it with the other cash in his pocket.

"That's two thousand down for Mr. Holmes," he said, making a note in the book. "I'll get your keys, not that you need 'em. Nobody disturbs anybody in my sphincter . . . I mean my sector," he chortled. "Must have forgot to take my Metamucil with lunch."

He escorted us to the front door, handed us a map with our adjoining cottages circled, tipped his hat, and wished us a very good night.

Ginny and I hopped in the Jag for the last time that day and slowly wound our way down the gravel driveway to our rooms; I gripped the wheel tighter than normal, feeling a much-heightened awareness of her presence next to me.

We extracted ourselves and our belongings from the car to the sound of pounding surf. The cottage was set among the trees, divided in two, with weathered siding, a split-level roof, and brick chimneys on each side. An Abe Lincoln special, or a Cape Cod condo.

I'd left the headlights on so we could see what we were doing. A cool breeze rustled the foliage, blowing a wisp of hair across Ginny's moist lips. The thin fabric of her dress clung to her, showing the outline of her hips. I imagined tossing the keys into the woods, tearing her clothes off, and ravaging her right there in the headlights till the battery went dead, or I did.

I extended my palm, both sets of keys in it. "Which will it be, Ginny," I said as casually as I could, "Same Time or Next Year?"

Ginny covered my hand with hers, a question in her eyes.

I stepped back involuntarily. She closed the distance, sliding the fingers of her free hand into my pocket, pulling me closer to her. Her knuckles pressed against my hip. My pants felt too tight.

I raised my eyes skyward, saw moonlight, dappled leaves. *Stay clear. Get to the jungle.*

My eyes met Ginny's. "No," I uttered, pulling away.

Her face pinched down. Tears welled up in her beautiful eyes. She wiped them away.

"Give me Same Time," she demanded, sticking a hand out. "I don't know if I'll be alive next year."

I couldn't breathe. Just stood there stonelike.

Silently, I let go of the key.

twelve

I was wrong about the Abe Lincoln thing. For one, the cottage had electricity. Running water, too. Half-shell sconces and brass lamps. Light-blue wallpaper, Berber carpet, and cushy chairs with braided piping. The place was furnished with a king-size bed and a velvety couch with embroidered pillows positioned in front of a black marble fireplace. Old books and stubby round candles were parked on the white wood mantel on either side of a rectangular wicker basket of silk flowers. An oval tin wood bin near the fireplace was stocked with split and seasoned birch. Abe would have liked it here.

I called Mona, waking her up to tell her we'd arrived safely. She asked if I'd met Pop. I said yes and inquired how she knew him. She laughed a laugh that has no age.

When I apologized for rousing her, she said the stars would have anyway, and besides, she wasn't dreaming yet. We rang off. I washed up, feeling confused and ungrounded. After climbing into bed, I lit a candle.

The image of *The Repentant Magdalen* flashed before me, making me melancholy. I thought of Ginny next door.

"Swell dreams and a peach, Ginny," I whispered, my eyelids falling.

The next morning I awoke to rapping on my door. My eyes pried themselves open and squinted across the sunlit room. Out the sliding glass doors to my back porch, I viewed a small Renoir-like flower garden and what looked like the entire West Coast.

We were on a bluff, all right—about two hundred feet up. And below it, deep blue—blue-whale blue—as far as a gummed-up eye could see. It was stark and serious, as if God had looked down his nose over his half-glasses, waved a finger, and thundered, "Okay, now put that there," and sploosh, the entire Pacific Ocean got dropped right at the border of Little River.

"You awake?" Ginny yelled.

My candle had burned down in the night, leaving a hole in the middle surrounded by a vampire's cape of wasted wax. Gone was my candle and the comfort of sleep.

My mind flashed on the hang-glider stunt I'd done a few days earlier, diving unparachuted and unafraid. For a second I wished I could fly off the back porch and sail out over the vast Pacific, a faceless shadow to a lounging whale, too distant for it to know or care what I was.

It was eight A.M. I pulled my pants on and stumbled to the door, the coarse carpet tickling my bare feet. I hesitated for a second before letting Ginny in. One more knuckly knock. The flip of a latch, the turn of a knob, and there she was, freshly scrubbed, keen-eyed, and lovely.

She thrust a bacon and egg sandwich and a container of coffee at me. "I assumed you hadn't *gotten* any," she said sardonically.

I didn't answer, just stood there devouring the food. We stared uncomfortably out the sliding doors at the view. The only sound was the surf below and my occasional swallowing.

"Tell me something," Ginny said. "When you think of isolation, what painting comes to mind?"

"*The Mill*," I replied reflexively, referring to the Rembrandt of a lonely windmill up on a bluff overlooking a dark river.

"Mmm," she said. "*The Mill*. I'm not surprised."

I tossed the paper cup in the wastebasket, my stomach strangling my breakfast. "Ginny," I said. "About last night . . ." I reached for her. She pulled away, turned her back to me, and started sobbing.

I handed her a tissue from the box on the nightstand. She snatched it, leaving me with a torn piece.

"You hurt me," she said.

"Please . . . let me explain. The last thing in the world I want to do is—"

Ginny slapped me across the face. "Wake up!" she cried, as I stumbled back two steps. The sting of shame hurt more than my cheek.

"What a waste of mascara," Ginny sniffled, inspecting her Kleenex.

Then she looked past me out the open front door. "There's Pop. Let's get the directions to Mona's."

I slid the big Baggie with the two Leonardo pages and the translation under my T-shirt, tucked it into my jeans, threw on the double gun rig and my leather jacket, and followed her out.

Pop was standing in front of the main house with a woman dressed in waitress garb. He spotted us and waved us over, shouting, "Holmes, Watson, front and center.

"This is Sue Ann," Pop announced. "Help me out. She's bringing up two kids by herself. What do you think, I should give her a nice raise, right? Of course."

He noisily chewed a piece of candy from a gold box of Godiva chocolates. "She gave me these to butter me up and it worked." He grinned. "Smart broad. I mean girl. Aw hell, I don't know."

"Broad," Sue Ann jumped in, smiling at Pop. She looked sturdy, but worn. Up near her collar, she wore a stickpin—a ceramic pig in a black top hat, smoking a stogie. I asked her where she got it.

She told me she made them, sort of a side thing. "I sell them for twelve-fifty," she said.

"Will you take twenty bucks for him?" I asked.

"Um . . . sure."

I handed her a bill. "Andy Jackson says hello."

Sue Ann passed me the pin and I carefully threaded it through Ginny's lapel. She actually blushed.

"Well," Sue Ann said to Pop, tucking the bill in her vest pocket. "Must be my lucky day." She strolled off toward the restaurant.

Ginny pulled on her collar and went eye to eye with the pig. "Is there some cruel significance to your choice of gift?"

"Not at all," I said with utmost sincerity. "I may be a lot of things, but cruel isn't one of them."

"I coulda told you that, Watson," Pop said to Ginny. "Look at his peepers. It's always in the peepers. Now have a chocolate. Both of you. Go on. Who cares if it's morning."

Ginny fished one out of the box and popped it in her mouth.

"Chewy, huh?" Pop said.

"Mmm."

"Holmes, pick one out for yourself. The ones with the Rice Krispies are good."

I did as he instructed.

"Now, how about a stroll through the garden. I'll go fix a fire in Watson's room."

"Good idea, Pop," I said. Ginny looked undecided.

"Have it cracklin' in fifteen minutes," the old codger added, ambling away.

"But we need directions, Pop," Ginny shouted after him.

Pop pointed toward the garden. "Elementary, Watson. You can't miss it."

Ginny peered at me thoughtfully, a smudge of chocolate in one corner of her mouth. I headed into the garden. She followed.

The path was bordered by large, pink-blossomed trees interspersed with just about every kind of flower a person could imagine. Pop's garden was lush and sweet-smelling, a place where a hummingbird could make himself a good living, with a path just wide enough for two people to walk next to each other, arm in arm.

The morning light blanketed us, its warmth soaking through the back of my jacket, massaging my tense shoulders. Underneath, I felt the cool steel of guns, waiting. In the distance, a lawn mower started up.

Ginny stopped about twenty feet in and knelt down to smell a cup-shaped, pinkish flower. I took two steps past her and turned around.

"I want to know about the fire," she said to the flower.

The taste in my mouth switched from sweet to acrid. I inhaled deeply, deliberately, hoping the perfume of the garden would over-power the olfactory memory of curling smoke. A moment passed. Ginny pivoted, still kneeling, and looked up at me, her vitreous brown eyes owning me.

"No you don't," I replied weakly, my energy focused on prying myself from memory's grip.

Ginny held out her hand and I helped her up. She pulled me close.

"Why are you doing this to me?" I whispered.

"Because I need you whole," she answered.

Whole. My hand began to shake. *She needs me. Whole.*

We stood silently among the flowers, each one an offering to the caterpillars and the calendar. My eyes wandered over Ginny's beautiful face.

A flock of birds flapped by overhead. She looked up for a second, then back at me.

"I know you're scared," she said. "Not as much of what's out there, but of what's in here." She firmly placed her palm against my heart.

"There's nothing in there," I uttered, my eyes misting up.

"That July night in 1980," she said softly. "You let go of that win-dowsill and never touched ground. You've been orbiting in the gravity of your own past, too terrified to reenter your own atmosphere. But, listen to me, Reb. This journey has forced you down. The Circles of Truth—they are *your* truth. *You're* the traveler. The twenty-circle path is *your* path. Wherever Leonardo meant for it to lead, it's led you to me and it's leading you back to you. I don't know why, but I'm your Ginny, your earth."

She closed her eyes and tilted her head back slightly. "Kiss me, Reb." Her moist lips parted expectantly.

She was my ground—my soft place to fall. This . . . girl from the crowd outside the Danieli, the girl driving the boat in the lagoon, the da Vincian translator, the snorer, the drooler, the voracious Venetian.

My chest was warm where her hand had touched me. I felt giddy and grateful. I kissed her—a slow and gentle kiss; the tips of our tongues touched and the sensation lit me brighter than a shooting star.

"*Un bacio,*" Ginny whispered.

"One kiss," I answered.

"I want to feel you inside me," she said. "Now."

The warmth in my chest spread south. Still holding my hand, she led me back down the path toward Same Time. I pulled my earlobe and grinned.

We emerged from the garden. A Japanese pickup truck with a metal mesh trailer full of landscaping equipment idled off the side of the main road, twenty yards away. Its doors were open, the back gate down, and two men were loading up a big John Deere riding mower. A new black Suburban with tinted windows was parked at an angle in front of the main house. Suburbanites checking in.

Seventy-five yards down the private road to Same Time and Next Year, I noticed white smoke streaming skyward from Ginny's brick chimney. I was figuring out how I was going to shoo Pop out of the room politely when I saw a man passing inside my open doorway; it wasn't Pop.

My mind drew into focus. I glanced at Ginny out of the corner of my eye. She was looking at the ocean, humming the theme from *Beauty and the Beast*. I unsnapped my jacket.

The landscapers' tailgate slammed. The two cab doors closed one after the other and the truck pulled onto the road, slowly descending the hill toward the exit. I grabbed Ginny firmly by the upper arm; she quit humming midphrase.

"Ouch!"

"Ginny," I said, "run to that truck right now and jump on the back." She looked at me, confused. "What?"

"Right now. Run as fast as you can." I pushed her hard. She stumbled into a jog as the truck pulled away, her look of puzzlement morphing into fear. She lifted her skirt and began to run.

I crisscrossed my hands inside my jacket and drew out both guns, then moved across the lawn in the direction of the cottages, keeping one eye on Ginny.

She was hauling now, closing on the truck as it picked up speed. Twenty yards, fifteen. A few feet from the trailer, she took two big strides and jumped for it. Grabbing the top steel rail, she vaulted over it onto the springy tractor seat. The truck vanished around the bend.

I scrambled behind some high bushes, my pulse throbbing in my ears, fingers tingling against the curves of the triggers. I sucked in sea air, filling my lungs for the fight. How many in the cabin, I wondered. After the party in the lagoon, after Milan, there'd be more than two, for sure.

How'd they find us? Damn! I made the reservation from the car phone. I wasn't thinking. Think now. Money's in the car, notes under my shirt. Get out of here.

I was a few feet from the Jag when I heard Pop's voice cry out from the cottage. "You peckers are in a heap of trouble!"

I couldn't let them hurt Pop.

"Shaddap, old man!" a gravelly voice yelled in a German accent. Glass broke with that shrill sound it makes when it hits a fireplace.

"That lamp cost two hundred smackers in '68, sonny!" Pop shrieked.

I heard an "ooofff," followed by Pop's muffled, "Ho boy." Two male voices chuckled.

A dark figure passed in front of the open side window of the other cabin—a balding man with an Aloha shirt, sporting a scrawny yellow ponytail. I recognized him from Venice: the guy piloting the yacht. Was Tecci in there? I hoped so.

I ducked low and reached the side of the cabin, pressed my body against the shingles, and tried to listen to the voices over the crash of the surf.

Somebody spoke in German to someone named Rolf. Another voice, a high one, said something I didn't understand.

I slinked around back and squatted by the deck. The sliding glass door was closed, the drapes drawn. I eyed my boots mournfully, slipped them off, wishing they were sneakers. I crept up the stairs, hoping Rolf and his buddy wouldn't see my shadow through the curtain and open fire.

I plastered myself against the house between the edge of the sliding glass door and the deck rail. With my guns shoulder-high, I reached a stockinged foot out and gave an Adirondack chair a tiny shove, then waited.

One of the men approached the door, mumbling. I held my breath. He pulled back the drapes and slid the glass open. He wasn't holding a gun.

Stepping out onto the deck, his eye immediately took in the view. "*Ser schön, Hans!*" he shouted, admiring the panorama.

I stuck a Sig in his ear, whispered into it, "*Guten tag, Rolf.*"

He stiffened. I spun him around and stepped behind him. Hans was kneeling on the far side of the bed, the mattress jacked up in front of him. All I saw were two hands with dirty fingernails. I aimed my other gun midway between them.

I thumbed the hammer. Hans exposed a pockmarked face.

"How do you say 'bang' in German?" I said.

Then a third guy—a real muscleman—stepped from the bathroom, an Uzi slung over his shoulder. He caught sight of me and retreated. A second later, a barrage of bullets cut through the bathroom wall, taking out Hans, two framed watercolors, the telephone on the nightstand, and just about everything along the front half of my cozy cottage.

I yanked Rolf back onto the deck. He stumbled and threw his hands up, knocking one of the Sigs from my grip. It scuttled along the wood floor onto the lawn.

Pivoting, he threw a good right hook that landed on my chest and knocked me against the deck rail. He followed it with a left, but I blocked it, smacking him with the other Sig on his nose. He cried out in agony, blood spurting from both nostrils.

Mr. Muscles emerged from the bathroom, letting loose another burst from the Uzi which splintered the Adirondack chairs and caught Rolf in the back. As his chest erupted, he plunged forward with a look of total surprise, smashing into me, sending me right off the deck.

Muscles ran toward me, a look of maniacal joy on his chiseled face. Rolling to my right, I heard Pop yell from inside Same Time, "Goddamn you peckers!"

The big man fired another short burst, weeding the yard right next to me. I kept rolling. When the shots stopped, I aimed at his center and squeezed off three rounds. He fell back, crashing through the sliding glass door.

As I scrambled to my feet, I heard Pop's assailants leave Ginny's cottage and bang open the front door of mine. Before they could see me, I dashed up the steps to Ginny's porch. Tucking the Sig into my pants, I hopped on the narrow wooden rail and boosted myself to the roof. Crawling like a lizard up the asphalt shingles, I crouched by the smoking chimney, assessing. Three down. Off in the distance, guests and employees were running in every direction. To my left, the Pacific yawned at the drama, spitting surf at ancient rock.

Duckwalking across the roof, I moved silently toward the hubbub emanating from my shot-up cabin.

I was at the edge when the two guys who'd laughed at Pop stepped onto my deck, side by side. The one on the left had a shock of red hair with a lot of goop in it. He gripped an Uzi with both hands, poised to fire.

The guy on the right wore wraparound sunglasses and a porkpie hat. He was packing a silver automatic with a black rubber handle. Though I had the edge on them, I didn't want to shoot them. Not yet. I needed to talk to them first.

Just then, someone near the main house shouted, "There, on the roof!"

The two guys looked off toward the source of the sound, then started to turn toward me. I jumped, and the three of us tumbled to the deck floor, amid the remnants of chairs and broken glass.

I scrambled to my feet. Red stayed down, but Porkpie was made of strong stuff. He'd lost his gun, but took a swing at me that landed square on my jaw. I fell back and tripped over Mr. Muscles's legs sticking out from the living room. My shoulder blade hit the jagged glass of the broken sliding door.

I lurched forward and threw a straight jab at Porkpie's grim face. Blocking it with a forearm, he spun to back-kick me in the stomach; I saw it coming and lunged at him to close the distance.

His kick was still partially in the chamber, but the force of it, combined with my forward motion, sent us through the railing onto the grass.

I leapt to my feet and reached for the Sig, but it had fallen onto the ground next to Porkpie. Behind me on the porch, Red was on his knees pointing his gun at me. I saw his finger squeezing the trigger, knew I'd had it.

Then I heard the sound of a gunshot from off in the woods and Red collapsed. Three more rounds kicked up the grass and dirt around Porkpie as he rolled over and out of the line of fire.

He picked up my Sig and pointed it at me, grinning.

A millisecond later, a yellow streak smashed him in the back of the head with a fireplace poker. Porkpie crumbled like dry cake, his hat flopping off when he hit the turf.

Pop flashed me his pearly white dentures. "Better'n Mickey Mantle," he chuckled. "Huh, Holmes?"

I looked back to the woods where the shot had come from. Nothing but the diminishing rustle of retreating feet on leaves and branches.

Thanks, Archie.

thirteen

I felt Porkpie's wrist for a pulse. He had one.

"Did I crack his melon?" Pop asked.

I checked and shook my head.

"Aw shucks. You know that bastard punched me right in the pancreas? And look at my place. Jeepers! What the hell did these fellas want, Holmes?"

"Pop, Ginny's gone and the cops are going to be here any minute."

"Damn tootin', if they don't get lost on the way over. Now what the Sam Hill . . . ?"

"I've got to get out of here," I said, heading for the Jag, forgetting my boots and guns.

Pop grabbed my sleeve, stopping me cold. "Holmes," he said gravely. "You look me in the eye." He gave me the discerning gaze of a wise old man—a good man who'd carved maybe sixty Thanksgiving turkeys, seen wars, buried friends. He said sternly, "Tell me something good. Right now."

"There's almost two million dollars in the trunk of my car," I said.

Pop raised his wiry silver brows, held my stare and my arm.

"No," I told him. "I'm not a thief."

He let go of me. "Well, then I'm stumped," he said, smoothing my sleeve.

"Here it is fast, Pop. I'm trying to do the right thing for Leonardo da Vinci."

"Leonardo da Vinci! Why, he's older than me! You joshing me?"

"I'm telling you the truth, and I'll tell you the rest later if you help me get out of here."

He peered at me a half-second, then grinned. "Well, that's gotta be a hell of a story. Hot damn! I guess you'll be needing the Baby Face Nelson Suite now. Get your stuff—what's left of it." He looked down at my stockinged feet. "Starting with your hoofs."

My boots were waiting for me by the deck steps. I slipped them on and searched the yard for my guns. I located them in the freshly mown grass.

I raced into Same Time and Next Year and grabbed our belongings, while Pop stayed outside to guard Porkpie. I had everything in the trunk in less than a minute.

"What about this pecker?" Pop asked, kicking him.

"He's coming with me," I answered. I picked up his brown hat and stuck it on his head. "We're going to have a little chat."

Pop helped me drag my still-unconscious prisoner over to the Jag. Together we hefted him into the passenger seat.

Pop gave me the combination to a lock that barred a road leading to a cabin at the far end of the property. He said he'd keep an eye out for Ginny and point her in my direction, and he'd come by later after ironing things out with the police.

I pulled down the driveway, leaning forward to keep my sore shoulder blade away from the seat. As I made a left onto Highway 1, I could hear the sound of sirens wailing from the south. I worried about Ginny, wondered where she was.

Following Pop's directions, I headed north a quarter of a mile, then pulled off to the left by a chain suspended between two moss-covered trees that blocked what looked like an old logging path. I got out of the car and opened the combination lock. It was just like the one on every gym locker in the world.

The rounded steel in my hand, the ridged black plastic dial and small, indented white lines and numbers, felt so familiar to me.

Touching them stimulated something more powerful than school memories, but I couldn't stop to let the thought coalesce. The lock opened on the first pull.

Back behind the wheel again, I drove twenty feet down the overgrown path, stopped, then ran back to replace the chain.

Porkpie was slumped against the seat, just coming to, when I returned to the car. I pulled out one of the Sigs and stuck it in his face, keeping one eye on the barely discernible road and the other on him. I wanted to pounce on him, break his neck with my teeth, tear him apart, and howl with fury.

For a full five minutes I drove through weeds, shrubs, and assorted fauna at a pace that barely kept the speedometer needle bouncing off zero. Porkpie was fully awake now, eyeing me like a rabid Doberman.

We emerged from the woods and entered a little field, at the edge of which stood a small, one-story, split-log cabin. Tiny porch, one window on either side of the low door, fieldstone fireplace, and a lopsided lean-to shed. An inch behind the cabin was a hundred-foot cliff and the cold Pacific—the classic Hollister House view. I stopped the car and turned off the motor. The surf resounded against the rocks below.

"I'm going to get out and come around," I told Porkpie. "Put your hands on your head. If you move, I'll shoot both your knees."

His contemptuous eyes followed me to the passenger door. Opening it, I stepped back and instructed him to get out. He obliged. The crook of my arm was stiff from holding it in one position.

I told him to put his hands down.

He lowered them, clenching and unclenching.

"Tell me where Krell and Tecci are," I demanded.

Porkpie reached behind his head to touch the lump, winced, and hunched down like he was going to be sick. He dry-heaved once, and, as he straightened back up, threw a lightning-fast front-kick at my hand, knocking the gun into the web of tall grass.

Positioning himself in a karate stance, he whipped a roundhouse kick that I barely pulled away from. In a fluid move, he shuffle-stepped in and launched another right at my chest. This time he connected, sending me flying backward about six feet past the house, knocking half the wind out of me.

I grabbed my gut and felt for the other Sig, but before I could get it out he was on me, driving a heel into my ribs.

I covered up, rolled, and scrambled out of the way and to my feet. He closed the distance again and threw another kick that connected, propelling me closer to the cliff and the angry ocean below.

"A kickboxer against a stuntman," he hissed, grinning at me through yellow teeth. "Let's see some stunts, boy."

Again I reached for the gun; again he drove his foot into my aching gut. I stumbled backward almost to the edge of the precipice, arms out, gasping for breath. Slipping on the rocks where the field gave way to the cliff, I struggled to regain my balance. I couldn't catch my wind; my diaphragm was paralyzed.

"Ready? Action!" Porkpie shouted, setting up for the kick that would send me over the edge. As he threw his leg out, I dropped to one knee, ducked, and punched him right in the sack with everything I had. He grabbed his crotch and cried out. I put a hand on the ground for support and swept his feet out from under him. He fell back, his hat falling off, and slipped on the same rocks that had almost gotten me the moment before.

Arms flailing, Porkpie tried desperately to stay upright. I reached for the gun. As I pulled it from the rig, he slipped and tumbled silently off the cliff.

I lay back on my elbows and stared, saucer-eyed, at the cloudless sky until I was able to draw a steady breath. I continued to lie there, half in the tall weeds, half on the cold rock, for maybe ten minutes before I finally sat up.

My stomach hurt, my shoulder blade hurt, I'd killed two guys, my would-be informant had just turned into pâté, and Ginny was starring in *Gone with the Landscapers.* All I had was an aching heart and a crunched-up porkpie hat.

With a quivering hand, I picked the damn thing up, inched over to the edge of the precipice, and tossed it over the cliff.

I shrugged out of my jacket and inspected it. There were two four-inch tears to the left of the mid-back. I reached over to feel my shoulder blade where it hurt. Two big slivers of glass protruded.

Painfully, I plucked them out with my thumb and forefinger. Each piece was triangular, from the sliding glass door Mr. Muscles had shattered. I flung them at the ocean.

I couldn't very well cruise into town looking for Ginny; if the cops got me, I'd be no good to her. I had no choice but to wait for Pop. I trudged up the stairs to the Baby Face Nelson Suite.

I entered the cabin, expecting to walk into a faceful of cobwebs. Instead, I found Pop's quaint private little hideaway.

In the center of an oval, braided rug stood an old easel with an amateurish watercolor of a bird in a tree taped to it. A padded piano stool—the kind you can lower or raise by screwing or unscrewing—stood in front of the easel.

A well-made rocking chair sat in the corner by the fireplace, a neatly folded Mexican blanket draped over its back. A handsome oak pirate's chest was placed next to the chair; on top of it sat a tall kerosene hurricane lantern and an open box of kitchen matches. In the far corner of the room was a sink with an iron-handled pump.

I cranked it a few times to get the water running and splashed some on my face and the back of my neck. The cool water refreshed me. I pulled Leonardo's notes out, soaked my shirt, and dabbed my wounds.

I didn't see a mirror so I went outside and looked over my shoulder at the reflection in the window. I crossed my arms as if I were doing some chest warmup exercises to see how far the cuts opened. Both needed stitches. Though I kept a fully stocked first-aid kit in the trunk of my car, it wouldn't do me much good by myself.

I slipped my jacket on and sat down on the front steps and pulled Leonardo's pages from my pocket. To my relief, they didn't look any worse for the wear.

I peered long and hard at the drawings. A hoisting system? A harness? What about those nested tubes? They could be connected to each other, or to the Dagger. But maybe not. Probably not. And those Circles. Twenty rings of what? And would they lead to the Dagger?

The afternoon sun bowled its lazy way across the western sky while Leonardo and I camped on the porch, rocking back and forth together, alone at the edge of the earth.

I was ruminating over how cruel the moon looked as it rose in the gold-spotted heavens when Pop appeared, driving a golf cart through a narrow clearing I hadn't even noticed. As he pulled up in front of me and parked, I tucked Leonardo's notes back in my jacket.

"Pop!" I shouted. "Did you hear anything about Ginny? Have you seen her?"

"Nope and nope," he said, extricating himself from the vehicle.

I felt crushing dismay.

"Saw a bunch of coppers, though," he added. "They had a regular party scooping up the stiffs. Don't get much mayhem around here that isn't on TV."

"What'd you tell them about me?" I managed.

He pulled a brown paper grocery bag out of the floor well of the cart, shot me a grin. "Oh, forty-five, five-eight, two-ten. You know, short and squat. Now come around here and get these sleeping bags."

I did. They were the green ones with the red flannel liners.

"Where's that pecker who punched me? You find the rope in the shed? Got him tied up there, or what? I'm gonna kick his ass."

I told him what had occurred.

"You're kidding me," Pop said, hobbling up the steps and into the house. "He tell you what you wanted to know first?"

"No."

"Well, that's too bad," Pop said, setting the groceries down on the pirate's chest.

I dropped the sleeping bags, lit the lantern, and slipped off my jacket.

"Whoa, Holmes," he said. "Those cuts need attention. I better go get some stuff to fix you with. I patched a few guys up in my day, you know."

I told him about the kit in the car and stepped out to get it. The firewood must have been well seasoned; Pop had a blaze going when I got back.

He had me pull the piano stool over in front of the rocker and sit down with my back to him, while he broke out a bottle of Cuervo Gold and two shot glasses. He poured me one.

"Drink this," he urged. "It won't make your back hurt any less, but it'll take your mind off of Watson."

"Nothing could do that," I told him.

"Then drink it 'cause you're sitting on my piano stool."

I took it and knocked it back while he poured one for himself. Then he cracked open the first-aid kit and went to work.

"Gee," he said, sitting down on the edge of the rocker seat. "Betadine, sutures, Lidocaine, syringe . . . What are you, a spy or something?"

"Actually I'm a stuntman."

"Well that clears everything up, don't it. You were just practicing over there at the inn. Now let me see here, I'm gonna poke you with the needle and then stitch you up like a mattress. You pour us each another slug of apple juice. It'll boost our doctor-patient relations."

I did as he requested. Pop took a snort. "Ooh, that's tasty," he said. "Okay now, Sherlock, I'll knit and you'll tell me the tale like you promised."

Pop took his time sewing me up while I told him the whole

story—my parents, Greer, Tecci, Krell, Venice, Archie, Ginny, Beckett, Gibraltar, Leonardo, and the Circles of Truth.

When I got to the part about Mona, he let out a hoot. "So you're the one she was talking about! You're Mona's Reb."

He dressed the wounds with sterile pads and adhesive tape.

"As far as I can tell there's three possibilities," Pop said. "One, my hearing aids have been picking up an Orson Welles broadcast; two, you just laid twenty miles of the sweetest-smelling shit that ever came out of a pucker; or three, this is a genuine case of truth being a whole lot stranger than fiction. I can't come up with a reason why it's not number three."

I fished the Leonardo notes out of my jacket.

Pop regarded them carefully, squinting to bring them into focus. "By goddamn jingo . . . Number three it is."

By the firelight I saw his smiling eyes taking in the mystery and wonder of it all, like a kid looking at a Buck Rogers comic book.

"Leonardo da Vinci," he uttered slowly, the tequila making each word glisten. "Mona have the slightest inkling the kind of hellacious pandemonium's following you around?"

"Haven't told her a thing. Just that I was coming."

"I didn't figure, because she would have said more than 'oh baby' when we were in the sack night before yesterday." He wiggled his eyebrows at me. "Yup," he said. "Me and Mona. Right over Viagra Falls. No barrel."

The old guy pulled out some roasted turkey sandwiches. "Have one of these," he offered. "Fresh bird."

I refused; the nagging worry over Ginny wrung out my stomach like a wet mop. I slugged another tequila.

"Some people are diamonds and some are glass," Pop said, taking a bite. "The average Joe wants to tell them apart, he just hits 'em both with a hammer. Me, I'm a specialist. I can feel a fine-cut facet through an oven mitt, see the real thing shining through the blackest night. It's a gift, I guess."

He turned his gaze from the fire to me. "After hearing your story, seeing these pages, and watching you in action, I figure you weigh in at about forty-six carats. That's a half-carat more'n the Hope Diamond.

"Now, Watson, I can't say how many she is, but I figure a lot, by the way she's shimmering in your eyes. I'm telling you she's out there somewhere right this minute, safe and sparkling. I'd bet my eyeteeth on it—if I still had them."

Pop took another bite, his cheek stretching out over it as he chewed. "Now here's the thing, Reb," he mumbled. "You don't have to turn off Ginny's shimmer to eat."

He shoved my sandwich at me.

I took it and munched it down, grateful for his words. He was right about Ginny. She was precious. And I was going to find her, and keep her.

We sat in our respective seats and ate by the fire, wading further into the Cuervo.

After a while I said, "I apologize for bringing this on you, Pop. About your place getting ruined, and you getting hurt."

"Aw hell, kid," Pop snorted, "I liked it. You think I'd be here if I didn't? And about the money, I don't want a goddamn nickel. As far as I'm concerned, that sumbitch Krell owes it to you for what happened to your folks."

I poured him another shot. He sipped it like nectar. "You know, I'm an orphan, too."

A lump rose in my throat.

"Yup," he said, "my old man was in the bootlegging business. You know what that was, bootlegging?"

"Transporting black-market booze when it was outlawed."

"Uh-huh. Made a nice dollar doing it. Lot of bad seeds, though, in that line of work. My dad was one of 'em. He had some wheat in him, I suppose, but he was mostly chaff. That's what my mother said. Her name was Beatrice. She had a bakeshop in town—doughnuts, pastry, cinnamon buns that smelled so good they'd make you pant. Everybody wanted those buns. Bing Crosby even came through one time when he was getting to be real popular. Said he'd heard about 'em from somebody down in Hollywood. Bought eight boxes."

Pop sipped some more tequila. "Mm, I like this stuff," he said. "Anyway, where was I?"

"Bing," I reminded him.

"Oh . . . you see, my old man was using the back of the bakeshop for stashing booze. He had a guy named Drymouth Dan Hollister helping him, would keep things sorted out when my dad was making deliveries. Dan always sounded like he'd been sucking on a Sugar Daddy for two weeks. Made a clicking sound like he was out of saliva, ya see? That's where he got his moniker. But he was a handsome bastard, maybe as good-looking as you, without all the muscles. How's your back, anyway? You sore?"

"No," I lied, and prodded him on. Pop's voice and the rhythm of the rocking chair had a soothing effect.

He continued. "Old Drymouth, he got a taste for my mom's buns, too, only not the ones came out of the oven, you understand. And I guess she liked the way he combed his hair. He had wavy hair slicked back with lots of Vitalis, like Victor Mature, remember him?"

"Yeah," I said, sipping, "wavy hair, lots of Vitalis."

"That's the one. So, my dad walks in on them while they're docking, so to speak, near the deep-fat fryer, and surprises the living piss out of them. In a fury he lunges at them and knocks over the hot oil and it splashes right in my mother's face. She screams and grabs the nearest thing she can find, which is a kitchen knife, and stabs my old man. He stumbles out of the room and into the front of the store where everybody's lined up for the sweets, and croaks right on the floor next to the cruller case. My old lady realizes what she's done and that her face is ruined so she grabs Drymouth's Saturday-night special and blasts herself right in the ticker. And that was that. Put a dent in the bakery business, I'll tell you."

Neither of us laughed.

"So, anyway, Drymouth felt sorry for me and ended up taking me in. I saw my share of shot-up guys—that's how I knew how to stitch you up. Like a bicycle, you never forget. Or is that an elephant? Anyhow, Dan went legit in the liquor business when prohibition was repealed. Over the years, he stashed away a bundle, which he passed on to me and I used to buy the inn when I got out of the service. Named it after him."

"What'd you do in the service?" I asked.

"Engineer. Army Corps of Engineers. Bridge builder."

He picked up a log, poked the burnt ones with it, and tossed it on top. The crackle of the revived fire and the distant pounding surf made me long for Ginny.

Pop eyeballed me for a second, reading my face. "So," he said, picking up the notes, "you're back on Watson. I mean Ginny. Damn! Antonia."

"All three of 'em," I answered. "I've got to figure out the Circles of Truth. Without Ginny's help. I'll need Mona more than ever now."

"I could go for Mona myself right now," he said. "Or a doughnut."

"Ginny's a mountain tiger." My tongue was thick with alcohol.

"Mountain tiger? What kind of bullshit is that?"

I was in the clouds with Ginny when Pop mumbled, "Doughnuts and mountains." Then he hiccuped. "Nerts!" he swore. "I hate the hiccups."

"What'd you say?" I asked, picking up one of the pages of Leonardo's notes.

"I said, 'Nerts, I hate the hiccups.'"

"No," I said, staring at the Circles of Truth. "You said 'doughnuts and mountains.' Doughnuts and mountains . . ." Searchlights flickered in my mind, illuminating what?

"Yeah, well, you know, tequila's good," Pop said, his speech slurred.

I pointed to the Circles, excitement prickling as the outline of a concept emerged. "Say these rings here were tossed onto a mountain; you know, like that Fisher-Price kid's toy with the different-colored plastic doughnuts in graduated sizes?"

"Yeah, sure. Look like dildoes with the rings off."

"The point is that the plastic rings are parts of a puzzle. A simple puzzle. In order to solve it, the kid has to line them up in the right order so they're touching. Do you get me? The doughnuts . . . have to touch. They have to *touch*." Thrill radiated through me.

"Hold it," he said, trying to catch my wave of Cuervo insight. "What're you saying?"

"Here," I said, tapping the page. "Maybe Leonardo's rings are all pieces of the same circle, only sliced apart and shrunk to ever smaller sizes, and each set of ten of them makes up one complete Circle of Truth, whatever that is—a code or something. So in order to solve it you have to blow each inner ring up until they all touch, forming one circular message. Two in this case, because there are two sets of them. I'm on to something. I know it."

Pop let out a gush of air that smelled like turkey and tequila.

"I think maybe you are. Hard to tell, though. I'm pretty much in the bag." He closed his eyes, laid his old head back. "In the morning I'll take you to Mona's."

"Do you know if she has a scanner?" I asked.

Pop folded his hands over his belly. "Course she's got standards, Holmes. Got high ones. She's seeing me."

fourteen

I dreamt I was a fresh cruller in a brightly lit case in a doughnut shop, clad in nothing but a sugar glaze, lying back, feet crossed, hands covering my groin, in a line of other crullers. Outside the case, a crowd of people looked in, pointing at me, singling me out. Mean-looking, wavy-haired men in zoot suits; women with full lips and hats with netting over their faces; children with comic books and cowlicks, eyeing me with lip-smacking hunger.

The crullers to my right were perched up on sugary elbows, gawking at me: Krell, the maniacal treasure hunter; Tecci with his wriggling wraparound snake; ring-polishing, coldhearted Beckett.

To my left, Mom and Dad reached glazed hands out to me. Next to them was Ginny, also reaching—to take me in her arms. And next to her was Leonardo—the only one not looking at me. The Dagger was between his teeth, and he was wearing a harness attached to a long rope. He slowly pulled it, eyes on something above him at the top of the case. I tried to see what it was, but couldn't make it out. It surprised me that he didn't seem to care he was a cruller.

I heard the sound of water splashing and momentarily panicked. If you're a cruller and get soaked, it's all over.

More water, like the drip from a turned-off hose. Then singing—terrible singing. A cross between Ethel Merman and a wounded raccoon. It was Pop crooning "It Had to Be You."

I opened one heavy eyelid, facedown on the sleeping bag. The door was open, Pop standing at the edge of the front porch, zipping his pants. He'd been serenading his dick. Behind him, the morning coastal fog spread out like dingy carpet.

"Top of the floor to you, Pop," I croaked.

"Morning, Reb. You hungry? I brought some breakfast from the inn." He waved a finger at a round picnic basket.

Springing up, suddenly fully awake, I asked him, "You went to the inn? Any sign of Ginny?"

"Afraid not. Manny the landscaper, he said him and Kurt just about crapped in the truck when she jumped onto the tractor. They pulled over right away to find out what the heck she was doing up there, and while they're pumping her for information, they hear gunfire. So they hop in the cab and take off, and don't look back for a couple of miles. When they do, she's gone."

"Damn," I said. "She could have spent the night in the woods, for all we know. Or Tecci could have snatched her."

"Don't go thinking the worst," Pop said. "It won't help." He sat down in the rocker beside me, handing me a biscuit. I chewed it absently.

"Do you think it's possible she could have found her way to Mona's?" I said.

"Shit, no. I'd have heard about it. Did she have any money?"

"Some."

"Well, see, that's good," he said.

"Yeah," I agreed, my brain clearer now. "If Tecci or Krell were up here, they wouldn't be lurking around on Highway One. They'd be in some hotel nearby, not cruising the coast road, right?"

"I suppose so," Pop said. "They'd be waiting for word from those peckers you laid out. You've got to think positive. Now turn around so I can check my knitting, make sure you're not getting infected."

I let Pop take off the bandage. "Looks clean. I believe I missed my true calling. Should have been a tailor." He removed fresh dressings from the first-aid kit and applied them.

Think positive, Pop had instructed. I was positive I didn't know where Ginny was. I was also sure I'd had some sort of insight into Leonardo's Circles last night. I desperately wanted to find her, but didn't know where to look. I had to do what I could, not what I wanted. And what I could do was try to unravel the code.

That meant Mona.

Pop had driven back from the inn in his Range Rover. I slipped into the rear seat and lay down out of sight, knowing better than to show my face. We headed down Highway 1, me feeling a tad queasy. I never liked riding in the backseat, even sitting up, and certainly not with a hangover. When we got off the main drag, Pop instructed me to hop up front, which I gladly did.

"Where are we?" I asked.

"Ukiah Road on the way to Comptche. Be at Mona's in a minute."

"How'd you get to know her, anyway?" I asked, watching the scenery—tall, wise trees, happy squirrels with plenty of holes to climb into and not many tires to get squashed under.

"I know all the babes around here," he said, with a sideways grin. "I was a regular Sir Galahad. Plenty of steel in the little jouster. You know, making merry with the old maidens. Dispatched 'em all forthwith at one time or another. But none of 'em come close to Mona. Now she's a diamond, all right. I mean a night-sky-star kinda winker. That doesn't quite get the point across. She's celestial. That's it! Mona's celestial. Don't you think? Even if you were a youngster last time you saw her, you must have known that."

I remembered Mona, clogs clopping up the streets of the old neighborhood. She always paused at the house next door, if the lady was outside, to compliment her on the scrawniest yellow rosebushes in all of Berkeley. There was definitely something celestial about Mona. And I was the guy who hadn't responded to her cards.

"Yeah, Pop," I agreed. "Celestial."

"Damn tootin," he said. "Okay, here we are."

He pulled up a steep gravel driveway within feet of a tiny sky blue house with dark shutters. The front screen opened and out came

Mona, plumper than before, with long silver hair that used to be brown. She wore a flowery dress and cork-soled denim sandals.

I felt a flutter in my belly, a tug on my heart.

Pop jumped out of the car like he was eighteen and made his way up the porch with a sprightly step. Mona kept her eyes on me as I followed. Pop hugged her tenderly, then stepped away from her as I approached.

"Reb," she said, hands on her full hips.

"Sorry I'm a day late," I said self-consciously, stopping in front of her.

She cupped my face with age-spotted hands.

"You're not late," she said. "You're right on time." Then a look of sorrow crossed her face. "I feel guilty, as though I let Martha down. I tried to—"

"I saved your cards," I told her. "Every one. You didn't let Martha down. I did."

"Well . . . now is no time for regret. You've come to me with great urgency. And after some terrible trouble at the inn. Tell me how I can help."

Her little house was filled with the scent of freshly baked cookies. Mona guided us upstairs to a small, brightly lit office adorned with framed logos of what I guessed were local businesses. I pulled the two pages of Leonardo's notes from my backpack and handed them to her without a word.

She held them gingerly, staring at them with a puzzled look. "Oh my Lord," she gasped, her eyes opening wide. "Are these what I think they are? Am I holding something of Leonardo da Vinci's? Is this . . . could it be . . . the Circles of Truth . . . the Medici Dagger?"

"I can't explain the whole story now, but—"

"You owe me no explanation," she said, studying the Circles. "Just tell me what you know about them."

"They're some sort of code Leonardo devised to send a message. They go together somehow. I know that. Maybe they're a symbolic alphabet. Remember your Sherlock Holmes?"

"The Dancing Men!"

I told her about the insight I'd had the previous night and explained that I wanted to eliminate the spaces between the rings, enlarging each one until they all touched, forming a solid image.

Mona understood instantly. She examined the pages, looking from one to the other. Then, spinning in her chair, she switched on her computer and flatbed scanner.

"Let's find your dancing men, shall we?"

First Mona scanned Ginny's translation and each page of notes just to have them on disk, then captured the image of each Circle. Next, focusing only on Circle One, she scanned the rings of the design individually and put one within the next. I watched carefully as her fingers worked the mouse, clicking and dragging.

When Mona finished, all the rings touched. We sat shoulder to shoulder searching for a pattern, an obvious design, symbols—anything. No dancing men. Nothing distinguishable.

I was surprised at the level of my disappointment. As if Leonardo would invent something simple.

Mona didn't seem to mind. "They could still go together like that," she said. "But maybe they're in the wrong order. Maybe it's not outside ring to inside ring. Maybe it's inside to outside. Some other pattern. I think Leonardo was having a little fun."

Her eyes shone like blue beach glass. "You know what we've got to do now, don't you?"

"We've got to scan each ring and blow it up to every possible size so that each ring could fit in any position in the bull's-eye."

"Exactly!"

We set about printing out ten transparencies for each ring, one for each position in the circle, labeling them #1 through #10 and dividing them into piles by size, so each could be fitted together with the others in every possible way. When we were done, we had a hundred sheets each for Circles of Truth One and Circles of Truth Two. The first combination, outer to inner, hadn't worked. So, next we lined up the rings inner to outer, with the original smallest circle on the outside, largest on the inside.

Nothing. We continued to try different combinations as Pop sat nearby with a yellow pad and pencil, making copious notes, recording the results.

An hour later and still nothing. Frustration crackled in me. *What am I doing? Ginny's out there somewhere, and I've got a couple hundred Circles of Truth and no clue how they go together.*

Pop said, "I could very well be the hungriest bastard ever been to Comptche. I'm going downstairs, fix us all something." I looked at him, overwhelmed with anxiety. He patted me lightly on the shoulder. "She's sparkling out there, Reb. She's sparkling."

Mona looked at him quizzically. "There's tuna in the cupboard," she said.

I heard him hobble out and down the stairs. Mona laid a hand on my knee. Emotion spiked.

"Look at me," she urged.

She peered into my eyes, her gaze caressing every crevice in my rocky cave.

"Martha was a good woman," she said softly. "I knew her for a long time before she adopted you. Knew her husband, George, as well, and how you filled in the space after he died. I knew all about you and your parents. I watched you grow and then you were gone and I wondered what path you chose."

I started to choke up. "Leonardo laid a path for a mighty traveler to follow, Mona. I'm that traveler."

After a moment of hushed silence, she breathed, "I appreciate what it took for you to come to me after all these years. I feel your desperation. I want to help. It's my duty to help you. We're not making sense of Leonardo's shapes and we're missing his pattern. If these are Leonardo's dancing men, we must let them dance."

Her face next to mine, she whispered, "Close your eyes, young man, and tell me what their next step is."

I let my lids fall. Mona moved behind me. She whispered again in my ear, "Now try to clear your mind of all the past and all the future. You are alone with Leonardo. What do you see?"

I felt her fingers massage my temples and let my mind wander.

No clue. The past and the future. Leonardo. No clue.

Suddenly the master's words flashed before me. Ginny's flowing script of Leonardo's notes. "Out then in back and forth one to the other the seer will wander the path and the truth of the past will lead the wise one to the dagger." Out then in. Outer inner. Mona's fingers massaged my temples. In circles, back and forth. And there I was at the combination lock by the road to the Baby Face Nelson Suite where I saw a white-haired Leonardo kneeling, turning the dial. Something profound clicked inside. When I'd touched the lock, more than school memories had been triggered. I hadn't known what. Now I did.

"The Circles rotate."

A big smile crossed Mona's lips. "Of course," she said crisply.

She quickly marked a page with an X, printed it out on a transparency, and handed it to me along with a plastic-tipped pushpin.

Out then in. Outer inner.

I grabbed two transparencies from Circle One: #1 the largest, and #10, the smallest, but in the second-ring size so that it would butt up against #1. Placing the X transparency over them, I stuck a pushpin through dead center and slowly started rotating #10. Mona leaned in, her warm breath on my ear.

"Stop there," she gasped. "Do you see?"

The ice of recognition chilled me like a polar wind. The two rings lined up. They connected.

"Oh my God," I said, "they fit together. But what are they?"

"I know exactly what they are," Mona said. "It isn't symbols. Not dancing men, but calligraphy! It's Leonardo's alphabet. This is a circle of words! You picked the biggest then the smallest, #1 then #10. How did you know to do that?"

"Um . . . this is going to sound weird, but I don't know how else to say it. Leonardo told me. I don't mean I heard his voice say it to me. That would be crazy."

"Not to me. But I understand. You received the information."

"Yes."

"How far did you spin it? This can't be haphazard."

"Of course not. This is Leonardo."

"Right. Each Circle of Truth is comprised of ten rings."

"That's it, Mona!" I shouted. "Ten rings, three hundred and sixty degrees. One ring, thirty-six degrees." Another flush of excitement tingled my toes. "What's next in the layout if they're outer inner?"

"Well, outer inner would be one, ten, two, nine, three, eight, four, seven, five, six. The next would be number two in the third from the largest size."

I fished through the transparencies until I found it, stuck it under the pile, poked the pin through the center and spun it clockwise, thirty-six degrees past where the first one had stopped. The marks connected with the others. I swallowed hard, feeling my Adam's apple rise and fall like a pile driver.

Mona sat down next to me, a look of fascination on her wrinkled face. "Leonardo wrote a message, sliced it in horizontal pieces, put them in a circle, and spun them."

To Pop she shouted, "Rodney Norcross, get your old self up here. Don't miss this!"

I heard Pop creaking up the stairs as I rifled through the transparencies till I found the fourth-largest ring. I attached it to the others, spinning it another thirty-six degrees. It fit!

Pop entered the room carrying a tray of sandwiches. I started singing to the tune of "La Cucaracha": "I'm a gen-ius, I'm a gen-ius, I'm a really coo-ool duuude. I'm a gen-ius, I'm a gen-ius, and that's a winning attitu-u-ude."

Pop and Mona laughed as I fished out the fifth-sized ring with a clammy hand, stuck it on the back, and spun it what I thought was thirty-six degrees past the fourth ring, or one hundred and forty-four degrees. Yow! I sang my little tune again. Pop grabbed Mona and danced to it.

I was doing it. It was working out.

I dug out sixth-position #8, laid it on the back, fanned it out so it was at one hundred eighty degrees and . . . and . . . nothing. I moved it back and forth in small increments. Still nothing.

Pop and Mona stopped dancing.

"I only have the top half of the words," I said, thoroughly deflated. How fast I had fallen from grace. Pluto to Pittsburgh at the speed of stupidity.

Mona picked up the pad and read, "One-ten-two-nine-three, rings one through five, top half of a line. Try the same thing with Truth Two."

They went together as the others had.

"By jingo," Pop howled, "you got the outer halves of two messages. Nice work. Now all you have to do is solve the inside."

I puzzled it out. "The inside of Truth One should be eight-four-seven-five-six, but number eight doesn't work. They obviously go together some different way. What way?"

"Reb," Mona said, "what were you thinking about when I told you to close your eyes?"

"The combination lock."

"Go back there. Say aloud what you see, any pattern you detect."

I shut my eyes and drifted.

Up and down, light and dark, high and low. Happiness and sadness, strain and relief, man and woman, lift and separate.

Antonyms rained on me like wedding rice. My mind arrived back at the chained-off road to the Baby Face Nelson Suite as I unlocked the padlock. "Right, left, right, pull down, success," I said. "Right, left, right. Leonardo said 'back and forth, one to the other.'"

I opened my eyes. "Back and forth. That's it! Number eight from Truth One, Mona. I need it in the sixth size."

She quickly handed it to me.

Back and forth.

I attached it to the five sheets of Truth One already connected with the pin, but this time I spun it *counter*clockwise. Nothing. "I'm wrong," I said, dejection dripping from my tongue. "I can't get it. I'm not the mighty traveler. I'm nothing."

"Shh," Mona said, kneeling down next to me. "You also said 'one to the other.' "

I listened to her words—Leonardo's words. Of course. It had to be. One *circle* to the other.

I grabbed #8 from Circle of Truth Two and attached it to the sheets of Truth One. I spun it counterclockwise, making little adjustments. The piece fit! I quickly attached rings 4-7-5-6 from Truth Two to Truth One, fanning them out counterclockwise. They all connected. I was holding a circle of Leonardo's words.

Somewhere in the distance I heard Pop say, "By jingo," but I was no longer in the room. I was on the path with Leonardo. *We* were the dancing men. I repeated the process with Truth Two. The inner circles of Truth One fit counterclockwise with the outer circles of Truth Two.

I was holding a second complete circular sentence.

I had done it! Two sentences in Leonardo's backward script, from two separate notebook pages. Two circles, twenty rings, 720 degrees, outer inner, back and forth, one circle to the other. Leonardo's complex mind, his stunning intellect, at play. The twenty-circle path. The path to the Medici Dagger.

"I *am* the mighty traveler," I said to Leonardo.

"But what do they mean?" Pop asked.

"I'm going to find out. And when I do I'm going to tell you. Ginny," I said, my mind suddenly filled with her.

Pop said, "Oh nerts, where's my memory—Iowa? I just talked to Mary at the inn. Said she got a weird call from a dame who said nothing but 'Tell Pop A.F.B.B.' Said it sounded like she was in a phone booth. That ring a bell?"

"Jesus!" I said, jumping out of my chair. "It sure does. Archie Ferris. I knew it was him in the woods."

"Who the hell's Archie Paris?" he asked.

"Ferris," I said, "like the wheel at a carnival."

"Oh yeah, your buddy," Pop said. "Your guardian angel. How come he sounds like a broad?"

"He picked her up. Thank God."

"What's B.B.?" Mona asked.

"Big Bear," I told her, relief flooding my heart. "Archie Ferris, Big Bear. Why the hell'd they go all the way to Big Bear?"

"And who's Ginny?"

A smile crossed my lips. A hopeful smile. A Hope Diamond smile.

"Your sparkler," Mona said.

I nodded.

"I'd say it's time for you to go," she told me, packing the transparencies in a box. She handed them to me along with the original notes and asked if I wanted her to assemble the rings into the completed Circles on the computer.

"No time," I told her. "Just make a backup disk of the files. Besides," I said, waving the box, "I've got these."

Mona copied the files and gave me the disk. I wrapped her in my arms. She reminded me that it was still in her will to let me know when she died. "White it out," I said. She pressed her cheek to mine.

"Thank you, Mona," I said, brimming with emotion.

I turned to Pop. "The Baby Face Nelson Suite. And step on it."

We left Mona standing on the porch, grasping her hair in one hand to keep it from blowing in the breeze and waving to us with the other. Pop winked at me and said it would be inconsiderate of him not to go back there later to personally show his appreciation for what she'd done.

On the ride back to Little River it occurred to me that I didn't have Archie's address in Big Bear, nor was there a phone in the cabin.

There'd be no message leaving me directions; Archie was too smart for that. His cell phone number was in my car. All I could do was head for Big Bear and hope he had it with him. Worst case, somebody would be able to direct me to his cabin.

At least Ginny was safe.

Back at the Baby Face Nelson Suite I quickly packed. I removed fifty thousand dollars from the satchel and tried to force it on Pop, but he wouldn't have it. I stashed the money in the trunk of the Jag and had one foot in the car when I looked up at the old guy. There were tears in his eyes.

A rush of gratitude welled as my own eyes got misty. Pop held his arms out to me. I crunched across the gravel and hugged him. He patted me right on the stitches.

"Pop," I said, ignoring the pain. "Pop . . ."

He took out a hankie and blew his nose so hard I figured a flock of geese was on its way. "I like you way better'n Baby Face. And about you not having a place to live? Well, here ain't so bad."

fifteen

I made my way back down the rugged path and did the thing with the chain, stopping to plant a kiss on the combination lock. Easing out onto Highway 1, I pulled into the first gas station I spotted and filled the tank. I rang Archie's cell phone, but the call didn't go through.

At the fastest speed prudence would allow, I drove down 128 to 101, every fiber in my being yearning to streak through like a Japanese train, ripping up mailboxes and tearing down clotheslines with the sheer force of my wind drag.

The earth slowly rotated out of daylight. I pressed on through San Francisco and San Jose, down 101 to Highway 5, fighting off the inevitable effects of mental and physical overexpenditure. As my eyes grew heavy, thoughts began to flow like sailors' whiskey. *Noble purpose, Pop and Mona, Circles of Truth, Ginny and Archie, Big Bear, curly hair, Fred Astaire, debonair.*

Suddenly the ride turned bumpy and I jerked awake. I had crossed the breakdown lane and was barreling down the slope of a canyon doing seventy-five. I tugged the wheel, hoping to change direction without fish-tailing, but I was going too fast at too sharp an angle and lost control.

One option left. I countersteered hard right and yanked the hand brake, locking the back wheels, throwing the Jag into a spin. When the car was halfway around, I tromped on the gas. The tires smoked. Dirt and gravel kicked up all around me as the full force of the big engine battled my rearward momentum.

Don't blow, I prayed to the tires as I headed backward down the embankment, rubber squealing, motor growling. In three frantic seconds the tug-of-war ended, the Jag winning out over the sloping ditch.

I sat perfectly still, the smell of burnt rubber wafting through the window. My heart thumped like in a Betty Boop cartoon. I reached for the key; my hand was shaking. I had the heights, two feet from the ground.

Ginny's hand had steadied me in the garden—before I'd unraveled the secret of the Circles. Just a little tremor, I thought. I turned the key.

The big engine purred as if nothing had happened; the muffler masked the angry boom of sparking gasoline. I threw the Jag into first gear and edged back into the night as the radio played the Beach Boys singing "California Girls."

Pulling off at Magic Mountain, I ducked into a Safeway, used the facilities, bought a Boulder Bar and some juice, slammed them down, and tried Archie again.

Still no connection.

A well-groomed man carrying a bag of groceries passed by. His pager went off. Something in my head went off, too. Of course. Archie's pager!

I dialed, punched in the number of the pay phone, hit the pound sign, and slammed down the receiver. Now all I had to do was stand there and wait, maybe get an empty coffee cup and hold it out to the Magic Mountaineers. Alms for the idiot.

Twenty minutes later, the phone rang. I just about yanked it off the wound metal cord.

"Archie?"

"Gagmaster?" he answered in his familiar baritone. "Sorry to be so long. We had to get to a pay phone."

"Is she with you?" My heart beat fiercely.

"Affirmative."

"Is she all right?"

"Of course," he said. "She's with *me.*"

I sagged against the side of the phone booth, bursting with feelings I couldn't comprehend.

Archie said, "Hey . . . you all right?"

"I am now."

"Where are you?"

I told him.

"Okay," he said, "take Five to Fourteen North to Pear Blossom Highway to Eighteen to Thirty-eight to Fawnskin. We're at 2116 Fawn Skin Drive, just past the four-thousand-feet elevation mark. Look for the bear I made out of a tree. Got it?"

I said I did.

"Good," he said. "Here."

I heard the muffled sound of two voices, then one that made my knees weak, questioning, "Reb?"

"Ginny," I breathed.

"Thank God. What happened at Pop's?"

"Didn't Archie tell you? He was there."

"He was? That doesn't make sense."

"How did you hook up with him?"

"I'll explain when you get here. Hurry."

"Okay," I said. "I'm getting on the road."

"Wait. Have you still got the Circles?"

Pride swelled in me. "I most definitely do."

"What are you saying?" she asked, incredulous. "Are you telling me you actually figured them out?"

I let my silence answer.

"Oh my God, I can't believe you did it!"

"I'm coming to get you," I told her, my mouth suddenly dirt-dry. "Be there in a couple of hours."

"I'll be waiting for you," she whispered. "Bye."

I hung up, gently this time, totally intoxicated with emotion, but thirsting for more, dying to drink from her well forever, to gulp quenching heartfuls of her.

There was plenty of gas in the Jag, too much blood in my veins, and exactly enough grit in my soul.

Drive, Traveler, drive.

I passed roving headlights and billboards advertising blue jeans and breakfast specials. Satellite dishes prayed to the licorice sky, red-eyed fruit bats swooped, teenage lovers sweated, and me, the son of the museum curator and the woman with the acorn eyes, steered to where nature intended.

I felt a pull on the stitches in my back, triggering images of Pop and Mona—their tears and kindness. The two of them, maybe right this moment, under a well-worn quilt. Soft old skin touching soft old skin. Pop making merry with Mona the maiden. And afterward, chocolate-chip cookies. The stuff of Comptche, the husk of human life. *Life.* I was sticking my toe in the pool and it felt good.

Before long I was bucking and dipping on the ridiculous Pear Blossom Highway, a two-lane shortcut to Big Bear. The San Bernardino Mountains were on my right, the dead-flat desert on my left. The road was so wavy, the highs and lows so extreme, that cars driving toward me looked like they were sending signals in Morse code.

I clicked on a classical station. Mozart's Piano Concerto No. 25 lilted on the radio and a strange chaotic sensation contrasted with the sweeping harmonious music. My breathing became shallow, my thoughts as coarse as a cat's tongue. Disconcerted, I mentally administered a self-exam.

My back was definitely sore where Pop had sewn me up, my buns were barking, my knee ached from smacking the dashboard during the spinout, and my underwear had been up my crack for a hundred and fifty miles. Exam results: mental melee, physical foundering. Therapist's recommendation: Change life and underwear.

Archie's directions were precise. A hundred yards past the elevation marker, I saw his sculpted bear. It looked more like a fat wooden monkey. I could picture Archie out there on a summer day with the McCullough, yanking the saw cord, brrrrmmm, bup bup bup, bzzzzzzzzzz, whoops, fuck it, bzzzzzzzzzz, whoops, fuck it. Hacking on the helpless pine, sweat dripping onto the saw's rubber grip. Not exactly Michelangelo chipping away everything that wasn't David.

I drove down the long driveway till I spotted Archie's Hummer parked in front of a big A-frame cabin. The lights in the house were out; smoke drifted up from the chimney toward the pregnant yellow moon. I parked, grabbed the box of transparencies and notes, and groaned my way out of the car. *Why are the lights out?* Although the air wasn't brisk, I suddenly got goose bumps.

Then someone grabbed the back of my jacket and put a gun to my head. Instantly I dropped to the ground like a sack of stones, catching my assailant by surprise. I scissored his legs and he went over, his silver gun glinting in the moonlight.

Grabbing his gun hand, I twisted hard. I heard an ugly snap and a cry just before a bolt of lightning hit my neck and time stopped.

When I came to, I was sitting in a steel and leather chair in front of the hearth in Archie's living room. A nicely built fire crackled on the grate. When the heat reached a little air pocket in one of the split logs, it made a pop and sparks flew against the glass fireplace doors. The sound echoed in my head like a boom from the "1812 Overture," and was accompanied by considerable pain, which flared from my left eye back to what I assumed was a good-sized lump behind my ear.

Off to my right a familiar throaty female voice uttered, "Reb." I felt comfort, as though a soft blanket had been fluffed over me.

I painfully inched my head toward the sound. Only four feet away, Ginny sat in an identical chair.

A hand with manicured and polished fingernails touched her shoulder. She shivered in response.

"See, honey?" an ominous voice said. "I told you he'd be back."

My eyes followed a black kidskin sleeve up to a shoulder, to a collar, to the tattoo of a serpent. The snake seemed to undulate with each carotid throb.

I elevated my gaze to meet a harsh chin, then a sneering mouth and the tip of a Roman nose, then two black eyes seizing my stare.

"Flame Boy," Tecci called out, like a long-lost pal. "We meet again on terra firma."

The sound waves rippled down my spine, shuddering me fully awake. I took in the sight of Nolo Tecci, his disturbed face angular and Picasso.

Memory's ghosts sprang from their cots, their long arms reaching—the blaze, the screams, the falling ceiling. The sea horses on the doctor's tie reared, whinnying at the sight of the serpent in their path. Liquid fury flash-flooded my senses. I lurched forward, but my wrists and ankles were tightly bound to the chair with box twine.

Tecci let out a pull-the-wings-off-a-fly laugh. Ginny wasn't tied down. She made a move toward me, but he squeezed her shoulder harshly, forcing her back into her chair.

I steeled myself, sucked in a long breath through my nose and let it out slowly.

"Where's Archie?" I asked.

"Taking a little nap," Tecci answered. "He's a big one. Made a nice heavy-bag for my men. Gave them an excellent workout. By the way, my guy out in the driveway? I think you broke his wrist. He's in the kitchen, wrapping it in ice. He doesn't like you as much as I do. Hey, Jocko," he yelled, "are you a little upset with Flame Boy?"

An angry voice from the other room called, "I'm gonna break his fuckin' neck, Mr. Tecci. Just give me a minute."

Ginny gasped. Nolo dug into her shoulder again and turned his head toward the doorway. "Quiet now, Jocko. You're upsetting Ms. Gianelli."

I noticed the reflection of the flickering fire on Tecci's polished loafers. He looked down at them, too.

"You know, Flame Boy, labor's pretty cheap. The Krauts, the Wops, everybody's cheap. That's because they're ignorant." He shouted in Jocko's direction again, "You're incredibly stupid, aren't you?"

There was no answer from the kitchen. Nolo stomped the floor twice like a stage manager giving a cue. Jocko appeared in the doorway, a strong-looking guy with a blocky chin and male-pattern baldness, wearing a white Polo shirt smeared with dirt. His wrist was wrapped in a checkered towel. He cradled it delicately.

"Aren't you stupid?" Nolo prompted.

"Yeah," Jocko acknowledged reluctantly, eyes downcast. Then he disappeared into the kitchen.

"That was a very good answer, don't you think?" Nolo said, smiling at me. "Do you think that was a good answer, Ms. Gianelli?"

Ginny looked at me with fear. "Yes."

"It was a good answer, wasn't it, Joey?" Nolo spoke to someone behind me.

"Good answer," a deep voice replied.

"Do you like it, Lon?" Tecci said to someone off to my right, just out of view.

"I like it," he answered, sniffling like he had a cold.

Nolo picked up a handful of transparencies from a small pine table next to Ginny. The sheets were a total mess, most of them bent. They must have gone flying when I hit the ground.

"By the way, Flame Boy," Nolo said, sifting through them, "I really appreciate these righteous rings. The question is, how do they go together and what do they mean? Look at all of them."

I saw the killer's hands touching Mona's transparencies—my work, Leonardo's genius—leaving infernal imprints on everything, visible only to me through the infrared of my hatred.

"How did you find us?" I asked defiantly. "I got the Hollister House bit that you had my car phone, but how'd you get here?"

"Ma Bell. We checked out the main phone at the inn right after you had the party with the Germans. I told Krell we shouldn't use those boys, but he's a patriot, you know. I guarantee he never had a Nathan's hot dog in his entire life. Anyway, we misplaced you for a little while until the dear sweet cannoli here called with the A.F.B.B. business. That didn't sound like a reservation to me. And, of course, as you might expect, I have a source who's got the spread on you and everyone you ever met. So A. F., that was Archie Ferris in a heartbeat. And B. B . . . well, not too difficult. Tell him, honey," he said to Ginny, "how you got all the way down here from the North Coast."

"Don't call me honey," she snapped.

Nolo smiled at me. "I do like her," he said.

Kneeling down on the carpet, he placed his chin on Ginny's shoulder. She flinched.

"When I say do something," he whispered in her ear, "you must do it. Now tell him."

Ginny nervously licked her lips. "I took a cab," she said softly.

Nolo stood up and laughed. "She took a cab! The girl took a four-hundred-mile taxi trip. I love that." He stomped the floor.

Jocko came back to the doorway, as if on cue.

Nolo stopped laughing. "Get out," he snarled. "I didn't call you."

The man withdrew.

Nolo waved the transparencies at me. "All right," he said. "I repeat, Flame Boy. How do they go together?"

I let my face hang loosely, showing apparent ease while inside thoughts crashed into each other like bumper cars.

"I'm a stuntman, Nolo," I said. "What do I know about this kind of thing? I was just trying to figure it out myself."

"Well, that's good, Flame Boy, that's exceptionally good. Of course you don't know what it means. How could you? But you, darling," he said to Ginny. "You know what it means."

"I'm an art historian," she said. "The designs may have historical significance, but I have absolutely no idea of what."

Nolo mimicked, "I have absolutely no idea of what. You're quite a hot little condiment, aren't you? Here's what I think. Flame Boy was playing Dick Tracy and somehow he uncovered some sort of code that Leonardo da Vinci made up five million years ago."

Nolo brushed the edge of one of the transparencies against his closely shaved chin. "I'm going to get a dollar for every one of those years, once Krell's analysts crack the code. That's where you come in, art girl. In case whatever the eggheads find out needs some artistic interpreting." He caressed Ginny's hair.

I futilely twisted my wrists against the twine.

"Relax, Flame Boy," he said. "I'm just toying with her. We've got the two pages of da Vinci's notes and all these nice circles on translucent paper. Herr Krell is going to be blissful."

"By the way, where is Krell?" I asked. "I'd like to meet him, share the bliss with him."

"In his jet." Nolo shrugged.

"Well," I said, "if Wiener's at the airport, what are we waiting for? Let's go."

"Wiener . . . You're a card, a regular joker."

My stare hardened, the molten pool of loathing solidifying in my gut.

"I'm the Ace of Spades, Tecci," I uttered. "I always turn up."

"Oooh," he taunted, "I'm trembling like a twig in a twister. That's not bad, twig in a twister. Do you think? Ah, I have the muse in me."

Keep him talking.

"Hey, Nolo. How did you know we were taking the taxi to Torcello Island?"

"Ah, money talks, Ace. In fact it screams," Tecci said with a malignant leer. "Now the question is, will you?"

Nolo set the clutter of transparencies down on the table, reached into his inside jacket pocket, and withdrew something that looked like a silver garage door opener with a little gooseneck attached to it. A surgeon's laser.

"You won't be turning up, Ace. You'll be burning up. You and your pal," he said, stroking the apparatus like a piece of velvet. "But first, I've got to sign off on you."

I swallowed hard. The signature "N" in the nape.

"Not her," I said, my eyes locked on Tecci's.

"That's very touching," he smirked. "I really think he's soft on you, sweetheart. One never knows. It's conceivable I might even get stuck on you, myself. Ms. Gianelli comes with us. She's not a roaster, she's a coaster. A coast-to-coaster. For now."

Tecci pulled a two-pronged electric device for zapping muggers from his pants pocket and casually zapped Ginny with it; instantly, her arms and legs splayed out and she collapsed, limp as a scarecrow. So that was the lightning bolt that laid me out in the driveway.

Tecci replaced the zapper in his pocket and clicked on the laser. He took a step toward me. "Joey, Lon," he called to his goons. "Hold Flame Boy's head back for me. Are you ready to scream, Ace?"

I gripped the metal rails of the chair, bracing myself for the pain.

Somebody grabbed my hair and pulled. I heard pops as my neck bent back, gas escaping from between cervical vertebrae, like at the chiropractor. Tough hands with callused fingers held my forehead. I smelled Nolo's breath as he exhaled. It was oddly sweet—toothpaste-sweet.

"Now don't move," Tecci said. "I like to be neat." Dread surged in me as I felt the first sting of the laser on my neck and smelled the unnatural scent of burning flesh.

I stubbornly clung to a thimbleful of resolve not to howl in agony.

"Nice cursive N," Nolo said, like a grammar-school kid, "loop, down, and up and over the mountain." I pictured him with the tip of his tongue sticking out of the corner of his mouth, focused.

"I did it just like this to your father in his study while you and Mommy were upstairs sleeping," he whispered in my ear.

My mouth went bone dry. I shut my eyes.

"I was just making sure he didn't have the notes," he continued. "Actually, it was his time anyway. And it was my pleasure to take him. He wasn't as tough as you. He cried."

I pictured my dad, downstairs at his desk that last night; he never did come up to kiss me.

Cameron West

Nolo started singing to the tune of "Jingle Bells": "What fun it is to laugh and sing a . . . 'slaying' song tonight."

I inhaled deeply, the smell of my own singed tissue filling my nostrils. I swallowed, surprised that my throat still worked. *He's just singing me.* A whiff of hope drifted in with the noxious vapor. Then it occurred to me: the knife is next. Tecci is a stabber—a gasher. I wondered where I'd get it.

"Almost done," Tecci said. "There, A-plus. Let go of him." I leaned my head forward and peered at the man who had burned his initial into my throat. He winked at me. "You're very brave," he said sarcastically.

Tecci turned to the goons. "Okay, boys, drag Miss Venice out to the car, get the gas, do the hokey pokey and shake it all around. Jocko, collect all the artwork and try not to trip and break your other wrist. Come on, we've got a plane to catch."

So he wasn't going to stab me; he was going to let me burn.

Tecci and his men moved about the room in a menacing choreography, transporting my sagging Ginny out the door. I understood that they'd have no use for her after she translated the Circles of Truth. The thought crawled over me. I watched Lon and Joey reenter with gas cans, spilling clear foul fluid along the edges of the floor.

I fought the burning pain in my throat and heart, and quested for that place where the rhythm of my swift feet skimming the forest floor opened my eyes to everything. Low branch, fallen tree, slippery leaves, the jet black panther.

"*Arrivederci,* Flame Boy," Nolo said, standing at the open front door with a gold lighter in his hand.

He sparked it, knelt down, and touched it to the floor, igniting the gasoline fuse. As he closed the door behind him, the trail of flame instantly whooshed around the room.

Smoke began to fill the place. I yanked at the cord cutting into my wrists.

"Archie!" I called. "Archie!" No human sound, just the deadly gust of fire.

186

The drapes ignited; flames traveled up to the pine-beamed ceiling. A windowpane burst. *Glass. The fireplace door!* My ankles were tied as tightly as my wrists but I could still move my feet.

I shifted my weight against the back of the chair and got on my tiptoes, lifting the front legs a little way off the ground. Carefully balancing so as not to tip over backward, I lurched forward, scraping the chair several inches toward the fireplace. I did it again. The chair moved again.

Black smoke billowed toward the ceiling. Dry, angry heat whipped me like a slave. I sucked in the thick air, coughed, and repeated my move, one, two, three more times.

One more shuffle and the tips of my boots touched the hot glass. I kicked one of the panels as hard as I could with the tiny bit of freedom the ropes allowed. The glass rattled against the brass supports. I sucked in more air, clenched my teeth, and kicked again. This time the panel shattered.

Sweat poured down my face, stinging the incision in my neck. I stuck my foot right into the fire. I felt intense heat through the back of my boot and the leg of my jeans as the orange flames viciously chewed at the twine. I tugged with every ounce of strength in my quadriceps. The rope burned through just as my pants caught fire.

I stood on my free leg, hopped over to the kitchen, and frantically rubbed my jeans against the doorjamb till the flame went out. Then I hobbled to the butcher block next to the sink. I grabbed a long knife and cut into the cord at my wrist.

The goons hadn't doused the kitchen, but it was quickly filling with smoke. In two frantic seconds I sliced through the tight bonds.

"Archie!" I shouted. Nothing but the roar of the fire. I turned on the tap full-blast, soaked my head, grabbed a dish towel, drenched it, too, and threw it over me. Then I ran through the smoke-filled house in a crouch, looking for Archie.

I found him in a bedroom down the hall, faceup on the floor, tied at the wrists and ankles. Tossing the towel over his head, I grabbed him by the arm and moosed him up onto my back—all two hundred and twenty pounds of him—tearing out every one of Pop's good stitches.

Dashing down the narrow hall, I staggered through the roaring flames in the living room to the front door. I grabbed the scorching knob and flung it open. The fresh air combusted behind me, erupting like a volcano. I stumbled out to the driveway and laid Archie down in the grass.

I checked him over. No burns. I held my fingers to his thick neck, felt a steady pulse. His face looked pretty busted up, though, and he was still out cold. I cursed myself for what I'd put him through.

The back of my right leg stung, my hand was blistering, my shoulder blade was raw and wounded, and my throat and lungs felt like I'd swallowed flaming swords.

At the Jag, I used my cell phone to dial 911. I gave the operator Archie's address and said one more word: "Fire." Then I grabbed the satchel from the trunk, removed ten thousand dollars, and stuffed it in my wallet.

Fifty yards into the woods, I buried the bag behind a tree under some soft dirt, leaves, and pine needles. Then I forced my way back to where Archie lay, still unconscious, as his house was rapidly consumed.

They've got Ginny, I thought, then collapsed on the cool ground.

sixteen

When I awoke, I was in a hospital room with light pink walls. A nurse stood next to me, taking my pulse. Her watch read 9:18 A.M. *Good, I've only lost a night.*

I reached for the large bandage at my throat. The movement surprised her; she took an involuntary step backward.

"Oh," she said, "you're awake. I'll get them." She hooked the clipboard at the end of the bed. I saw that my right leg was elevated at the knee by pillows.

Daylight streamed in around flowery curtains I could see through a veil of pale nylon that separated me from the patient in the next bed. From his size, it looked like Archie. His face was heavily bandaged, and an IV dripped something into his left hand. Next to him a machine monitored his heart rate with a steady blip, blip, blip.

"Arch," I called. My throat felt as though someone had reamed it out with a wire brush.

"Mmm," he muttered.

"Are you all right?"

"Mmm."

"Thank you."

"Mmm."

"Arch, I've got to know something. That was you up there in the woods, wasn't it?"

"Mmm."

189

"I knew it."

Just then two men entered my room, one of them obviously a doctor, wearing a white coat and stethoscope, the other a gray-haired policeman with a big gut and aviator glasses. A young officer in a tan uniform appeared behind them and remained by the door.

The doctor picked up the clipboard, studied it for a moment. From his unshaven chin I guessed that he had worked the late shift.

"Mr. Barnett," he said, "I'd say you had one heck of a night."

"What are they doing here?" I asked.

"I'm sure the sheriff will explain that to you in a moment."

"What's my condition?"

"Well, you've inhaled some smoke, so your lungs may be sore for a while. You have first- and second-degree burns on your hand and on the back of your right leg, and a slight laceration on the underside of your right forearm. I restitched two recent wounds by your left scapula. You have what appear to be rope burns on each wrist and something extraordinarily puzzling on your throat. Either you're a precision masochist or someone burned the letter N into your skin with some sort of highly accurate tool."

Not someone, I thought bitterly. Some *thing*.

"How did you handle it?" I asked.

"I cleaned it and stitched it. I'm afraid it will leave a substantial scar, although plastic surgery may diminish that."

I indicated Archie. "What about him?"

"I wasn't his attending physician, but I've conferred with his doctor. He suffered multiple facial contusions, broken nose, several fractured ribs, concussion. He may have bruised internal organs, although there's no evidence of that."

"He's going to pull through, then?"

"I would say so, yes, in time. But he's not my patient, you are. How are you feeling?"

"He's my friend," I said. "I want the best for him no matter what it costs." I leaned forward painfully, looking the doctor in the eye. "Do

190

you understand what I'm saying? Best care, full-tilt, soup to nuts, all the clichés. That man gets supreme attention and care." I checked the doctor's name tag. "I want your assurance, Dr. Kluver, okay?"

"Yes, I understand. I promise you I'll pass that along. You have my word. Now . . . please tell me how you are feeling, other than resolute."

I didn't answer. I was thinking about how to get away from the police.

The doctor prodded, "May I ask you, Mr. Barnett, are you a member of some kind of cult?"

"That'll be it, Doc," the gray-haired cop said sternly, moving a step forward. "We'll take it from here."

"Yes, certainly, Sheriff." The physician retreated past the young cop who guarded the door like a boot-camp Marine.

"Excuse us, O'Toole," the sheriff said to his subordinate. "And close the door behind you. Nobody comes in."

"Yes, sir," the young officer replied, with military precision.

The sheriff swaggered over. "Mr. Barnett," he announced in a grave tone, "you are in a truckload of trouble. Someone matching your description, driving your Jaguar, participated in a shootout at a resort in Little River that resulted in the deaths of four persons. A fifth washed up on the shore nearby, but we can't pin that on you . . . yet. In addition, the Malibu Fire Inspector is interested in questioning you about the possible arson of your private residence.

"For icing," he continued, "at three o'clock this morning," he pointed in Archie's direction, "this gentleman gets the spanking of a lifetime, and his place lights up, and, what do you know, you—Smokey the Bear's worst enemy—are on the guest list for that, too. And the ten grand in your wallet. You didn't win that arm wrestling."

I heard another "mmm" from Archie.

"Now I checked you out," the sheriff said. "Occupation: stuntman—granted that doesn't come up every day—California carry license, no priors, not even a ticket for jaywalking. Till about a week ago, you're Dudley Dooright. I would really appreciate knowing just what in the solar system is going on here."

191

The sheriff cinched his belt a sixteenth of an inch and pushed his glasses back up his bulbous nose. "You're on my turf here," he said, jabbing a chubby finger at me. "And you're not going anywhere—not even to the toilet—till I get some reasonable answers. I've got a small jail cell and a big temper. You with me?"

As far as both of us were concerned I'd been apprehended.

The door opened behind him. Without looking, he barked, "I told you, no interruptions, Charlie."

"The name is Beckett," a voice from behind the sheriff said in an exquisite British accent. The sheriff turned around, and the inspector took a step in my direction.

He wore a charcoal double-breasted suit with a faint blue pinstripe, his Borsalino rakishly cocked to one side of his perfectly coiffed head. A cobalt tie and matching pocket hankie completed the look. He carried my suitcase in one hand and my jacket in the other.

"You're not allowed in here," the sheriff blustered. "I'm questioning a prisoner. O'Toole!"

He opened the door hesitantly.

The sheriff said, "Didn't I tell you—"

"Silence, Sheriff Gullerson," Beckett said, raising his small but immaculate hand. An emerald parallelogram cuff link glistened on his French cuff.

Sheriff Gullerson probably hadn't heard that before. "And just who the fuck are you, the Prince of goddamn Wales?"

"I would say, sir," Beckett said, "that if one added an 'h' to Wales, the title would be more fitting of you." He removed an immaculate leather ID holder from his pocket, flashed it in front of Gullerson's face, closed it, and replaced it in its home.

Then he pulled a neatly folded paper from his breast pocket and handed it to the sheriff. Gullerson's brow furrowed. From my vantage point, I could see an embossed blue and gold seal at the top of the letter.

"The White House . . ." Gullerson said with astonishment.

"Neither this man," Beckett said, pointing at me, "nor I have ever set foot in this hospital. Your total cooperation is expected, as is that of your assistant."

That sounded good to me. Not to the sheriff. His plug of seniority had been pulled.

"You will be rewarded for your silence in due course, sir," Beckett said. "And I must apologize for my earlier remark. That was unkind. I only wish I could regain a small percentage of the girth you would most likely give away with enthusiasm."

Gullerson eyed the official paper. "I don't suppose I can keep this."

"Correct," Beckett said, taking the letter back. "Now will you please excuse us, sir."

"Uh, yeah, sure." The sheriff glanced at me one last time before ushering O'Toole out the door.

When they were gone, Beckett took a step closer. Our eyes swapped as little as they could. I realized he wasn't after me; he needed me. My concern lessened. I wasn't the big fish, I was the minnow. I just needed some room to wiggle.

I struggled to a sitting position, dangling my feet over the side of the bed. I could tell I wasn't ready to stand yet.

"Liked my coat, did you? I recovered it at the Four Seasons."

"She's *gone*, Beckett. Tecci kidnapped her."

"I see. Listen to me. I've gone to considerable personal risk to free you. Think of it as a very magnanimous gesture on my part following the thrashing my underlings and, particularly, I took in Milan. I ask for no apology, but at least acknowledge your misjudgment."

"What you told me about Krell, that was all true."

"Your cynicism got the best of you. Me as well, I admit," he added, rubbing his chin where I'd nailed him.

"You know about the gunmen in Milan?"

"You mean the bus incident? You are remarkable."

"How would Tecci have known where we were?"

"An excellent question," Beckett said. "But I'm afraid I can't answer that for you. Consider it a mystery."

I wanted to smash him for toying with me, but then I'd have to deal with Gullerson.

"Okay. How did you find me here?"

"Originally I placed a tracking device under the lapel of your jacket when we collided at the Accademia. That led us to the Gritti and then to Milan, although we lost you when you slipped out of the country without going through customs. Neat trick.

"We were watching out for you and learned of the fire at your residence. So unnecessary. We guessed you had returned to California, which is where we picked up your signal at the Hollister House."

"People change jackets. What made you think I'd keep mine on?"

"People do change coats, don't they, but when they're on the road they generally keep their belongings with them. We found the bloody transmitter in the grass by a cottage in serious need of repair. It must have come off during your fracas."

"We could have been killed there," I said angrily. "And now Tecci's got Antonia."

"Yes, that is unfortunate. However, don't forget who abandoned whose ship. And watch your tone with me. I'm your life preserver, so to speak."

He pulled the backup disk Mona made for me from his pocket. "Found this in the glove box of your car. Had a chance to look over your work—the two hundred separate rings—and Leonardo's notes. I know you're on to something exceptional, although I confess I'm utterly mystified at this point."

"That's why you're here," I said, stretching my neck, which tugged at the bandages on my throat. I heaved my suitcase onto the bed, dressed, then pulled back the curtain and went to Archie's side. Beckett followed, his gaze bearing down on me. I wasn't going on Gibraltar's hook. But I was going back in the water, and I knew which direction to swim.

"Archie," I called. "You're going to be all right, my friend."

He opened an eye and grabbed the front of my shirt with surprising strength.

"Wha haffen Ginny?" he mumbled.

"They took her," I said, gently placing his hand on the bed. "But I'm going to get her back. And you're going to help me," I said to Beckett. "I know how the Circles work."

Beckett's eyebrows raised slightly. He smacked his lips.

"Splendid."

We stepped through the Medical Center's automatic doors into the fresh air.

"Tell me you have a jet nearby," I said.

"Of course. At the Big Bear Airport," he answered. "One of the privileges of being well funded."

"You saw the files. You must have a computer handy."

"My laptop in the car is loaded with CorelDraw and all the files that are on the disk." He pointed to a silver sedan in the parking lot, Mobright at the wheel.

"Then all I need is a program that'll translate Italian into English," I told him. "You wouldn't happen to have that in the car, too, would you?"

"Actually, I am an expert Romance linguist. My Italian is flawless. So you see, Gibraltar is your friend."

"I'm not doing this for Gibraltar."

"I'm clear on that," Beckett said as we reached the car. "Your focus has shifted—you are after Ms. Gianelli, and the Dagger is your bargaining power."

"Exactly. You and I still have different agendas."

"Quite. Nevertheless, I dazzled the sheriff so as to extricate you from his meaty clutches. Quid pro quo. Getting into the car instead of mugging me, stealing the disk, and vanishing in the mist will be a good start."

He held the rear door open and I climbed in. Mobright squinted his beady eyes at me in the rearview mirror.

"Now," Beckett said. "Let's find the Dagger, shall we? Any idea where to begin?"

"Rome," I told him.

seventeen

*A*t Big Bear Airport we boarded a private plane that looked similar to Dracco's. Beckett and I buckled into presidential-class leather seats in a large private compartment. I snugged my belt with shaking hands. It was one part heights, ninety-nine parts pulling away from the continent where I'd last seen Ginny.

That was a particularly cruel kind of torture, finally having someone to live for, but not knowing if she was still alive. The Dagger was a ransom I would gladly pay to free her. I had to follow it and work with Beckett to unravel the mystery of the Circles of Truth.

Once we were airborne, Beckett said, "Well, then . . . I suspect we have some work to do over the course of the next thirteen hours. Please begin with an explanation of the Circles."

I plugged the laptop into an AC bar just above the bird's-eye maple table in front of me, and turned it on. Beckett watched with keen interest as I opened the CorelDraw files, located the proper rings of Truth One, put them in the correct order, and rotated them to fit together, repeating the process with the second circle. Beckett studied the results carefully.

"So," he stated, "inner and outer alternations, thirty-six degrees per ring, flip flop from one circle to the other. Positively ingenious. How the devil did *you* arrive at this?" He heard his tone of superiority and blanched. "Do forgive me," he said. "Let me rephrase that. How did you arrive at this?"

"Tecci's got these, too," I said, ignoring his question. "Krell's people will figure this out. And they've got Ginny to translate them. Can't you find out where they are?"

"I'll have Mobright extend Gibraltar's reach, but Krell will most certainly wish to remain behind the curtain for now. Not only are we on his tail, but of course there is also Soon Ta Kee. Krell is a slick fish, albeit a sick one. And Tecci . . . well, there is only one Nolo Tecci."

I took stock. Just because I had the Circles of Truth laid out didn't mean they were directions to the Dagger. What if they were some cryptic message or a laundry list or a love letter to Ginevra de' Benci, for that matter?

I wiped the sweat off my upper lip with the back of my unbandaged hand and pulled up the scan of Ginny's translation on the computer. Beckett peered at the document as I explained how the notes led to Rome.

"Absolutely brilliant," he said. "Belvedere Palace, the Vatican. I believe you're right."

"You believe Antonia's right. All I did was the ring toss, here."

"Honorable of you to say so. Yes, of course, Ms. Gianelli is to thank for the Rome connection, but do not sell yourself short on the Circles. What you've done is miraculous."

Beckett smoothed his Windsor-knotted silk tie. "Now bring up the Circles again and let's find out what they say."

I shifted my focus to the computer screen and the drawing program. Opening the file containing the completed Circles, I mirrored each image. Truths One and Two were now written left to right and presumably legible, except that they were still circular.

"Excellent," Beckett said. "I trust you can utilize the program to break them apart."

"I think I can do that, but where?"

Beckett studied Truth One carefully for a full minute, tracing it with a slim finger. Then he pointed to a place where one of the letters had a tiny handle sticking off it.

"Try here," he said.

I broke the circle at that point, clicked a few commands, and snapped it into a straight line. Watching Mona work had paid off.

Beckett took a pen and a small leather-bound notepad out of his pocket. He started jotting.

"What does it say?" I asked impatiently.

He ignored me and kept writing. Several more minutes passed.

Finally I said, "Can you do this or not?"

Again he ignored me, deep in thought. He continued to avoid me for another half hour.

I settled uncomfortably back in my chair. There was nothing to do but wait and think.

I pictured Tecci and Krell and Ginny on Krell's jet. That was an image I couldn't allow myself to linger on. I looked out the window. We were above the clouds. No birds, no bugs, no lost balloons. Just freezing cold hypoxic air. Killing air.

"What have you got?" I finally asked.

He scribbled one last note, shaking his head in puzzlement, then tapped the page with his pen. He frowned. "Are you ready for this?"

"I'm more than ready."

"All right then, here it is," he said, taking a deep preparatory breath.

> "Soar with love me my each friend and thing you will of be the this new guardian world of the for dagger above you the tangle all of the are sleeping carver's its mighty whorl keepers."

I said nothing. What could I say?

Beckett repeated the garbled sentence.

I let out a sigh. "Mighty whorl keepers? Who taught you Italian—Dr. Seuss?"

"I accurately portrayed my skills at translation," Beckett replied confidently. "The message Leonardo wrote is the one I just read to you."

"Are you sure you broke it in the right place?"

"I believe I did," he said, pointing out the little knob again. "This is a marker. I chose the break based on my substantial experience with cryptanalysis. The question now is, what the devil does he mean?"

We looked at each other silently for a moment; then I leaned my head back and ran my tongue back and forth across my teeth. "Mighty whorl keepers . . . mighty whorl keepers," I repeated.

"This is obviously a scrambled message, Reb. A transposition code." Beckett rhythmically tapped the pad. "Perhaps every other word drops out or every third, but of course that would be in Italian, and we've already got the correct English."

"I'm thinking here," I said.

"This is no time to be silent," Beckett urged. "Share your ideas. So far, with the exception of punching me in the jaw, they've been good."

It was my turn to ignore him, and I took it. "Mighty whorl keepers," I mumbled to myself. "What the hell's he talking about, 'soaring with love'?"

The phone on the maple table beside Beckett rang. He answered it without hesitation. "Yes, bring it." He hung up. "Lunch."

In short order, Mobright pushed an elegant cart into the cabin.

"Bravo," Beckett said.

"Yes sir," Mobright answered deferentially. "May I ask whether you've made any progress?"

"You may, but you won't get an answer yet. Be a good chap and close the door behind you."

Neither Beckett nor I made a move for the cart, although the aroma of Mexican food emanated from the table. The image of Beckett in a sombrero entered my mind, providing me with a temporary respite from the burden of thought. I pictured him and Mobright strumming guitars and singing "Guantanamera."

Beckett pointed at Truth Two on the computer screen. "Since you choose to be silent," he said, "be a good man and break this one here and straighten it out for me."

I did as he requested, then got up to check out the trays on the cart. One plate of tamales with refried beans and saffron rice. The other, filet mignon. Beckett looked up from his work.

"Which one do you want?" I asked, hoping he'd pick the steak.

"One moment, one moment," he cautioned, holding the notepad six inches in front of his face, fingers gripping the tip of his pen. After a few seconds he mumbled, "Mobright cooked the tamales for you."

"He did? Mobright?"

"Yes. At my instruction. Vegetable. Your favorite."

"How do you know they're my favorite?" I asked, carrying my plate back to my seat.

"Please . . ." he said, annoyed.

"Mobright, a chef?" I muttered to myself.

"No one is merely who he seems to be," Beckett said. "No one. There, I've got it!

> "The lion I God and offer the languid future man
> share people the secret my the bearded heart man will
> and never know soul.

"Equally cryptic," Beckett said. "Just as I'd suspected."

"Wonderful," I muttered. "Languid future man."

"Yes, quite."

My companion poured himself a glass of water from a silver pitcher, pulled out his pill organizer, and swallowed some capsules. He chased them with a sip and picked up his meal.

I watched him carefully tuck a corner of the white linen napkin into his collar, then slice off a small piece of the meat. He put his knife down, placed his free hand in his lap, and chewed inconspicuously, as though he'd gone to finishing school with the Queen. He pushed his plate aside, apparently through with his meal.

I cut off half a tamale with my fork and stuffed it in my mouth so my cheeks puffed out. Beckett eyed me.

I studied the garbled messages on his notepad.

"Listen to both of them," I instructed.

"Please finish chewing first," Beckett said.

I swallowed and read the two lines aloud. Then I inhaled the second half of my first tamale. The son of a bitch Mobright could cook.

"You know what I think?" I said, looking at Truth Two.

"Mm?"

"I think there is no such thing as a bearded heart man, that's what I think."

"Good point."

"Uh-huh. So we'll take that 'heart' out of there."

He thought about that. "All right then. We'll do that."

"You know what else? 'Share people the secret'?"

"Yes?"

"Take 'people' out and you've got 'share the secret,' " I said. "What do you think of that?"

Beckett regarded the notepad with growing enthusiasm. "You're really quite amazing."

His flattery didn't touch me. What I felt was gratitude for having gotten as far as I had, and determination to push on further.

"I'm going to finish this tamale," I said, "and use the facilities while you type these sentences. Then we're going to start tugging words till we find out what is exactly what with the Circles of Truth. How much time before we touch down? Eleven, twelve hours?"

Beckett checked his Oyster Rolex. "About that."

I shoveled the last chunk into my face. "Well," I said, standing up, "start typing."

When I returned, Mobright was in the room staring over Beckett's shoulder with a pad and pen.

"No one is who they seem to be," I told him.

Mobright looked taken aback.

"You're not only a smirking prick," I offered, "but you make a very nice tamale."

The look of puzzlement faded, replaced by his familiar glower.

I pushed past him. "Aren't you supposed to be coordinating the search for Krell?"

"But I'm only—"

"Get back to it," I interrupted, taking my seat. "We're busy."

Mobright retreated and Beckett slid the laptop toward me. "You don't like him, do you?" he said. "The man is a tad squirrelly, I think."

"Forget that. Truth Two. We took 'people' and 'heart' out of there. Let's see what that leaves."

Beckett turned the screen in his direction and read it. " 'The lion I God and offer the languid future man share the secret my the bearded man will and never know soul.' Take 'my' out of the 'secret my the bearded man.' "

I clipped it out and pasted it down between "people" and "heart."

"That's good," Beckett said. " 'The secret the bearded man will and never know soul.' Never know soul . . ."

"I'm taking the 'and' out of there," I said. I clipped it and pasted it down after "heart" in the same order as the sentence.

"Take 'soul' out, too," Beckett commanded.

"Why?"

He pointed at the four words I'd pasted at the bottom. " 'People my heart and.' Tell me 'soul' doesn't follow." His gray eyes gleamed.

"You're right," I admitted. "Heart and soul, just like the tune."

"Look at this now, Reb," he said, pushing my hands away from the keyboard. "What at the beginning of the sentence would Leonardo do to 'people my heart and soul'? If this is the correct order, then a verb would naturally precede those words, would it not?"

"Right," I said. "The verb is 'offer.' "

"So take 'offer' and put it in front of 'people my heart and soul.' Now what have we got up top?" We both looked down and saw:

> The lion I God and the languid future man share the
> secret the bearded man will never know.

I said, "Somebody has to offer people, right? There's only one word that's singular and that's 'I.' I offer. Are you certain 'offer' is singular?"

"Positive. *Offro*. Singular. You needn't question my skills."

"Okay, then, 'I offer people my heart and soul.' What's sticking out here?"

"The lion God?" Beckett asked.

"Yes, that, but also 'future' is sticking way out. This is a message. Leonardo wasn't talking to his peers in the present. This was meant for the future." I cut "future" and pasted it before "people."

"Absolutely," Beckett confirmed. We stared at the two lines.

> The lion God and the languid man share the secret
> the bearded man will never know.
>
> I offer future people my heart and soul.

"What the devil is 'the lion God'?" Beckett mused.

We both puzzled over that for a minute and then it occurred to me. A smile crept over my face as I felt the thrill of discovery. "It's not 'the lion God,' Beckett," I blurted. "It's 'the lion, comma, God, comma, and the languid man.' Leonardo didn't use punctuation."

"By Jove, you're right," Beckett said. "Then who is the lion?"

Tingles of excitement tap-danced on my stomach. Back and forth, in and out, I was walking the master's path.

"It's Leonardo himself," I stated with certainty. "Leonardo is the lion. Leonardo, God, and the languid man share the secret the bearded man will never know. I'm sure of it." A wave of sadness washed over me as I read the next line.

"He's offering us his heart and soul," I whispered.

"So he is," Beckett said, shaking his head in amazement. "So he is."

I took a deep breath. "Now who the hell are the languid man and bearded man?"

"Excellent question, my good man. Perhaps it's in with the mighty whorl, eh? Incidentally, how in the world did you get so bloody good at this?"

"I'm enigmatic," I said.

"Quite right," he replied with a smile. "I suppose the same could be said of me."

With Truth Two solved, we stepped into Truth One, side by side, ready to explore the rest of Leonardo's lush and mysterious path.

Beckett read it out loud.

> "Soar with love me my each friend and thing you will of be the this new guardian world of the for dagger above you the tangle all of the are sleeping carver's its mighty whorl keepers."

" 'Soar with love me my' doesn't sound right," I said. " 'Soar with love me'? I'm pulling 'love.' "

"Why? 'Soar with love' sounds right."

"Not with 'me my' after it," I said. "Watch this."

I clipped "love" out and put it below. Now it read "soar with me my."

"Granted, the lack of punctuation would allow it," Beckett said, "but it still looks strange."

"I'm grooving here," I said. "Watch this." I cut "each" and pasted it to the right of "love" below.

"Now read it," I told him. "Please."

" 'Soar with me my friend,' " Beckett read. "Good show."

" 'Thing you will be,' " I said. "Sorry 'thing,' it's moving day." I dropped it down next to the words "love" and "each." The bottom line now read "love each thing."

Beckett began to read what remained on the top line.

" 'Soar with me my friend and you will of be the.' 'Of' has to be next," he said.

I pasted it below.

"Now 'this,' " I said, moving it.

Beckett read the bottom line excitedly. " 'Love each thing of this . . . world'—it has to be 'world,' Reb." He removed his handkerchief from his coat pocket and mopped his brow. "My word . . ."

I clipped "world" and pasted it at the end of the bottom line. " 'Love each thing of this world,' " I said softly.

Beckett read the top line. " 'Soar with me my friend and you will be the new guardian of the' . . . 'for,' Reb, pull 'for.' "

I was already doing it.

" 'Soar with me my friend and you will be the new guardian of the dagger.' Goddamn," I said. "We are getting into the sweet stuff now. Can you smell it?"

"With both nostrils," Beckett said exuberantly, pointing at the top line. " 'Dagger above you the tangle.' Dagger above you? 'Soar with me my friend and you will be the new guardian of the dagger above you.' That makes sense somehow."

"No," I said. "Look further. 'The dagger above you the tangle all.' 'All' shouldn't be there. I'm pulling it." I moved it to the end of the bottom line, which now read, "Love each thing of this world for all." "Hmm," I said, "I've lost it. 'For all' what? After that we've got 'of the are sleeping carver's its mighty whorl keepers.' We're in the mud here. Give me a second, give me a second. 'Are' would have to come next, right? 'All are'?"

"Definitely," Beckett said. "Do that."

I dropped the word "are" down below next to "all." Then I read the remaining top line.

> "Soar with me my friend and you will be the new guardian of the dagger above you the tangle of the sleeping carver's its mighty whorl keepers."

Beckett and I looked at each other blankly.

After a concentrated moment he pointed at a line on the screen and said, "What if we have a sentence break here? Then it would read, 'Soar with me my friend and you will be the new guardian of the dagger above you. The tangle of the sleeping carver's its mighty whorl keepers.' Doesn't hold up, does it?"

I shook my head. "What if we clipped the second 'you' out of the first line and stuck it in the bottom? Then that would make it 'you all are.' That would be okay."

"My dear American friend, I'm afraid Leonardo wasn't from Alabama," Beckett chuckled.

"I'm serious." I took the "you" out of the first line and laid it in before the word "all." "Now read the top line."

Beckett complied. " 'Soar with me my friend and you will be the new guardian of the dagger above.' "

"Continue," I prodded, "don't read it as two lines."

Beckett sighed. " 'Soar with me my friend and you will be the new guardian of the dagger above the tangle of the sleeping carver's its mighty whorl keepers.' Goodness," he said. "Take 'its' out of there."

I did, pasting it into the bottom line. I read the new line, my pulse quickening. " 'Love each thing of this world for you all are its.' " My eyes met Beckett's.

We both whispered, "Keepers."

I clipped that word from the top line and placed it at the end of the bottom one. I read it.

"Love each thing of this world for you all are its keepers."

I looked at what remained on the top line with a mixture of awe and concern—that I wouldn't get it, that I wouldn't grasp Leonardo's meaning.

I read.

"Soar with me my friend and you will be the new guardian of the dagger above the tangle of the sleeping carver's mighty whorl."

Beckett and I sat back, enthralled, exhausted, and bewildered. The stitches in my back hurt. So did my leg and hand, not to mention my mind. Outside, red and orange scarves of sunset unfurled as daylight faded into early evening.

After a moment, Beckett said, "I understand the second part of each line, lines two and four, if you will. They are quite straightforward.

"Love each thing of this world for you all are its keepers.

"I offer future people my heart and soul.

"Both very powerful messages," he said. "Without question. But the first two:

"Soar with me my friend and you will be the new guardian of the dagger above the tangle of the sleeping carver's mighty whorl.

"The lion God and the languid man share the secret the bearded man will never know.

"I am baffled by them," Beckett said. "My brain is porridge at the moment. I'll just jot this down and confer briefly with Mobright. Perhaps the stretch will help."

"How much time do we have?" I asked, my eyelids putting on weight.

"Roughly five hours. In the interest of prudence, I'll make some preliminary demands in Rome. Isn't power intoxicating? I wonder what progress Krell's people are making."

I laid my head back on the soft leather seat and began to fade. "No one outpaces the mighty traveler."

"Yes, well, we will see, won't we?"

I dreamt I was a slice of Wonder bread lying on a tile counter. A beautiful girl in sunglasses appeared with two jars and placed them next to me, the glass of the jars clinking against the ceramic glaze of the tile. I listened with interest to the familiar sound of lids unscrewing. The girl took a whiff of each, a grin crossing her full lips. She picked up a silver knife.

From the jar on the left she scooped out a slab of peanut butter and spread it all over me, sweeping the knife neatly back and forth the way they do on Jif commercials. The peanut butter felt cool and soothing.

Then she dipped the knife into the second jar, digging out a glob of marshmallow which she spread on top of my peanut-butter blanket like a skier carving fresh sweet snow.

As the girl looked down at me, her waiting "fluffer nutter," a slice of pumpernickel bread—shaped just like me only dark as a crow—flew into the room. My anger made me hot and my peanut-butter-and-marshmallow spread began to melt. Suddenly the slice of bread landed on me, suffocating me.

I struggled against its force, heard its perverse laugh. I couldn't speak or scream because I was bread. Then it occurred to me that I wasn't ordinary bread, I was Wonder bread.

The evil slice laughed again and pressed harder, squishing my peanut-sugary coating till it spilled over my crust and onto the white tile. I peeked around the enemy and glimpsed the horrified girl. Not to worry. I'll save you. I began to spin myself, clockwise then counterclockwise, the thick spread a welcomed emollient.

My anger and confidence swelled with each gooey turn, generating more and more heat. Giving myself a final clockwise spin, I roared to life like a propeller, rotating with such speed that centrifugal force flung my wicked attacker off me, across the room, and into a dog dish. I heard the four-legged clicking of a hound's nails on linoleum as I hovered in front of the astounded girl. "Soar with me," I said.

Then I awoke, panicked, desperately wanting to stay in the dream state, to follow where my unconscious might lead. I knew Ginny was the fluffer-nutter girl. We were about to soar. *Where?* Above the tangle, came the response. *What tangle?* Of the sleeping carver's whorl, of course.

Then I was lost. *The sleeping carver. Carver of what? Wood? Marble? Could it be marble?* Leonardo used to say that sculptors covered in their marble dust looked like bakers covered in flour. *Oh my God.* I remembered Ginny's translation: "He is gone now, back to dust." I'd thought it was Francesco Melzi, going to dust the furniture—just a simple note about a common task. It wasn't. In a blast I knew who the sleeping carver and the bearded man were. They were one and the same.

My eyes popped open. "The sleeping carver, the bearded man. It's Michelangelo!" I shouted.

Beckett was back in his seat. Mobright stood behind him.

"Oh my . . . how in the blazes did you arrive at that?" Beckett asked.

I told him.

"Fantastic!" he exclaimed, practically dancing in his seat. "Now go on. The exact location is above the tangle of the mighty whorl, Reb. Where *is* the mighty whorl? Where did Michelangelo go back to his marble dust from?"

A prickly second, then another blast. "The Sistine Chapel. The tangle of the mighty whorl is the ceiling of the Sistine Chapel. I know it."

Beckett gasped. I continued.

"Michelangelo interrupted his work on the ceiling of the Sistine Chapel to do the statue of Moses for Julius's tomb."

"Reb, you've brought us to the brink of discovery," Beckett exalted. "Now where is it in the Sistine Chapel? Don't dally. We have less than two hours till touchdown."

I began massaging my temples.

"What are you doing?" Beckett asked.

"It helped me think once before when somebody did this."

"Here," he said, quickly stepping behind me. "Allow me."

His gesture surprised me. So did his gentle touch. I imagined his fingertips were those of the silver-haired Mona. Instantly I envisioned her, urging me to clear my mind of both the past and the future. "You are now with Leonardo da Vinci," her voice echoed in me. "You are now with Leonardo . . ."

Sandals on the Sistine Chapel floor, eyes lifted to the ceiling. I scanned the frescoed sea of color and serpents and ancient people, twisting and fleeing, perching and hovering.

"Where are you, languid man?" I demanded, my mind wide open, scrutinizing Michelangelo's tumultuous whorl. "Who are you?" Then the enormous ceiling went blank, with the exception of one spectacular scene—the apogee of Michelangelo's masterpiece—God reaching his awesome hand out to touch the extended fingers of . . . a languid man.

"It's Adam!" I shouted. "Adam is the languid man!"

"The *Creation of Adam,*" Beckett uttered. "That's it!"

"Yessss!" I replied with steely certainty. "The Dagger is between the outstretched fingers of God and Adam. Just above it. In the ceiling. I'm positive."

"My Lord," Mobright gasped. "The ceiling of the Sistine Chapel!"

Beckett pulled out his hanky again, dabbed his brow. "I'm awestruck," he whispered.

I grinned and winked at him, giving my earlobe a little tug.

Mobright departed to get us some tea.

"I have just one question for you, Reb," Beckett said. "How the deuce did Leonardo get the Dagger up there? The ceiling is nearly sixty-five feet high. Did he use Michelangelo's scaffolding?"

"No, he couldn't have. That was taken down immediately after he suspended work so the ceiling could be viewed."

"Well it's not possible that he went up from the ground. He must have gone down through the floor above."

"You mean the roof?" I asked. "How would he do that?"

"No, not the roof. Though you know your history, you're obviously unaware of the layout of the chapel. It has four levels. Two below, the chapel itself—which is designed rather as a fortress, with high windows—and then above it a guards' room which leads to a machiolated gangway."

"What's machiolated?"

"Walls with holes cut in them, firing slits. The point is, Leonardo could have first paced off the exact spot below God and Adam and then gone above to the guards' room, paced it off again, and dug down."

"That's very good. But how would he do that if the guards were there?"

"My question, exactly," Beckett sighed, tapping his pen against the tip of his nose. "Even at night, and we can be sure he must have done this at night because—"

"He called Michelangelo 'the sleeping carver.' "

"Right. And the 'gone back to dust' bit. If Michelangelo had stopped his work on the chapel to take up a sculpture, that would have given Leonardo the opportunity. But if he took it, he most certainly would have had to go after dark."

"Still," I said, "that leaves the problem of the guards. No chance they would have taken the night off, huh?"

"Guarding the pope? This *was* the Vatican in the Renaissance. No one turned his back on anyone. Swiss guards and all that." Beckett chewed on the end of his pen for a minute.

"So, then," he said, "how did he do it?"

Mobright entered carrying a tray of Danish and tea. "A selection of pastry, sir," he announced, then retreated once again.

"Blueberry twist?" Beckett asked, offering me the plate. I declined; then it smashed me—the dream I'd had at the Baby Face Nelson Suite. Leonardo on the floor of the cruller case, staring up, in a harness attached to a long rope. Of course.

I pulled the laptop to me, furiously tapped the computer out of sleep mode, and opened the two files with Leonardo's pages. My eyes darted to the drawings—not the Dagger, not the Circles, but the harness, the nested tubes, and the hoisting system.

"Include me, please," Beckett said.

"What if these particular drawings aren't randomly placed on these pages like so many of Leonardo's other sketches?" I said.

"Go on. I'm with you."

"What if these three nested triangular tubes with the rope and pulleys are really a telescoping mast that could be mechanically raised to the ceiling?"

"Of course! Then the harness was for him, the hoisting system a differential he used with a rope attached to the mast to raise himself to his rendezvous with God and Adam. Brilliant! You do lift your mental weights, don't you?"

I barely heard Beckett's words. Time stripped away and I was there with Leonardo in the dark chapel as he raised the mast, with the aid of the differential. I watched him step into the harness and pull himself arm over arm, up the long rope, carrying in his cloth backpack a drill, a bag of wet plaster, his paints and brushes, and a dagger.

Who else could have done this but Leonardo? Who else could have conceived of it? Melzi could have helped him carry the equipment. Short hop across the courtyard from the Belvedere. Maybe they took an underground route.

Leonardo *had* carefully paced out the floor. He knew *exactly* where to go. In the black of night, in the hollow stillness of the Sistine Chapel, by the singular light of his massive genius, he ascended to the ceiling, cut the hole, and slid the Dagger vertically between the outstretched fingers of God and Adam. Then he sealed the opening and repainted it, supremely confident that not even the brilliant Michelangelo would ever know.

Finally, he descended, while the guards above the thick ceiling paced in their uniforms, slapping their thighs to keep warm in the chill night air. They never learned of the intruder below. Neither did Michelangelo—the sleeping bearded carver.

"Well . . ." Beckett said, patting his lips. "My goodness. I guess I'm on again. I suppose I should grease the Vatican wheels, shouldn't I? Do excuse me."

I was rebandaging my leg and contemplating the odd juxtaposition of pain and the electrifying tingle of discovery when Beckett returned.

"Have you gained us access to the chapel?" I asked.

"Naturally, albeit with significant difficulty. The pope's away just now. We'll go in from above, of course."

"Of course," I repeated. "There's no way Krell's people could know this. Even if they do, they'd have to make arrangements to get Tecci into the guard room. You'd know about that."

"We'd know, yes," Beckett concurred. He removed his hanky, mopped a few beads of sweat from his brow. "How is your leg, anyway?"

"It'll be all right."

"How about your neck? The middle of the bandage is dark with blood. It doesn't look very good." He looked genuinely worried. Tired, too.

"Neither do you," I said. "What about all your pills? You said they don't help. With what?"

"Tennis elbow," he replied with a half-smile. "Afraid I won't make Wimbledon this year. Now, about your neck . . ."

"I've been hurt a lot worse than this. Tell me, please, any word on Ginny?"

"Nothing so far, I'm afraid. Mobright has our best men on it."

"This is terrible, Beckett. All of this is meaningless if she's hurt, if she's . . ."

"I understand your concern, but you simply must not think the worst. Where would you have gotten if you'd been preoccupied with her when you were soaring? You'd have crashed for certain."

"All right. So . . . we get the Dagger and then what? We let Krell know that we've got it, that we want to trade it for Ginny?"

"You want the Dagger, too," Beckett said, strapping himself in. "Your father wanted it, you want it. Remember the noble purpose."

"If she's alive and there's a breath left in me, I've got to save her. That's my noblest purpose. Everything else comes next."

"Of course. I comprehend you now much better than I did before," he sighed, patting my hand lightly. "You're not the crass ruffian I first believed you to be."

"And you," I said, "are not the arrogant . . . well . . . yes you are."

Beckett laughed. "That's the spirit. A little jocularity. Now, I've given this some thought," he said. "I believe we can meet both our objectives. Once we're in possession of the Dagger, we'll make it known to Krell. He will have to respond. He's trapped. The man is an angstrom away from acquiring the Medici Dagger, the very thing he believes will ultimately save him. He'll have no choice but to negotiate. And when he does, we will have him, and then you will have Ms. Gianelli."

Beckett sat back in his seat and smiled. "Relax, young man," he said. "You've done the impossible. We are now in the golden chair."

eighteen

$\mathcal{F}$ear and excitement had been my daily bread since I'd become a stuntman. But yearning, caring, passion, purpose, connectedness, they were all new to me. Something extraordinary was happening—the reweaving of my torn fabric, thread by thread.

I looked at Beckett. One thin leg was draped over the other. He bobbed it confidently. The bottom half-inch of an ankle holster was intermittently visible below his pant cuff.

Weapons. I needed them.

"I want my guns back," I said.

His leg stopped bobbing. "Oh yes. I've been meaning to ask you about that small one. Very interesting."

"Where are they?"

Beckett turned away, leaned toward the window to catch the view. "You're an unofficial guest. No name, no nationality, no guns. There is no latitude with this."

I heard the usual shrill sound of tires hitting tarmac as we touched down at Leonardo da Vinci Airport.

We were met by a black Mercedes sedan chauffeured by the wide-shouldered Pendelton, whom I had last seen when I stripped off his blazer in Milan. Mobright climbed in the passenger seat. The two exchanged a brief blank glance.

No baggage claim, no customs, no waiting. The A12 Highway along the Tiber, left on the GRA, right on Via Aurelia to Mussolini's wide road into St. Peter's. Past the basilica, Michelangelo's monstrous dome, and Bernini's four-deep colonnade, we zipped with grave officiousness around the throng to the Sistine Chapel.

Pendelton parked in a place where it seemed you'd either get a million-dollar ticket or be condemned to eternal damnation. He exchanged words in fluid Italian with a man wearing the cassock of a high-ranking official.

The priest shook hands hesitantly with Beckett and introduced himself in English as Cardinal Gaetano Lorro, the Vatican secretary. In his worldly eyes was the look of anguished anticipation, which no amount of formality could disguise. I was not introduced.

Pendelton waited by the car as Lorro led us through a huge doorway up a staircase to the large guardroom. The sounds of our footfalls on the marble reminded me of the resplendency, the immeasurable importance, of the surroundings. I rose closer with every step to the imminent future and my appointment with Leonardo.

A thin man sporting wire-rim glasses and work clothes stood a few feet from the center of the floor, where nine blue chalk lines intersected. He held a translucent schematic in one hand.

A ten-inch-square marble tile had been pried up where the snap lines crossed and a high-powered, five-inch hole cutter stood over it mounted on a precision drill press.

We converged on the spot. "You're sure this is the location, Elverson?" Beckett asked.

Elverson held up the schematic. One side showed a detailed outline of the ceiling below, the other displayed the layout of the room in which we stood. "Absolutely," he said.

"And there is no possibility of causing structural damage?"

"None whatsoever. The area you wish to expose is right next to a floor joist." He pointed to a dot where the fingers of God and Adam met. "There is approximately a two-foot space above the arc of the ceiling, which is itself rather thin. We won't touch the ceiling though. As you see, I did some minor preparatory work in the interest of saving time, but Cardinal Lorro refused to allow me to drill until your arrival."

"Hah!" Beckett laughed. "No drilling till the inspector's arrival. I like that. Most excellent. Let's proceed."

Elverson fired up the drill. Mobright and the cardinal stepped back as Beckett and I inched closer.

Angular morning sunlight cut through the galaxy of mortar dust that instantly surrounded us as Elverson carefully drilled down.

I waited impatiently, totally focused on the bottom end of the bit as it disappeared into the antiquated floor. I prayed to God—a last-chance prayer.

Then, with the sudden loss of opposing force, the drill poked through. Beckett said, "Be a good man, Elverson, and step aside."

I knelt down and peered into the hole. Total blackness.

I carefully reached into the opening, almost elbow-deep, until my fingers brushed the ceiling. My saliva evaporated.

Mobright and the cardinal moved in. "*Sia accurato,*" the holy man pleaded, "*per la causa di Dio.*"

"He's telling you to be careful for God's sake," Beckett translated, hovering over me.

I tried to moisten my lips with a dry tongue. "*Glielo prometto,*" I said softly. "I promise."

The ceiling felt cool and rough against my fingertips as they lightly brushed the surface, moving right then left, then a little farther left, and right again. Then my pinky made contact with something metallic. I crept my other fingers over and touched hammered metal. Then a corner. A box.

"Anything?" Beckett whispered.

I could smell his Old Spice, could feel his breath on my ear, but I couldn't speak. My fingers ran along the side of the box. A clasp. I walked them over the top. Irregular surface. I grasped the box and lifted it. It was surprisingly light. I pulled it up through the hole and laid it on the floor.

A beat-up, hammered-tin box.

"*Mio Dio!*" Cardinal Lorro gasped as he, Mobright, and Elverson crowded in.

I opened the latch. Inside was something wrapped in a piece of finely woven red cloth. Lifting it by its thicker end, I was shocked at its near weightlessness. I felt cool sleek metal through the delicate fabric. With the thumb and forefinger of my bandaged hand, I pinched the cloth at the narrow end and in one quick move disrobed the artifact like a magician.

I was holding the Medici Dagger.

Though faintly aware of the utterances emanating from the small crowd huddled tightly around me, I was not with them. I was with Leonardo, somewhere in a velvety fold in time where we two had kept our strange, preordained appointment. I had found him. He had called to me and I had found him, to repay some inexplicable debt—to the world, to him, to my mother and my father.

I slowly rotated Leonardo's creation in the dust-sprinkled light, noticing how quickly the intricately molded handle warmed in my hand, how the faultlessly symmetrical double-edged blade rose to a miraculously sharp point eight inches from the shaft.

I turned it till it glinted in the sunlight that spilled in through the square openings in the brick walls, walls by which smartly dressed guards in steel helmets had dutifully marched so long ago, to protect Pope Leo and all his treasures—none more valuable than the man he ignored in the Belvedere Palace.

I gently touched the metal tip; a tiny drop of blood instantly appeared, as though I'd been pricked by a Red Cross lancet. I marveled at the incredible precision of the almost weightless object.

"Reb," Beckett said from somewhere very close by. "Reb," he said again, this time touching my shoulder.

It was a touch through time, a ripple in the universe, nudging a solitary star out of its tiny galaxy. I felt myself pulled slowly toward the sound of his voice, felt the slight sting in my finger, the gauze on my hand, my knees on the tile, the stretching of burned skin at the back of my right calf. I heard my breathing, and faint voices, and shoe leather pivoting on dusty tile as the others in the room shifted positions. I slowly turned my face to Beckett.

"You have indeed done it," he beamed.

A door clicked shut across the room behind us and a familiar voice said, "Yes you have, Flame Boy."

Everyone spun around to the sound; I crash-landed back in the present. Nolo Tecci stood just inside the door wearing his kidskin coat, black gloves, and a vicious grin. In his hand was a Glock 17—leveled at us. He was flanked by Lon and Jocko, who also had guns with silencers drawn and pointed in our direction. Jocko's wrist was in a cast. Everyone froze.

"Nolo," Mobright uttered. "You're early." *Mobright the confederate? Shit!*

"What exactly do you mean, he's early?" Beckett asked.

Mobright cleared his skinny throat. "I meant . . . that . . . I just didn't expect him so . . . soon." He flashed me a worried glance before returning his gaze to Beckett's.

"Do you have something you'd like to share with us?" Beckett said coldly.

"No, sir. I was merely saying—"

Tecci sang, "That's liffffe, that's what all the people sa-ay," snapping his fingers like Sinatra, taking two casual steps into the room. He pointed his gun at Beckett. "Those are nice words, don't you think? Here come four other nice words: Hi honey, I'm Rome."

Beckett stood, dusting off his hands. Tecci strolled over to him.

"Arlen . . ." Tecci said dispassionately. "No kiss?" He ran the barrel of his gun down Beckett's cheek.

There was a moment of taut silence; then Nolo jutted his chin at me. "Ah, Flame Boy . . . you are the fucking ace. I thought you died."

"I rose," I replied, starting to get up.

"Ah, ah, ah. Stay where you are."

I put my knee down.

"I see you kept my autograph," Tecci said.

"I've been meaning to thank you for that," I said, glancing down at the Dagger. Cool steel in my hand. A quick toss . . .

"Easy there, Ace," Tecci cautioned, "don't go getting magnificent on us." He jerked his head at Jocko. "Get the knife from him and whatever else he's got. Lon, relieve these other citizens of their guns."

Lon passed by Beckett and collected Elverson's handgun. Cardinal Lorro wasn't carrying. Jocko stepped over to me and frisked me quickly, then held out his hand.

I gripped the Dagger tightly, muscles tensed. Jocko and I exchanged a long fierce look. He reached for the Dagger.

"I know you two have a little thing going between you," Tecci said offhandedly. "You annoy everyone, Flame Boy. Be brave, don't be brave, it's all the same to me."

I broke away from Jocko's gaze, looked over at Tecci. "Where is she?" I said between clenched teeth.

"She's tart, that one," Tecci chuckled. "Very smart, too. Tart and smart. She was busy as a bee unscrambling da Vinci's poetry when we got the call. You should have seen her."

Mobright must have called him from the plane. He dies. Then a thought snagged me: Tecci had said, "She *is* tart." *Is.* Present tense. Ginny was alive. Sounds of tourists drifted up from the streets below.

I slowly opened my hand and let the Dagger rest freely in my palm. Jocko picked it up by the shank and presented it to Tecci.

Tecci pointed the Dagger at Beckett's breast, a half inch from his suit coat, then patted him down in a strangely sensual way. Tension bristled through the room. Beckett didn't flinch when Tecci slid his hands down his thighs. Nolo didn't reach his ankle holster. I wondered when Beckett would make a move for it.

"This is a very nice suit, *Arlen,*" Tecci said. "Just as nice as your sheets. I like nice sheets, don't you Flame Boy? You know, I wonder what happens to freshly pressed sheets when their owner doesn't come home? Do they get lonely or do they just lie there like cats who don't care?"

Tecci flicked the Dagger, catching the inspector's monogrammed pocket handkerchief with the tip. "AB, now that is dashing," he laughed, wrapping the blade in the fine silk.

He stashed it in his coat pocket, his eyes never leaving Beckett's. Then he grabbed the knot in the inspector's tie, leaned in, sniffed him, and kissed him gently on the lips like a lover.

"There," he said, then stepped back toward the door.

Beckett stood perfectly still, arms at his sides, with a slightly bemused expression. I figured he must be calculating the right moment to make his all-important move. We were dangerously close to now-or-never. If he went for the gun, I'd follow his lead, make the most of it . . . somehow. Seconds ticked to the throbbing pulse in my ears.

To Lon, Tecci said, *"Lei ragazzi ammazzare tutti."*

I recognized the words *"ammazzare"* and *"tutti."* Massacre everybody.

"We meet on the rolling palace as planned," Nolo said. "Then everybody gets their cash. Now if you'll excuse us, we've got a helicopter to catch—at the papal helipad, no less. Any last words, Arlen?"

Beckett turned to me slowly.

"Reb," he said sadly. "You were indeed a mighty traveler."

Then he casually smoothed his lapels and stepped over to Tecci. "And a devilishly handsome one, too," he added with a smile as he walked past Nolo and out the door.

I felt as though a switch was flipped, the light blazing me blind. I was stunned, from my aching knees on the tile to the sweat-soaked brow on my hollow skull. *Beckett and Tecci? How did I miss that?*

Nolo winked at me, turned, and strolled out of the room singing to the melody of Streisand's hit "People": "Papal . . . papal who need papal . . ." I heard him cackle as his voice faded down the stairs.

Cardinal Lorro's knees quivered, shaking the folds of his elegant robes. His lips moved in silent prayer, racing for salvation after a life spent in service of Christ, or art, or both.

Jocko looked comfortable. Lon chuckled. Mobright gaped at me, shaking his head, and I knelt, the heat from the core of the earth on a one-way trip through the floor beneath my knees, to power my thighs, my balls, my belly.

Jocko grinned at me through crooked teeth. Then he stuffed his gun into the front of his pants. He reached into his back pocket to pull out a switchblade, flicked it open, and approached me, rubber Wal-Mart soles squeaking on the cold tile. I watched his movement, preparing for either a stab or a kick.

Jocko leaned forward, low, for a punt. Too close for the face. I tensed my abdominals. He kicked me. I faked like it knocked the wind out of me and fell forward clutching my stomach.

I rolled to my right and grabbed the loose tile Elverson had pried up, came out of the roll, and flung it at Lon's face. It caught him high on the cheekbone, leaving a gash, and he stumbled backward against the wall. Cardinal Lorro sprang for the door and Lon shot him in the back.

Elverson sprang for Lon, but a second too late. Jocko fired. Out of the corner of my eye I saw Elverson crumple. I scissored Jocko's legs and he went over. I threw him in a full nelson and rolled him on top of me as another gunshot split the air.

I felt the shock of the blast through his body; he shuddered, then went limp. I grabbed his gun, aimed vaguely at Lon, and fired off three quick shots, missing each time. Mobright dove for him. *Mobright on Lon? Why?*

Then two shots rang out from behind me. Lon buckled, leaving a smear of red on the brick wall. As I turned to look at the shooter, Mobright picked up Lon's gun and dropped into a crouch. I took two wild shots at him, missing him in the gun smoke and the urgency.

"No, Reb!" Mobright shouted, dashing to take cover behind an oak desk. I flashed on the drill four feet away. I snatched up the heavy tool as a voice from behind me shouted, "You've got the wrong man, Reb!"

Already in full motion, I heaved the drill with all my might at Mobright. Just as he reached the desk, the tool smashed him in the side, knocking the wind out of him.

"Stop!" someone shouted.

I spun around in total confusion. Inside the far door a man who looked oddly familiar pointed a smoking handgun loosely at the floor. He was the one who had shot Lon.

He dropped his gun and raised his hands. "Don't shoot, Reb. Please don't shoot." He turned to Mobright. "Are you all right, Timothy?"

"No," Mobright gasped.

"Who the hell are you?" I shouted at the man.

He moved swiftly toward me, his arms still raised.

Stopping three feet from me he said, "You know me as Henry Greer—the courier."

"Greer?" My mind reeled. I saw an image of the withered, dying man at The Willows, heard the rasping voice. The person in front of me was sixty, full head of gray hair, lean, clear-eyed. But Greer had died in the nursing home, hadn't he? "Greer?" I repeated.

"Yes," the man said in the rasp. "Henry Greer." He cleared his throat. "But my real name is Arlen Beckett."

Jangling shock. "What are you talking about? Arlen Beckett just left with Tecci."

"No he didn't. Beckett just arrived, because I am he."

This was too much too fast. "Everybody's a goddamn liar here!" I shouted. "Jesus, if you're Beckett, then who—"

"His name is Jack Heath," Mobright groaned. "He was Inspector Beckett's second-in-command. He's been using Beckett's name with you for some twisted reason."

Keeping my eyes on the new Beckett, I said, "You think I'm listening to you, Mobright? A minute ago you drew on me. You were going to shoot me."

"No, I wasn't. You tried to shoot *me!* God, Reb. The inspector shouted to you that you had the wrong man. I think you broke my ribs. And after I picked off that redheaded German for you in Mendocino."

"What?" I desperately tried to cling to unchallenged facts. There was me, there was Ginny, there was Archie. I thought it was Archie in the woods in Mendocino. He said it was him when I asked him in the hospital.

"I saved your ass in Mendocino," Mobright groaned. "Took him out a second before he was going to plug you."

"What the hell's going on here!" I shouted.

"Give me two minutes to explain," Beckett said.

"Make it one. Talk fast."

The man took a breath.

"I met Heath at Oxford when I was on a fellowship. He was biding time until he could take over the family empire. We became friends. One night over too much brandy he confessed he'd had a homosexual encounter, something that wouldn't have been approved of by his father or British society at that time. He made me swear never to tell anyone."

"So what?"

"After completing my studies, I returned to the States and was recruited into the Central Intelligence Agency. Not long after, Heath called me, literally out of his mind, screaming that his father had found out about his secret and that he'd been totally disinherited. He accused me of breaking my oath. I reiterated my loyalty to him and offered my help.

"I arranged for his emigration to the U.S.; then, at his request, I sponsored him into the organization. As Mr. Mobright said, Heath moved up the ladder right behind me, and we moved together to Gibraltar. While investigating Nolo Tecci's part in Krell's organization, I discovered that Tecci had been implicated in blackmail years ago. One of the victims was Jack Heath's father."

"You're telling me Heath's college affair was with Nolo Tecci? Jesus."

"Gibraltar doesn't allow for skeletons in closets, Reb. The bones tend to rattle. I had to investigate Jack—privately. I found journals in his house, dating back to just before he joined me in America, detailing his hatred for me, his unwavering belief that I was the one who had betrayed him, though it had to have been Tecci.

"I couldn't believe it," Beckett went on bitterly. "Our relationship had been a complete sham. All along he was planning his retribution, just waiting for the right moment. What an *idiot* I'd been! What a fool."

"So what does this have to do with me?" I urged.

"There was more," he added. "Jack has AIDS."

"AIDS," I repeated, picturing Heath's gaunt face, remembering how at the Big Bear Hospital he'd said he wished he could put on some of the sheriff's weight. Heath was slated for death.

"*And*," Beckett continued gravely, "he *was* in recent contact with Nolo Tecci."

His eyes flashed to Mobright's and then to mine.

"I confronted him at his home."

"And?"

Beckett grimaced. "Heath pulled a spray bottle from his desk and . . . The last words I heard from him were 'All good things come to he who hates.' "

"Then what?" I asked.

"A few hours later, Tim Mobright here found me in my car. He told me I was being accused of stealing information with the intent of selling it to our adversaries.

"A copy of a file had been made from a computer which only I and my superior had access to. I remembered the day I'd left Jack alone in the room for a few minutes. I had no defense. I had to run to escape being removed by my own organization before I could vindicate myself. My one ally was Tim."

"That's what this is all about?" I spat. "Some fucking file?"

"Have you heard of the Passive Coherent Location system?" Beckett asked.

I remembered my first meeting with Heath in Milan. "I know what the PCL is," I said, getting pissed. "Tell me what's in the goddamn file!"

Beckett's face reddened. "An *equation* is in the *goddamn* file, Reb. An equation for an electronic countermeasure that would allow aircraft and weapons systems to be modified to mask the disturbance of the broadcast channels that the PCL works on. If Heath sells it to Soon Ta Kee through Werner Krell, then Ta Kee can dictate U.S.-Chinese policy."

Shit, I thought, for the first time comprehending the magnitude of the vortex Ginny and I'd been sucked into.

Mobright groaned. Beckett knelt by his side, comforting him.

"After I went underground," he continued, "Jack recruited Tim, who went along as my mole. Tim kept track of Heath, learned Krell had boxed himself in to an impossible delivery date with Soon Ta Kee, promising him a weapon which would be absolutely useless unless it had a housing that was ultralight and capable of withstanding the incredible temperatures generated by uncontrolled free-fall reentry through the atmosphere. There *is* no such modern material, but Krell is convinced there is; the alloy supposedly discovered five hundred years ago by—"

"Leonardo," I finished.

"You were my means of getting to Heath before he got to Krell with the disk," Beckett said. "It occurred to me to use you to roust him."

"It occurred to you to *use* me," I seethed. "To *roust* that lunatic."

"This is much bigger than either of us, Reb. I had no alternative."

"So you played Greer, the courier. A crippled old man . . ."

"We can be whoever we need to be," Beckett said matter-of-factly.

"You were dying in a hospice. . . . The nurse said you were dead."

Beckett stood. "I believe 'is no longer with us' were the words I chose for her. Look, we're out of time," he said, turning to Mobright. "Tim, tell me what you know."

Mobright gathered his strength. "Reb found the Dagger in the floor," he said, "but Tecci showed up earlier than I'd told him to and took it away, spoiling our plan that you would arrive first. He and

Heath left just moments ago. They're heading for Krell's Pullman. They didn't give me the details. They expected me to come with Jocko and Lon."

"We've got to get to that train," I said, panic and rage rising. "Ginny's on that train."

Over by the door, Cardinal Lorro and Elverson were dead. Jocko lay still, a puddle of blood spreading under him. Just then Lon moaned. I'd thought he was dead, too.

"Wha . . . ?" he mumbled.

I could feel precious seconds ticking Ginny's life away. I picked up the drill and stepped over to the goon, knelt and squeezed the trigger. The hole cutter whirred. Holding it an inch from Lon's shoulder, I said, "Where's the rolling palace?"

His eyes cleared. "Fuck you, Flame Boy!"

"You held my head while Nolo burned his initial in my neck. I'm going to like this more than you." I revved the drill.

"All right, all right," he groaned. "It's going to Zurich."

"Which train?"

"IC382."

"Where does it stop in Italy?" I moved the drill a quarter inch closer.

"Milan, I think," he muttered, leaning as far away as he could from the bit.

"Is Krell on the train?"

"Of course."

"Is Antonia?"

"Who?"

I clamped my fingers on Lon's thick jaw and snapped it toward me. "Miss Venice," I hissed. "Is she on the train?"

He nodded.

"Where are my goddamn guns, Mobright?" I demanded.

"On Krell's plane, the one we took here. In the cabinet to the right of the sink."

Police sirens wailed outside. "Tim . . ." Beckett said to Mobright.

"I'm all right, Inspector," the injured man replied, aiming his weapon at Lon. "You two best be going. I'll look after our friend."

Beckett said to me, "Well, then, let's go get your guns."

"What about the pilot?"

"Don't worry about Halliday," he said, withdrawing a small spray bottle from his coat pocket.

"Then who'll fly the plane?" I asked.

"We're taking Dracco's."

"Dracco? You mean that was you in Milan? You gave the card to Ginny?"

"Mm-hmm. I nailed those two by the bus for you, passed the business card to her. Let's move. Dracco's at the airport. We've got to get to Krell's train."

There was no time to ponder. I slipped into the hall behind Beckett and followed him to Pendelton's Benz, which he pointed out was closer than his own car.

The big-shouldered man was slumped over behind the wheel— dead. "He spotted me," Beckett explained.

We pulled him out and rolled him behind some bushes. Beckett took the wheel and we blasted for the airport.

Heath's pilot was in the hangar. He was surprised to see me and even more surprised to see Beckett. Two minutes after incapacitating him, I had the mini strapped to my arm and the two Sigs hanging under my jacket.

We found Dracco shaving in the bathroom in his hangar, his Gulfstream ready for travel.

"Hey, Beckett," he chuckled. "You hooked up with Hollywood Reb. How about that?"

"We'll be needing your services right now," Beckett told him. "Full fare. Milan. Linate Airport is closest to the Stazione Centrale."

"Linate it is," Dracco answered, toweling off his rugged face. "Let's boogie."

Once airborne, Beckett and I stared uneasily at each other from our leather seats. Thoughts and feelings swooped down on me like Hitchcock's birds. Four days ago I'd sat on Emily's carpet dents, crying homeless tears to my picture of Ginevra de' Benci. Since then I'd punched and shot and burned and bled and kissed and felt. I'd soared with Leonardo da Vinci, held his Dagger for my father, and all as the unwitting actor in Beckett's little drama.

My hands shook; I willed them to stop, grabbing the ends of my armrests. Beckett turned to me, but I spoke first, my eyes burning into his.

"You played me, you prick. I told you at the hospice nobody plays me."

He didn't have to answer.

"The night you called me with that raspy put-on voice, you said you knew my father. You didn't know him at all, did you?"

"I had a complete file on him."

"Why would you have a file on my father?"

"Because of what we found on Greer's plane."

"What?"

"The story I told you about Greer and Tecci on the train was true, except Greer didn't ditch his plane and his legs weren't broken in the fall. He did try to sell Leonardo's page and Tecci double-crossed him— slashed his arm badly and was going to throw him off the train at the St. Roddard Pass.

"Greer jumped early with the money and the notes, made his way back to his plane, and took off for America. He didn't get far; apparently he went unconscious from loss of blood and ditched. I picked him up in no time because I was tracking him."

"Why were you tracking Greer?"

"Because in addition to transporting Leonardo's precious page, Greer was carrying secret documents to a contact in Greenland. You see, he was a courier for hire. He worked for everyone from the

National Gallery to the KGB. My job was to make sure those documents never reached Greenland.

"I arrived at the plane, which was still afloat and not badly damaged, and removed Greer, the documents, and the satchel. Greer was unconscious and bleeding profusely. He never would have made it to Greenland, much less Washington, D.C.

"As I got him onto the ship, he revived long enough to tell me about the Medici Dagger and pass me the page of Leonardo's notes. My mission was, of course, secret. I couldn't let those notes surface; I certainly couldn't mail them to your father in an unmarked envelope. There was too much at risk. At that time a magic dagger and an eccentric munitions manufacturer didn't seem like much of a threat. So I sank the plane and the notes went into a vault, along with the satchel of money, to be buried forever beside a thousand other extraordinary artifacts."

I shook my throbbing head. "Buried forever . . ."

"Well, not forever," Beckett said. "Until two weeks ago. When the second page of Leonardo's notes surfaced in Italy, it brought back the memory of the incident with Greer, the satchel in the vault, and the page of notes. I knew the money would be an asset. I didn't know of what use the page would be, so I researched the Medici Dagger. Of course your father's file came up, along with the family photo that had run in the newspaper at the time of the fire. Without knowing why, really, I looked into what had become of you. When I found out you were a stuntman, well, that's when my plan gelled."

"I know the rest," I murmured to the window.

"You were the perfect appendage, Reb. My God, how powerful a force vengeance is," Beckett said to himself.

My hands were shaking again, not from the heights, but from pent-up rage, at the tragedy of greed and malice, the dominoes of death. Was it raw circumstance or preordained that my parents would die, that I would become Leonardo's mighty traveler, that I would be sitting now, at this moment, across from the man who'd rescued

Leonardo's first page of the Circles of Truth from being lost at sea only to imprison it in a steel vault until it was time to set it—and me—free?

I looked up to see Beckett staring at me with the same dispassionate grin he'd had on his face when I'd left him dying in his hospice bed.

He seemed to read my thoughts. "Survival of the fittest," he said. "I needed to survive and you were—"

"Fit," I finished.

"Yes. I couldn't conceive at the time just how extraordinarily fit you were. You actually found the Medici Dagger."

"And Tecci and Krell and Heath have it."

"For the moment."

"And they have the woman I love."

Silence over the whine of jet engines, wind over wings. I couldn't believe I'd said those words. The woman I *love*. Tears fought for their freedom. Turning my face toward the window, I blinked them back, but Beckett saw.

"If anything has happened to her . . ." I managed. "If she's in any way . . ." I couldn't finish the sentence. I faced him again. "There will be a reckoning. Do you hear me? If I'm not dead, there will be a reckoning."

Beckett looked at me solemnly. "If we don't catch them, Reb, it will be the Prince of Darkness himself who will reckon with me. So," he said, plugging his laptop into a modem. "Let's focus on the problem at hand."

Beckett dialed into the Internet and connected with the Ferrovie Dello Stato, Italy's national rail company. In short order, he had a printout of every train leaving Italy for Zurich that afternoon. He made an anonymous call to the FS office and confirmed that the IC382 was pulling a private car and that it was departing from Milan in an hour and fifteen minutes.

He told me it would take us at least an hour to get to Linate Airport, which was six kilometers from the Central Station, a dicey six kilometers; by car it could take a full half hour to reach the station once we touched down.

I asked if he could pull any strings to delay the train.

He said he couldn't, and that even if he could, a move like that would only alert them and cause them to flee. "Where would we be then?" he added.

He was right. I had to get my brain clear. The only way to get on the train was to catch up with it. To do that, I'd need speed. Jungle speed. I saw myself streaking for the IC382. Beckett wasn't in the picture. I felt the familiar sensation of resolve. One way or another, I was going alone.

I asked Beckett to print out a map of the roads that followed the train route. Inside a minute I was poring over them.

The train stopped in Lugano, about eighty kilometers north of Milan. After that, it was a straight shot to Zurich.

"Does Dracco have firepower?" I asked.

Beckett got up from his seat and opened a closet. "He's fairly well stocked, actually," he said. "Automatics, sniper rifle, an assortment of knives—"

"What's that?" I asked, pointing to a large futuristic black plastic weapon.

"This," he said, handing it to me, "is a Pancor Jackhammer. Hmm . . . loaded. It's a gas-operated automatic shotgun that'll turn anyone it's pointed at into a cave painting. Useful, but a little difficult to conceal. I can't see an application for it in this mission."

"Hand it over."

I leaned forward and stashed it down the back of my jacket, tucking the barrel into my pants. It fit. "How about transportation in Milan?"

"I'll check with Dracco," Beckett said, stepping toward the cockpit.

I closed my eyes, felt the muscles in my face tighten, the grit in my gut. Krell, Tecci, Heath—Old-Spiced and pin-striped . . . why hadn't I spotted him as a fake? "No one is merely who they seem to be," he'd said. "Isn't power intoxicating?" Heath was dying to tell me it was a sham. That son of a bitch had sat next to me, told me where to break the Circles. He'd massaged my temples, for chrissake. Then he'd sent me to my doom, standing next to his former lover. Damn! And Greer . . . I mean Beckett . . . he'd sucked me in with a cough and a phone call, had me dancing like a marionette.

When I opened my eyes, Beckett was sitting in his seat staring at me. "When I lay in that bed playing a dying American pilot, I admit I felt a pang of regret, and I feel it again now. By nature I'm not a panderer of men. Of course, you have no reason to believe me at this point."

It was my turn to not answer.

"I'm sorry for what happened to your throat," he said.

I ignored the statement. "What did Dracco tell you?"

"He's got an assortment of vehicles at his private hangar. One hell of an accommodating mercenary."

"We'll rent a car from him. That shouldn't cost more than two, three grand."

"Four. I'll cover it, of course."

"From Greer's satchel, right? When I got it, it had two million in it. How much when you got it?"

Beckett crossed his legs, folded his hands. "Three."

We touched down at Linate Airport, taxied over to Dracco's hangar, and slowed to a stop. I deplaned first, while Beckett settled up with Dracco. Inside the hangar were a Bell Jet Ranger helicopter, a black Mercedes sedan, and a brand-new red Harley with the key in it. I looked back at the jet and saw Beckett stepping off.

I saw his jaw drop in the Harley's rearview mirror.

nineteen

In eighteen minutes the mauling city gave way to brown earth and bulging Alps. I screamed up E35 on Dracco's Harley, wondering what I'd face aboard the IC382. I'd killed I-don't-know-how-many on the boat in Venice; five bought it in Little River; Lon and Jocko were out of the picture. Who was left? Tecci and Krell and Heath? Had to be more than that.

I pictured Krell from the description Lois had given me by phone the last time I'd flown into Milan: bald, not bad-looking. What was clanking through his crazy head? He had the Dagger; he had Ginny; Soon Ta Kee was on his tail; and he was cruising through the Alps in a silver Pullman?

In Krell's eyes, everyone had to be dispensable. No way they'd hand Ginny the Dagger in Zurich and say they were sorry. I remembered the story Beckett told me about Greer. Tecci on the back platform, the high bridge, the rolling wheels, the double-cross. And then, with the force of an asteroid, a thought struck: Tecci was going to toss Ginny off the back of the Pullman at the St. Roddard Pass.

I checked my watch. It was going to be tight. They'd be pulling into the station in fifteen minutes. Followed by a ten-minute stop. That gave me twenty-five minutes. I could just make it.

I roared by the flow of traffic on the winding road, dipping into the breakdown lane, kicking up gravel and bottle caps. I was ahead of everybody, in the clear, until I tore around a corner and ran smack into the Swiss border at Chiasso.

I'd forgotten about the goddamn border! Instantly, I regretted having the Jackhammer. Too late. I slowed to a stop and sat up straight, arching my shoulders back to make space for the shotgun.

It was a small station: four uniformed guards, probably bored, certainly not waiting for me. I smiled at the young one who approached me and asked for my papers, hoping he'd have some sympathy for a hunchback. I wondered if I should say hello. Opting for silence, I handed him my passport.

The guard flipped it open, matching the picture with the face.

"American on a Harley," he said with an Italian accent. "I ride a Honda. Are you renting or owning?" He eyed the bike with admiration.

I told him a friend of mine had loaned it to me.

"Really?" he said, surprised. "It looks new. Must be a very good friend."

"Wonderful guy. Very generous," I assured him.

"Hmm, what is in the back of your jacket?"

Time ticked irrevocably by, steel wheels rolling for Lugano.

"It's a back support," I said. "I have a very, very bad back."

The guard scratched his chin with my passport. I checked his countenance from behind my shades. Curiosity or concern?

"What is this bump?" he asked, frowning. He called to a middle-aged guard who was checking a Saab. "Luigi!"

The man waved the car through to Swiss freedom. I felt envy, fear, anger. The guard walked quickly toward us, his hand moving to his holstered gun.

Ticking clock, pounding heart, sweating hands.

Luigi pointed his chin grimly at my back.

Time's up.

I squeezed the clutch, dropped it into gear, spun the throttle, and peeled out, lifting the front wheel a foot off the ground. Over the thunder of the Harley's huge engine, I could barely hear the shouts.

The bike hung in the air for a full five seconds before I let it fall. I snatched a look in the vibrating mirror. The two guards were jumping into a car.

A moment later I heard the *weeoo* sound of their siren. Shifting into third, I continued to accelerate around a corner in the winding road.

Think, think! Direction, roads. I'm on N2. They'll call ahead to Lugano. They'll send guys south to box me in.

I remembered the map I'd studied on the plane. SS340 cut east at Chiasso to Lake Como. I surveyed the terrain on my right. Chuckholey, tough going, but the highway had to be that way. It was off-road or nothing. Backing down to ninety, I pulled into the wilderness, churning up dust like a stagecoach. Dracco's Harley was now a monster dirt bike.

I dodged the big rocks, kicked up the little ones, and hauled ass toward a rise a half mile ahead. I no longer heard the siren, only the rumble of my engine and the ping of the stones. Felt them, too, smacking my shins.

I slowed as I reached the top, not wanting to catch unexpected air. What I saw was a hundred yards of low-sloping grass and the SS340. Ten seconds later I landed on my new route. No cops. But no Lugano either.

The tourists drive by Lake Como at a torturous five miles an hour. There are no back roads to take, no freeways to hop, nothing but nature, cheese shops, and oompah bands.

I inched along in wrenching frustration, wholly disjointed from the festive surroundings. Boarding the train at Lugano was a tragically missed opportunity. It had certainly left the station and was streaking for the St. Roddard Pass. All around me carefree people in sporty haircuts and hiking boots admired that iridescent, deep-blue lake.

The watery vision stilled my mind and I drifted, hooked to a line that dangled from memory's long pole.

I recalled my first trip through the pass, cruising south from Zurich in a VW bus. After crossing a bridge, we'd entered a tunnel. When it spit us out the other side, I'd noticed train tracks thirty feet below, running parallel to the road.

Suddenly I was back in the jungle. Clear vision, crystalline thought. Goddamn! *I know how to intercept that train!*

I cut west on the road to Gandria, then wound my way toward

Bellinzona, tooling as fast as the snaky road would allow. If the police were looking for me, they'd be on Highway N2. Checking my watch, I calculated when the train would reach the tunnel. Twenty minutes, tops. I cranked the throttle; my burned hand throbbed. Anger snacked on the pain.

At Bellinzona I got back on the main road at last. Passing everyone as if they were still-lifes, I watched for cops and prayed for train.

I blasted through Giornico. The mountain loomed ahead in the distance—a chunk of rock with two gaping holes.

As I careered around a hairpin turn, my foot peg scraped along the coarse pavement. I was losing the split-second battle for control when I heard the screaming whistle.

With all my strength, I forced the bike up and onto the straight-away. And there it was! At the back of what looked like thirty cars, Krell's silver Pullman glinted in the afternoon sun.

Ginny!

Hunching down, I gunned the Harley up the ascending parallel road as the locomotive barreled into the tunnel.

Sirens wailed behind me.

I'm on that train, I resolved. *One take.*

Speeding past the Pullman, I saw the curtain pull back and glimpsed Krell's bald head. The mountain towered above, its open mouth waiting to devour me. *Not today. Time it . . . time it . . . Go!*

I jerked the bike hard right. The ground fell away as I launched for the rapidly disappearing train. I leaned forward, keeping my body loose, anticipating the impact.

The rear wheel landed first, square in the middle of the car in front of Krell's. Tromping the back brake, I laid the big bike down, taking the hit on my right hip and elbow as I slid by the air-conditioning unit, just managing to grab hold of it. The eight-hundred-pound motorcy-cle screeched across the roof of the car, plummeted off the side, and crashed into the brick wall at the face of the tunnel.

Steel fingers and iron will kept me clinging to the train as it hurtled into the darkness. Wind battered me like a cat-o'-nine-tails, deafening me to all but my inner charge, my mission. I was chin down, spread-eagled, unable to do anything until we emerged from the mile-long tunnel into the sunlight that filled the cavernous pass.

I was about to crawl around the air conditioner toward the Pullman when five men rushed like ants out of a hole onto Krell's front platform.

I pulled out the Jackhammer, flattened myself against the roof, and squeezed the trigger; the force of the kickback jumped the shotgun out of my hand and off the side of the car as one of the guys exploded like a piñata.

I drew out one of the Sigs, a weapon I knew I could count on, and let loose, directing my fire side-to-side like a lawn sprinkler, emptying the magazine. I heard screams over the sound of the thundering train, then nothing, which gave me a moment of hope, till about a hundred rounds tore through the air conditioner, ripping it to shrapnel.

I fell away, covering my face with my arms, and slid to the side of the car, grabbing the gutter rail. Drawing the mini from my sleeve, I frantically pressed the button for full automatic as the next burst of machine-gun fire ripped the rest of the air conditioner from the roof.

I squeezed the trigger, firing most of the clip of pellets at the two remaining men. A microsecond later, tiny explosions popped like firecrackers. I lifted my head up slowly. Carnage.

I slipped the gun back into the armband; the heat burned my skin. Spidering over the edge of the car, I leapt down into the litter of bodies. I pulled the other Sig from its holster and burst through the door in a low crouch. No one in sight.

"Ginneeey!" I yelled, searching the car.

"Reb!" she screamed from the back platform.

I sprang through the rear door, all rational thought deserting me. Tecci stood behind Ginny in the corner, the Medici Dagger pressed to her throat, his Glock 17 aimed at my heart. Two feet away, Werner Krell leaned against the railing, sweat pouring down his face, eyes wild and darting. Heath wasn't there.

"Ace . . . you do always turn up, don't you?" Nolo said. "Say hello to Herr Krell."

My chest heaved, breath rasping in my smoke-scorched throat. My eyes locked on Ginny's. The wind blew her hair across her terrified face.

"Ginny," I whispered.

Nolo nodded at my gun. "Put it down."

I laid it on the platform floor, my mind racing.

"Boot it over," Tecci ordered.

I kicked it into the ravenous gorge. "Where's Heath?"

"He took a little stroll," Tecci smirked. "Missed all the fireworks."

Krell clasped his hands together and looked up. "If there was a heaven, neglected fruit would sail skyward instead of crashing to the dirt to molder and reek. So you see, Newton's law of gravity is really God's precept of the plummeting souls of fruit and men. And my bombs . . . my bombs, which will carry their souls in their skin. Each one consecrated by the blood of the Medici Dagger." He flashed a smile that oozed madness.

I felt boundless rage. "You're fucking insane," I seethed.

"The time for talk is over, boys," Tecci said.

Krell cackled, "Ah, time. Time, time, time. What time is it, anyway?"

"It's later than you think," Nolo said.

The smile dropped off Krell's smooth face. "No it isn't," he snapped. "It's exactly when I think! You told me, 'Time is a desert.' Well, this is *my* time. I am God's camel, and your only purpose is to fill my hump. And now I have the Dagger and the desert is mine! So, do what you have to do," he ordered, waving his hand at me. "I've got history to make."

My skin prickled.

"Werner," Nolo said quietly, almost reverently. "Welcome to history."

He turned the gun on Krell, shooting him between the eyes. The blast sent him over the railing into a tumbling free fall. Ginny screamed as he pointed the smoking gun back at me.

"I'll miss him quoting me," he said.

"You just killed Werner Krell," I said, stalling. "When did you decide to do that? Really, I'm interested."

Nothing.

I tried again. "You never cared about the alloy, did you? About Krell's plans or Soon Ta Kee. What were you and Heath up to?"

"That depends on when, Flame Boy," he said.

"You blackmailed Heath's father, way back in merry old England," I said, "didn't you?"

He looked surprised for a second, then amused.

"You told him about you and Jack, and threatened to spread the news."

Nolo laughed again. "How'd you figure that out? Jack never did."

"And you didn't like it much when Krell and Ta Kee paired up, either."

"Flame Boy, do I look like someone who socializes with people who take rickshaw rides? When Werner connected with Ta Kee, in my mind, his day was done. You see I'm really quite a free spirit. Freedom—that's what satiates my appetite. Werner, he was way different. His gut was full from grazing in his personal pasture of horrors for so long. Hey, that's a good line; I should write that down. So, satellites, bombs, who cares? I get to enjoy the smell of fresh air again."

"You mean flesh air," I said, anger spiking. "Burning flesh."

"It's true. I do like that, too. The smell of blood isn't bad either, or the scent of a man . . . or a wet woman. Oops," he said, pressing the blade against Ginny's throat. "She's starting to tremble."

"She's a *major* pain in the ass, isn't she?" I blurted.

Ginny gaped at me.

"You mean pain in the neck," Nolo chuckled. "Literally. You know she tried to stab me in the throat with her little pig here?" He pointed to Ginny's stick pin woven into his lapel. "It was right after I told her about signing you. Personally, I think she has a crush on you. Tell me it's true, honey." Nolo sang, "You've got a crush on Ace . . . sweetie piiiie . . ."

Tears trailed down Ginny's cheeks.

"She's a smart one, though," I said, barely containing.

"Oh yeah, a real Poindexter. You should have seen her figuring out da Vinci's poetry. It was beautiful, too, those Circles of Truth. She wanted this knife badly. And now," he said, laying the flat of the blade against Ginny's jaw, "she's gonna get it."

"No," Ginny pleaded, squirming against his arm. "Reb, please . . ."

"What, honey?" Tecci laughed. "You think Flame Boy's going to save you? Wrong. You're next. I'm the carver, babe, and you're going to do the sleeping. Down in the mighty whorl."

Ginny stared at me wide-eyed, locked in horror's grip. The vision of her, the wind, and the rhythm of the clacking wheels carried me exactly to where I needed to be—the jungle.

"Let me go first, Tecci," I said.

"What? Why?"

"I'm supposed to."

"Hah!" he laughed, but I could tell he was intrigued.

"It's meant to be this way." My gaze burned into his. "This is history— the end of five hundred years of it. Leonardo . . . my parents . . . me. That's the order. This is your poem and so far you've written it perfectly—like the N you carved in my neck. Finish it right. You can call it . . . 'Destiny Wept.' "

I could feel Ginny's desperation, but kept my eyes on Tecci as the train rolled along the track, high above the waiting river and crushing rocks.

"You're right, Ace. It is my poem. Up and over."

I breathed a sigh of relief as I turned to Ginny. "I'm so sorry, Antonia."

I leapt onto the gleaming brass railing and pushed off right for Tecci, launching a kick at his stunned face. Ginny ducked. Nolo blocked with the Dagger, slicing right through my boot into the arch of my foot. I grabbed his gun hand. He growled, thrusting the Dagger at me. I caught that wrist and twisted; the knife skittered across the floor.

Tecci head-butted me and squeezed off a round; somewhere behind me, Ginny screamed. Tugging his hand free of my grip, Tecci smashed me in the side of the face with the gun. I spun around and threw a back fist. His head smacked into the wall of the Pullman. Blood spurted.

I punched him in the face; the sound of teeth cracking punctuated his scream. Sagging to his knees, he dropped the gun. I kicked him with my bloody foot, banging his head off the car again. He slumped forward in a heap.

At the other end of the platform, Ginny was bent over, holding the side of her thigh, blood seeping from between her fingers. I ran to her. She fell into my arms, sobbing.

"I've got you," I said softly into her hair. "You all right?"

She pulled away from me. "No, I'm not all right!" she shouted, punching me hard in the stomach.

I doubled over, thinking yes you are, Ginny Gianelli, yes you are. I felt her hand on my shoulder and straightened up.

"I save you and you hit me," I groaned. "Why do you do that?"

She bit her lower lip in a way that made me forget my gut. I lovingly touched her cheek, and she tilted her head back as she had in Pop's garden. Then her face went white as a cloud. "Reb!"

Tecci stood behind me, drenched in blood, raising the Medici Dagger to strike. I tugged out the mini and fired a burst. He jerked backward, pellets exploding. I fired again, emptying the clip.

I rushed to him, grabbing his throat, my thumb covering the head of his tattooed serpent. I wrenched the Dagger from his dangling hand and slipped it into my back pocket. Arching him over the railing, I plucked Ginny's pig from his lapel.

The demon's bloody lips quivered, red rivulets accentuating his hideous face. "Destiny wept," he gasped.

"Not for you," I said, and pushed him into hell.

I watched him rapidly diminish to an undistinguishable dot as relief quenched my adrenaline thirst.

Finally, it's over, I thought.

And then Jack Heath stepped onto the platform, his gun leveled at me.

"Where is it?" he asked grimly.

I hesitated; he aimed at Ginny.

"No!" I shouted. "I'll give you the goddamn Dagger! *If* you let her go at Zurich . . . unharmed."

Heath turned the pistol back on me.

"Young man, you are indeed valor itself," he pronounced. A torturous pause followed; then he said, "All right. Your lady fair lives."

I presented the Dagger to him in my open palm.

When it was safely tucked in his suit pocket, Heath thumbed back the hammer.

"Wait!" Ginny pleaded tearfully. "Let me kiss him goodbye. Please."

"Splendid idea," Heath said. "Be my guest."

Ginny took my hands, moved toward me.

"Ah, quite lovely," Heath said. "Now I can put a single bullet through both your hearts."

My soul sank through the earth, out the other side, and into the blackness of savage space. I had failed. Perfectly and completely. Ginny, my diamond, would shine no more.

I moved between her and Heath's gun in a futile attempt to protect the girl I loved. I pulled her close, felt our thighs touch, her full breasts against me as we enfolded, aligning our pounding hearts. In Ginny's almond eyes was a delicate and frightened invitation to forever.

Our lips met, warm and soft, gentle and sweet as summer, moist tongues entwining, stirring something wondrous inside me for the very first time—a breathless and blessed hello as we approached the piercing sound of goodbye.

Then beating helicopter blades rose swiftly from below as a Jet Ranger came into view, Dracco at the stick. Beckett perched next to him, a cold eye against the scope of a sniper rifle.

"Nooooo!" Heath screamed behind me. I threw Ginny to the floor as the rifle exploded. Heath clutched his punctured chest, then collapsed beside us, faceup, eyes open in permanent surprise.

The chopper stayed on the train's tail as Beckett lowered his weapon and gestured animatedly for me to search the dead man.

I quickly removed the Dagger from Heath's breast pocket. Next to it was a black computer disk. A corner had been shot off.

I struggled to a standing position and raised my two possessions for all of heaven and earth to see.

twenty

*I*nside the Pullman, Ginny lay back on Krell's leather couch and hiked up her skirt to inspect her wounded leg. Tecci's bullet had routed out a nine-millimeter-wide, two-inch-long half-pipe on the side of her upper thigh. Sutures would close it, but there would always be a scar, visible to the beach crowd—and to me.

I sat beside her, peeled off my neatly sliced boot. The gash on my instep would also require stitching, but I knew from experience that it and the rest of my body would heal in time.

Leonardo's notes lay under a crystal paperweight on Krell's Victorian desk. Next to them sat two hand-tooled leather satchels, brimming with cash.

Beckett and Dracco met us at the Zurich station and quietly removed us to the Hotel Arbial. A physician arrived shortly thereafter. He worked quickly, didn't say a word, and had the best tan I'd ever seen.

I presented the disk to Beckett. Neither of us thanked the other.

Dracco flew Ginny and me back to California, during which time we both slept like stones with the aid of pain pills and the absence of worry. Under a hazy morning sky that held the promise of sunshine, he dropped us off at the Big Bear Airport.

Ginny and I took a taxi to Archie's house—ex-house really; it was mostly charcoal. The bushes were still green, though, and Greer's briefcase was still buried under the cool dirt. I left it there again. The Jag was in the driveway, too, and fired right up, purring eagerly.

At the Medical Center we found Archie reading. He looked at us in stunned delight and laid the book in his lap, holding his place with his finger.

Most of his bandages were off except for a nose splint, and he looked a little puffy and purple. But his eyes were as clear as china glaze. I sat on the bed next to him. Neither of us said anything for a while.

"That really wasn't you in Milan, was it?" I said.

"Nope."

"Or up in the woods?"

"Sure I was in the woods. That's where my cabin is."

I thought back to when we lay next to each other in the hospital the morning after the fire. I hadn't mentioned Mendocino when I'd asked if he'd been in the woods.

"Archie," I said.

"Yeah?"

"No one could replace my father."

"I know that."

"But I could use a big brother."

His eyes got watery. Mine, too.

Ginny joined us. She thanked him for taking her in when he did, and kissed him on his ear—the only place, he said, that didn't hurt. I kissed him on his other ear and he cracked a smile that filled the whole room. He held up the book he'd been reading: *Leonardo,* by Robert Payne.

I told him about the present I'd left buried for him behind the tree. He said he liked presents.

It was four in the morning when Ginny and I pulled down the driveway to the Hollister House. We rang the buzzer at the main building and a light switched on. When the door eventually opened, Pop was

246

standing there in a robe and sleeping cap. He rubbed his eyes and peered at us for a moment, his perfect false teeth gleaming in the hall light.

"By jingo, it's Holmes and Watson," he said. "Come on in, you two."

We hobbled in like a couple of Yodas. He sat us down on the couch and stared at us, like we'd appeared out of a lamp he'd rubbed. We stared back, vibrating from the trip, soaking in the sight of him and the sweet stillness of the night.

Pop left the room, reappearing in a couple of minutes carrying a round wooden tray which held four stoneware mugs, drifting trails of tangerine-scented tea steam. As he handed us each a cup and took one for himself, Mona stepped into the room in a long blue robe and slippers, her face wrinkled from sleep. She didn't say a word, just sat on the edge of Pop's chair.

Pop pushed his hat back. "So . . ."

Even though it was damn late or damn early, it was time to tell the tale. Ginny and I pieced the whole thing together, for them and for each other. Pop and Mona listened eagerly, his old head cocked to one side, her hair draping loosely down her lapels. Pop exploded more than once with "What happened next?" and "By jingo."

Chirping birds were ushering in the dawn as we finished.

I withdrew the Medici Dagger and presented it to Pop. He cradled it in the palms of his hands, hunching over, gazing at the spectacle. He passed it to Mona, who held it up to the light, turning it till it glinted magnificently.

The four of us basked silently in the beauty of Leonardo's creation. When Mona returned the Dagger to me, the heat from her hands lingered in the mysterious alloy.

"What are you gonna do with it, Reb?" Pop said.

I found myself enveloped in sadness—sublime sadness. It was the blanket I'd been wrapped in since that tragic night in the summer of '80—the cover that had simultaneously provided me warmth and kept me cold as a tomb.

247

Ginny reached over and touched my knee, and that blanket fell away. I didn't need it anymore.

"The Dagger belongs in the National Gallery," I said softly, "with the Circles of Truth."

We sat for several fragile minutes, grasping our cups, breathing in the grandeur and tragedy—the strange symmetry of circumstances that had brought us together.

I nabbed a quick look at Ginny. She caught me and hooked me, and held me in her stare. Then she took my face in her hands and kissed me deeply, shamelessly, a low feral sound emanating from her throat. It was a ground-stomping, wall-pounding, whinny-if-you-can, fog-up-every-window-in-the-world kiss.

Most of me turned to warm taffy as Pop began to whistle "A Kiss to Build a Dream On." I opened an eye and saw that he and Mona were holding hands.

Finally, Pop announced, "Well, if you're looking for Same Time and Next Year you can have 'em—except Same Time's not altogether patched up yet."

With her lips still touching mine, Ginny said breathlessly, "Next Year will be just fine."

I gave my earlobe a little tug.

"By jingo," Pop chortled. "I believe you're right."

acknowledgments

Many thanks to Laurie Fox of the Linda Chester Literary Agency for her tremendous agenting and contributions to the book. Thanks to my editor, Mitchell Ivers, and the staff at Pocket Books, and to Sally Willcox and Laurie Horowitz at Creative Artists Agency. Thanks to Linda Michaels, my foreign rights agent.

Special thanks to Paula Wagner and Tom Cruise for sharing the vision of Tom as the perfect Reb. Thanks also to Gaye Hirsch at Cruise/Wagner Productions. Thanks to Marsha Williams for her enthusiasm and support of this book.

Thanks to Seamus Slattery, my partner, my best friend, a creative genius. It is my great fortune to be able to collaborate with you. Thanks to Jane Slattery, a true friend, and to Mike and Katie Slattery for their patience and support.

To my wonderful wife, Rikki, I thank you for the gift of your love, your fine ideas—including the name for the Circles of Truth—for your excellent editing, and for your unsurpassed culinary touch.

To my beloved son, Ki, I am delighted by your musicality with so many instruments and awed by your writing talent. I am so grateful to be able to watch you grow into such a fine human being.

Last, thank you to all my guys. Without you, I would not have survived. I especially thank Clay and Wyatt for allowing me to use some of their really cool phrases in this book.

There is comfort in the comfort room.